AUG 2 4 2015

D0779898

AUG 2 4 2016

MONDAY MORNING JOY

TIA McCOLLORS

WHITAKER HOUSE

Publisher's Note:
This novel is a work of fiction. References to real events, organizations, or places are used in a fictional context. Any resemblances to actual persons, living or dead, are entirely coincidental.

All Scripture quotations are taken from *The Holy Bible, New International* Version®, NIV®, copyright © 1973, 1978, 1984, 2011 by Biblica, Inc.® Used by permission. All rights reserved worldwide.

MONDAY MORNING JOY
Days of Grace ~ Book 3

Tia McCollors
www.tiamccollors.com
tia@tiamccollors.com

The author is represented by MacGregor Literary, Inc., of Hillsboro, Oregon.

ISBN: 978-1-62911-569-6
eBook ISBN: 978-1-62911-591-7
Printed in the United States of America
© 2015 by Tia McCollors

Whitaker House
1030 Hunt Valley Circle
New Kensington, PA 15068
www.whitakerhouse.com

Library of Congress Cataloging-in-Publication Data

McCollors, Tia.
  Monday morning joy / Tia McCollors.
      pages ; cm. — (Days of grace ; book 3)
   ISBN 978-1-62911-569-6 (softcover : acid-free paper) — ISBN 978-1-62911-591-7 (ebook)
1. Mate selection—Fiction. 2. Man-woman relationships—Fiction. I. Title.
PS3613.C365M66 2015
813'.6—dc23
                          2015021571

No part of this book may be reproduced or transmitted in any form or by any means, electronic or mechanical—including photocopying, recording, or by any information storage and retrieval system—without permission in writing from the publisher. Please direct your inquiries to permissionseditor@whitakerhouse.com.

1 2 3 4 5 6 7 8 9 10 **ᵾ** 21 20 19 18 17 16 15

Dedication

To Rhonda McKnight,
a woman I'm blessed to call my friend and confidante,
for walking this journey beside me, for pushing me from behind,
and for encouraging me from ahead.
Thank you for being my Proverbs 27:17 sister.

1

My fiancé walked out on me six months ago. Yes, he took a piece of my heart with him, but evidently other people thought he'd also taken my hearing.

"Isn't that her?" the woman whispered. "Isn't that Rae Stevens?"

Her voice was raspy. She sounded like my tenth-grade social studies teacher, Mrs. Swift, who chain-smoked cigarettes and guzzled diet colas like a cactus thirsty for water. It was hard to concentrate on the Civil and Spanish-American wars, listening to Mrs. Swift. So, I blocked her out. I did the same to the woman trailing behind me in the produce section of the grocery store.

"I don't know," the woman with her said. "I've only seen her in pictures with him. Never in person."

What did they know? I'd recovered as quickly as any woman who'd just had her heart crushed. I picked up each container of fruit salad, searching for one that was heavy on the pineapple and light on the honeydew melon. *Ignore them*, I told myself, even though I could see them in my peripheral vision. They were craning their necks to get a better look at my face. I turned away, making it hard for them to see if their speculations were correct. They took a step closer while they pretended to be interested in the prepackaged cantaloupe slices.

"No ring on her finger," one of them whispered. "I bet that's her."

"But she doesn't wear glasses, does she?"

Not usually, I wanted to turn around and say. But I'd ventured outside for a brisk stroll through the tree-lined walking paths at the park, and the pollen ending up getting the better of me. By nightfall yesterday, my eyes were red, puffy, and watery, so I'd had to ditch the contacts. Wearing my studious-looking eyewear, and with my hair piled high on my head in a ponytail, it was a wonder anyone recognized me at all. And why would they? Why should they care?

Seemingly satisfied, my spectators pushed their shopping carts to the opposite end of the refrigerated display. Yet they carried on like they were professionals at dispensing gossip.

"Do you have to give the ring back when you get dumped?" I heard one of them say.

"If it were me, I'd sell it and go on a shopping spree."

"Well, it's obvious she didn't do that. Not on clothes, anyway."

I couldn't believe they were having a conversation about me while I was in earshot, as if I was invisible. The nerve of some people. The nerve of *women*. Didn't the bonds of sisterhood prohibit us from spouting hurtful words about and at one another? Almost every woman experienced a devastating heartbreak at some time in her life. Did these two women forget what it was like to be reminded of an ex by the slightest trigger, even if it was six months after the breakup? A special song. A favorite restaurant. The passing scent of a man wearing your ex's signature cologne. Soon enough, all memories would fade away.

I tugged my wrinkled shirt down over my jeans—the pair from my closet that was a size too big instead of a size too small. I wished Farrah was by my side. My best friend wasn't as tame at bridling her tongue. She would've put those women in their place for being so rude. I had promised to help Farrah with her personal resolution to speak the truth in love and to exercise more control over her mouth; but, just this once, I would've given her a pass to do what I didn't have the guts or personality for. Instead, I kept ignoring them.

I was tired of being everyone's sympathy case. You'd think the gossipers would've gotten over it by now. After all, it hadn't been *their* emotional turmoil to deal with. But sometimes it seemed that all of Greensboro had a vested interest in my happily-ever-after with Trenton Cason. He was the city's most popular sports broadcaster—and, up until our fourteen-month-relationship, a very eligible and sought-after bachelor. He'd since reclaimed that title.

I was moving forward with my life. I would never be Mrs. Trenton Cason, and I was finally fine with that.

Lord, keep me, I prayed silently. Three simple yet powerful words that had helped me to make it from one day to the next. Prayers and Farrah, my closest confidante of eight years.

I pulled out my cell to phone her. She answered on the fifth ring, just as I was about to hang up.

"Greetings," she chirped. As long as I'd known her, Farrah had never answered the phone like a normal person. A simple "hello" wouldn't do.

"Hey. Are you and hubby all lovey-dovey tonight, or is Casey still out of town?"

"He'll be back on Wednesday," Farrah said. "And I'm counting down the hours. I miss my boo."

"I know you do," I said. "Wednesday will be here before you know it."

Farrah and Casey were approaching their third wedding anniversary. Even after three years of marriage and a year of dating before that, Farrah missed him like crazy when he was on the road. She'd fallen madly in love with the truck driver who'd changed her flat tire at a gas station.

He'd rumbled into the parking lot of the adjoining truck stop to buy a pack of peanuts and a soda to give himself a caffeine kick. Farrah—dressed in the black cocktail dress she'd worn to her niece's graduation party in Charlotte—had been in bare feet as she muscled the lug nuts from her back wheel. Casey had come to her rescue, and he'd been her knight in shining armor ever since. I'd dutifully and happily served as the maid of honor in their wedding. I'd gained a brother in Casey, and he depended on me to keep Farrah company while he was on the road, away from home.

"I need my best friend," I said as I dropped a bag of red delicious apples into my cart.

"I know that tone," Farrah said. "What happened?"

"Oh, you know. Just some inconsiderate, insensitive women."

"Who don't matter," Farrah inserted.

"I know. But I was actually having a good day—a good two weeks, honestly, of actually enjoying myself and focusing on me. Even this morning, when I heard the song we'd picked for our first dance at the wedding reception, I was fine. But these women have me flustered."

"Don't let them steal your joy." Farrah spoke abruptly and with authority, but with a caring softness in her tone. She let me cry whenever I needed to and had consoled me more than once with Rocky Road ice cream and glazed doughnuts. But in the early months, she'd also pulled me out of bed and made me live my life. On my worst day, she'd treated me to a hot stone massage, a milk-and-honey manicure, and a sugar body exfoliation that I was sure removed ten years' worth of dry skin. I glowed, inside and out. On another depressing day, she'd dragged me to the rinky-dink carnival in the mall parking lot, where we spent a ridiculous amount of money trying to win a huge plush giraffe. We left with a stuffed frog, instead.

"I won't let them," I assured Farrah, snaking slowly through the aisle of organic cereal and whole-wheat flour. "I'm just having a moment."

"I was going to call you, anyway. I need to practice my smoky eye look on someone with your complexion. Want to volunteer?"

Farrah had a growing fascination for all things beauty. She'd recently expanded her part-time gig as an independent cosmetic sales rep and had begun soliciting clients for makeup consultations and applications for special events. When she wasn't recreating the looks she saw in the latest magazines, she spent her time training as an esthetician. Microdermabrasion, glycolic peels, sea salt facials—she could do it all, and do it well.

"Only if you give me a facial first," I insisted. My skin needed to be refreshed, and Farrah's anointed hands always revealed a glow that I could never achieve with the drugstore products in my makeup stash.

"Five thirty good?"

"Perfect," I said, distracted by my favorite gourmet yogurt-covered raisins. "Should I bring food? I'm at The Fresh Market right now."

"Ooooh," Farrah crooned. "Bring some of those yogurt-covered raisins. I've been craving them for a few days. You never should've gotten me hooked on those things."

I tossed two packages in my cart, hoping all her recent food cravings meant that I'd soon have a little niece or nephew. "Are you sure you aren't pregnant? This isn't the only craving you've had lately."

"Not pregnant yet," Farrah confirmed. "But I'll work on that on Wednesday."

I scooped some flaxseed into a plastic baggie. "There are some things I just don't need to know about."

"Hey, I'm married. I have rights."

"Including the right to privacy," I teased. "I'll see you later, girl. And thank you for being there."

"Anytime, all the time," Farrah said before hanging up.

I rounded the corner and accidentally crashed carts with one of the women who'd been assessing my love life in the produce section. I took a deep breath. "Excuse me," I said. As I maneuvered around her, I looked her and her companion in the eye with a gaze that was meant to say, *I heard you. And you were wrong.*

They both turned and hurried in the opposite direction. Their hushed conversation started again, but I was relieved that I couldn't hear their words this time.

I pushed my cart into the express lane, which ended up not being too "express." An elderly gentleman in front of me used his arthritic fingers to pinch the coins from his palm—one penny, two nickels, two dimes, another nickel, and so on—until he'd paid for his red onion, two sweet potatoes, and three lemons with exact change. He seemed to move in slow motion as he picked up his bag and shuffled out the door.

My purchases zipped forward on the conveyer belt. *Beep. Beep. Beep. Beep.* The clerk slid them across the scanner before I had the opportunity to pull out my wallet.

"Fifteen dollars and forty-nine cents," the clerk said as she bagged the items.

I opened my purse and fished around hurriedly for my wallet. Where was it? My mind flashed back to that morning, when I'd used my credit card to pay for a new laptop adapter cord I'd ordered online. I must have left my wallet on the kitchen table beside a half-empty—make that half-full—glass of orange juice. *No joy stealers*, I told myself.

"Sorry," I apologized to the antsy clerk. "There's probably something in here."

If I can scrounge up enough for one bag of raisins, I'll be satisfied, I decided as I unfolded a receipt from the office supply store. *Voila!* Two bills—a five and a ten. I handed them to her victoriously.

"Hold on a second," I told the woman. "Let me just find some change." I shook my purse but heard only the clink, clank, jingle of my car keys. Where was Mr. Penny Man when I needed him?

I turned at the light tap on my shoulder to see an open hand holding two quarters. "Here you go, sister," the woman said.

I breathed a sigh of relief, even though I felt the warm rush of embarrassment across my face. As I took the coins out of her palm, I tried to make eye contact, but her peepers were shaded by dark lenses the size of two saucers. Her smile, however, was like a warm hug.

"Thanks. Forgot my wallet," I explained.

She dismissed me with a slight wave of her hand. "I did the same thing last week, when I had an entire cart of groceries. Needless to say, we ordered pizza for dinner that night. Which was what my son wanted, anyway."

"I think I know what I'm having for dinner tonight," I said. "Veggie pizza."

"I love a good veggie pizza. With extra olives," she added.

I felt better. It was amazing how much a kind person had changed my day. All it had taken was a warm smile, fifty cents, and a brief back-and-forth about food.

I dropped the two quarters in the clerk's open palm. She handed me back a dull penny.

"Here's your change," I said, holding out the penny to the woman behind me. "Next time, the forty-nine cents is on me."

"Keep it," she said, adjusting her Hollywood-style shades. "Let it remind you that all you need is *one* on your side. And *God* is on your side. I'm Quinn, by the way."

"And I'm Rae. Nice to meet you."

"I never did like Trenton Cason, anyway," the cashier blurted out of the blue, as if she felt obliged to offer a word of condolence. "He smiled too much for me. I've never seen a man smile that big unless he was up to something. You'll get back on your feet."

I didn't need a man in order to get back on my feet. I was standing just fine.

"Have a great day," I said to both of them. I scooped up my bags and left with a feeling of hope, thanking God for the message He'd sent me. With God on my side, how could I lose? God's love was greater and worth more than anything that I'd lost. He *was* my joy.

⌒

I pulled my car onto Battleground Avenue and enjoyed the stress-free ride to the offices of the *Greensboro Ledger*. My editor, Shelton Hayes III, preferred to meet on Monday afternoons to review the editorial schedules and follow up with our small, ever-dwindling staff.

Although we sometimes grumbled about the meetings, I didn't mind attending. It gave me a chance to get out of the house at the beginning of the week instead of being holed up inside with my laptop. Freelancing afforded me a steady paycheck without snatching away my liberties, like late nights, later mornings, and the freedom to determine my daily schedule.

Dating and then being engaged to a high-profile, seasoned sportscaster had expanded my professional network and enabled me to build my portfolio. I'd secured some profitable assignments on Trenton's name alone. That was about the only positive remnant of our relationship.

At one time, I had considered spreading my wings in a larger city, like Charlotte, Atlanta, or Miami, where there'd be plenty of large companies more apt to contract writers instead of keeping them on staff full-time. But Greensboro was more my speed. Here, personal and professional life moved at a slower pace compared to the metro areas where most of my media-driven Aggie alumni friends had ended up planting themselves.

Whenever my college girlfriends returned to the city to visit, they invariably pointed out what they perceived as a scarcity of men—more specifically, eligible, gainfully employed men who embraced the same values and earned the same pay grades they did. In some respects, they were right.

Maybe that was why it had been so easy for me to fall for Trenton. Fall *on* him was probably a more accurate description. I was attending a black-tie event for local journalists at the Grandover Hotel, floating through the corridor in a floor-length red gown, trying my best to look engaging and comfortable, even though soirees like that weren't my thing. I would rather have spent that night stretched out on my bed eating popcorn and doing crossword puzzles. But since I'd been in need of lucrative freelance assignments, that hadn't been an option.

Across the room, I'd eyed an old college professor studying the platters of cheese and crackers on the banquet table. I'd headed his way, but somehow my high heels—borrowed from Farrah's extensive shoe collection—had gotten tangled in the hem of my gown. Down I went. Trenton had been a few steps in front of me, and I'd instinctively reached for him, the nearest person, during my stumble. His knees had buckled from the unexpected weight of me falling against him.

"My mother always told me women would fall at my feet one day," Trenton had said as he helped me keep my balance while I readjusted my shoe. He'd flashed his set of whitened, polished teeth—a grin that was always camera-ready. That smile that everyone seemed to love roped me in. I'd recognized him immediately, although I pretended not to.

And here I was now, pretending not to see him, and hoping he wouldn't see me stuffing yogurt-covered raisins in my mouth.

We were stopped side by side at the traffic light. I blinked to be sure the pollen hadn't left a haze over my eyes. Removing my glasses, I took another quick glance. Different car, same man. He must've gotten that salary increase he'd wanted.

2

Trenton was so engrossed in conversation with the lady sitting in the passenger seat of his new ride that he didn't see me. She was wearing a strapless shirt of some sort, maybe a bandeau, that revealed toned shoulders. When she began to snap her fingers with an exaggerated sway of her upper body, I realized they were singing together. *Are they serious?* First her, then him. A duet, accompanied by obnoxious gestures, like they were the king and queen of karaoke. Sonny and Cher. Captain & Tennille. Peaches and Herb.

I unclipped my shades from the visor and slid them on. *Come on, green light,* I thought as I focused on the road. *Green. Green.* It seemed that two decades passed before the signal changed. I hesitated before accelerating, wanting to let Trenton's sparkling, midnight-black foreign sports car zoom at least two car lengths ahead of me. Displeased with my stall tactic, the driver behind me blasted his horn. I wasn't moved by the man's impatience. He shot me a rude middle finger when I looked in the rearview mirror, then maneuvered dangerously around me, so close that he nearly clipped my side mirror. He gunned past me and had just cleared the intersection when a flash of blue lights appeared.

That put a smile on my face. *Serves you right.* Like my grandma always said, *"God don't like ugly."*

I tuned in to the city's gospel station for the remainder of my ride to the office and let the music lift my soul.

In less than twenty minutes, I pulled into the parking area outside the newspaper's office, dodging the growing pothole at the front of the driveway. It was a residential property that had been converted to house the *Greensboro Ledger* before I was born.

I parked in my usual space to the left, shaded by a dogwood tree. I popped the trunk, lifted out my laptop, and carried it into the aging building. An old brass bell announced my arrival, just as it did for every visitor. There were very few, but the ones who came frequently knew us all by name. The librarian, Lois, who was also a Greensboro historian, brought doughnuts on the last Monday of every month. Wallace lived in the neighborhood behind the newspaper office and visited at least once a week to dote on our part-time volunteer receptionist, Ms. Bessie. The sixty-seven-year-old retiree gathered information about church and community events, and she adored bright red lipstick, which she applied liberally to her full lips. Then there was Mason, a longtime Greensboro resident, whose sole purpose it seemed was to complain about something, anything, or *everything.*

The *Greensboro Ledger* was far from being a technologically advanced newspaper. There were two desktop computers that looked like they had been rescued from the recycling bin approximately ten years prior. But Shelton, the current publisher and editor-in-chief, wasn't concerned about the latest upgrades. Like his grandfather and great-grandfather before him, he was focused on the paper's mission to instill a sense of community and conscience.

"Hi, Ms. Bessie," I said, picking a peppermint out of the glass bowl on her desk.

"Hey, baby," she said, surveying me from head to toe. "So, you rolled out of bed and decided to come in?"

"Do I look that bad?" I asked.

"You don't look that *good*," Ms. Bessie said. "But I still love you. What if your Mr. Right walked in to this office today?"

"I'm not concerned about Mr. Right. I'm not concerned about Mr. Anybody."

"You don't have to be concerned, but you should be ready." Ms. Bessie studied her reflection in a heart-shaped compact mirror, pressing her lips together, then snapped it closed. "It's summertime. People are coming alive and crawling out of their caves. The sun is out. Vitamin D makes everybody feel better, and the men start looking."

"So, that's what I need," I said. "Vitamin D and a veggie pizza."

Ms. Bessie shook her head and rubbed her plump belly. "Enjoy that pizza while you're young. I'm too old for that to sit well with my stomach."

Nothing sat well with Ms. Bessie's stomach. "I'll look better next week," I promised her.

Working from home had also done another thing for me: It caused me to choose comfort over fashion. With the exception of Sundays, investing in the extra effort to get dolled up like most women wasn't a daily necessity for me. My best work was produced in the comfort of my pajamas and fuzzy slippers. I hadn't had a reason for wearing mascara and lip gloss Monday through Friday when a freshly scrubbed face and some ChapStick suited me just fine.

"Do it for yourself, if for nobody else," Ms. Bessie said. "When you look good, you feel good." She whirled around in her black ergonomic office chair. It was the newest thing in the office. She'd convinced Shelton to purchase it for her by complaining about consistent back pain.

"Yes, ma'am," I said, knowing Wallace was much of the reason Ms. Bessie had stepped up her game. Over the last two months, she'd had several appointments with her new hairstylist, who'd been curling her tresses into soft ringlets. I'd never realized her hair was so thick and full, since she'd always kept it tucked into a tight bun. Wallace had convinced Ms. Bessie to let her hair down in the literal sense.

I followed Ms. Bessie down the short hallway to the open area of desks. Shelton's oversized mahogany desk was the centerpiece of the room. It was wide. Like him. And it was the very desk that had been delivered to the office the day his grandfather had opened the newspaper's doors.

"Good afternoon, Shelton," I said. He refused to let me tag "Mr." to the front of his name. When I did, he ignored me.

Ms. Bessie walked in with a folder and a handful of pencils. It was her routine, even though I never used my #2 hard lead pencil. She was a former educator who had joyfully taught kindergarten for forty years, and she believed in being prepared.

"Are you ready to get cracking, Shelton?" Ms. Bessie asked. "I've got tons of church announcements to sort through. You know your church folks are serious about getting their events printed in the paper." She walked over to the small, rickety table in the corner, where the coffeemaker sat, and dumped some grounds from the tin into the filter.

I was the only one in the office who didn't drink coffee, but Ms. Bessie made sure everyone else could get an afternoon jolt before the meeting. After fifteen minutes of waiting, we assumed we were going to be the only ones in attendance.

"I'm so glad our paper focuses on the positive things happening in the community," I said, scanning the news Web sites for the top headlines from most of the major newspapers. "Leave the murders, robberies, political scandals, and other stuff to everybody else."

Shelton leaned back in his chair and splayed his sausage-shaped fingers on his stomach. "Unfortunately, that's the way of the world these days. Sad, but true. That's why we do things different. That's not to say we don't care about the corruption that's plaguing the world and our city; but if we raise the issue, I believe we need to offer a solution. When we're better informed, we make wiser decisions."

"Amen to that," Ms. Bessie chimed in.

Shelton tipped his chair forward again, and it squealed in pain. Its wobbly legs looked as if they could barely hold the weight of a preschooler, and they creaked whenever Shelton leaned over and favored the weight on his left side. If that chair had a mouth, I was positive it would scream for mercy.

"Thank you, Ms. Bessie," Shelton said when she handed him a Styrofoam cup of steaming coffee. He blew across the top before taking a cautious slurp.

"One day, I'm going to follow your example and eat healthy," Shelton said, eyeing me as I snapped off the lid from my container of mixed fruit. He pulled an icing-glazed pastry from beneath the napkin covering the plate in front of him. "But not today." Then he opened his abyss of a mouth and stuffed nearly the entire thing into his jaws. Bits of white glaze sat on his fingertips like snowcapped mountains. He licked his fingers, wiped his palms with a napkin, and slurped again from his coffee. He set the cup on the edge of his desk, then grabbed his ample midsection like a prized possession.

Ms. Bessie rolled her eyes. "You need prayer," she teased.

"You've got that right," Shelton said with a laugh. "And while you're at it, pray for the paper. We are barely hanging on. People aren't spending the advertising dollars like they used to." His mouth formed a firm, straight line. "The numbers aren't looking good. Not at all. We need the help of Jesus and *all* of His disciples to stay afloat."

I was disheartened but not surprised by Shelton's announcement. The *Greensboro Ledger* had always been a low-budget publication, but I enjoyed the grassroots feel of the paper. Although I also penned articles for online media and national magazines that were definitely more lucrative, there was something special about the in-depth local pieces I wrote for this paper. It wasn't merely about the stories; it was about the people behind them.

"We'll make it if we dig in our heels and try to find some new advertisers," I suggested. Shelton needed to know we were a team. A family. "Maybe we each could commit to obtaining at least five this year."

"Five each?" Ms. Bessie raised her eyebrows. "I'd feel more comfortable shooting for two, but I can't speak on anyone else's behalf. It seems to me that the rest of our staff is pulling a disappearing act as it is."

Shelton rubbed his forehead. "Melvina and Stuart couldn't make it in today, but they're still on board, for the most part. We haven't lost everybody. Yet." In all seriousness, he added, "This is my family's legacy. If I have to write every article myself, I will. I can't let it die. This is history. History," he repeated. His voice was solemn, his expression downcast.

A lump rose in my throat. I didn't want to see the *Ledger* succumb to the fate of other small community newspapers, especially the ones that gave a voice to African-Americans. I would write until I had no more words left. I'd do whatever Shelton needed me to do.

Bessie dumped two personal-sized creamers into her coffee. "Maybe your letter from the editor for the next issue should address the state of the paper. Call the community to action. Sometimes, people are passive because they don't know what's going on."

Shelton shook his head as if he didn't see the benefit of Ms. Bessie's suggestion. "I see your point, but I'm not ready to take that route yet. Let's pursue advertisers first," he said, flipping over the first page of his yellow steno pad. He looked at me. "Rae, I've got to make your load heavier over the next month or so. Can you handle it?"

"Yes," I said, without hesitation.

I loved writing. Words gave me life. I had twenty-five journals that chronicled my life to prove it. There were countless pages of records of my awkward middle school years, as well as the ups and downs of those teenage years, when I had so-called friends who were as close as sisters one week, then as distant as archenemies the next. The most recent journal was the one I'd started after meeting Trenton. It contained the happiest of times—and the worst of times. The focus of my writing had changed from recording my personal problems to penning prayers.

I waited while Shelton drummed his pencil eraser on the desk.

He finally spoke. "One of your top stories will be on Malachi Burke. Ever heard of him?"

"His name sounds familiar," I said, trying to put a face with that name. I'd thought I knew all of the local politicians and major business leaders in the area.

"Major League Baseball player up in New York who grew up around here. He's had some bad luck with shoulder injuries lately, but he's headed back here to kick off his baseball summer camp."

I moaned inside. This was not the kind of story I'd been hoping to get. Professional athletes always thought they ruled the world, even if they never left the dugout or the bench. I'd been introduced to a few by Trenton, and I'd yet to meet one who wasn't conceited and who didn't expect everyone around to cater to his needs.

"What about Melvina for that story?" I protested politely. "She has grandsons who play baseball. She'd be perfect."

"Melvina needs a break to tend to her husband. If you haven't heard, he fell off a forklift last week at work and threw out his back. Have you seen the man? He's not exactly going to bounce back anytime soon."

"Shelton, I'd really rather not do anything sports related," I persisted. "With good reason."

Shelton tucked his pencil behind his ear and folded his arms across his desk. He looked me straight in the eyes. "You can't let that man rule your life," he said, picking up on my meaning. Since my breakup, Shelton had referred to Trenton as "that man," sometimes adding a few other choice words.

Was I wrong for not wanting to take on any assignments that might cause me to cross paths with Trenton? Baseball player, hometown hero—he would be all over the story. For the chance to become Malachi's best buddy, he'd camp out at the baseball field and put a nine-year-old bat boy out of a job.

"I seriously considered how you'd feel when I was thinking about it last night," Shelton went on. "I asked Lenora what she thought, and she said you might not want to put yourself in a position where you might encounter that man."

"Great minds think alike," I said. "Spoken from a woman with a compassionate heart." I'd always loved Shelton's wife, Lenora. I'd seen her thoughtfulness displayed in numerous ways to the staff. Last summer, after I'd had two wisdom teeth extracted, she had shown up at my place with a pot of homemade mashed potatoes.

Shelton should have listened to his wife. But he hadn't. I could tell. I pretended to be distracted, avoiding his gaze, so Shelton would reconsider.

"Malachi Burke isn't a local athlete, and this story isn't just about his career. No boring stats stuff. No game coverage. Just Malachi—who he is behind the baseball cap. The chances are slim to none that you'll run into Trenton," Shelton tried to assure me. "As a matter of fact, no one knows Burke's coming into town. They think he just dropped a few thousand to put his name on some banners. But he's coming to spend some time with his grandma, too."

"How did you find out?" I asked. Shelton was huge on building relationships, and he always seemed to be in the know.

"His grandma told me. Man, when you get that woman talking, she'll tell you her whole life's history. Lenora had me call to see if she would bake three sweet potato pies for the women's luncheon at the church. Before I knew it, she was whining about some doctor's appointment she didn't want to go to, and then she told me that Malachi was coming."

"Malachi Bush, huh?"

"Burke," Shelton corrected me.

Ms. Bessie shook a finger. "I think my niece dated him when they were in high school. Not for very long, though. I think he had a girlfriend at every school in the city."

"So, his reputation precedes him?" I wasn't surprised.

"That was high school. No teenage boy is trying to tie himself to one girl. People change," Shelton said.

"And not always for the better," I said, snapping the lid back on my fruit salad. I started tapping the plastic fork on the top.

Shelton looked at his watch. "Malachi's flying in today, probably landing as we speak. I scheduled you to interview him on Wednesday," he said, his decision final. He'd exercised his editorial pull.

"Wednesday?"

"Eleven o'clock. That was the time his assistant suggested. Maybe you can treat him to lunch. We'll reimburse you for any expenses."

"Well, you have yourselves a fabulous meal at Mickey D's," Ms. Bessie teased. "We might even be able to afford an apple pie and an ice cream sundae for dessert."

Shelton crumpled up a piece of paper and threw it at Ms. Bessie, then turned back to me. "You should probably spend a few days with him. This is going to be a center-spread feature. I'd rather you give me more than enough than not enough. This is Malachi Burke. Write a book on him, if you want to. We'll *make* it fit."

Ms. Bessie beckoned me to the desk where she was sitting. "I Googled him. He's handsome. Can you wear something besides *that* on Wednesday, please?" She pursed her ruby red lips.

I twisted my ponytail until it was wrapped into a tight knot. Wednesday was going to be interesting.

But I'd said I would do anything for Shelton. It was time to make good on my word.

3

Malachi

Malachi never thought he'd have to take the Scripture "flee fornication" so literally, but today, he ran from it on a one-hour, forty-nine-minute flight from New Jersey to North Carolina. Sometimes, you had to leave those demons behind, even when they looked as divine as angels—Krystal, Chanel, and Alexandria.... The list *used* to go on.

Malachi looked at the business card the flight attendant had given him. "Call me," she'd scribbled across the top, along with a smiley face. Even wearing a conservative airline vest and a knee-length skirt, the curves of her body couldn't be denied as she moved up and down the aisle in first class. She offered Malachi a glass of champagne. He declined. He wasn't a drinker. Never had been. His addiction had been women.

Malachi dropped the card in the first trash receptacle he saw after stepping off the plane. *No chance.* Temptation followed him everywhere he went, but he was learning ways of sidestepping it.

He hadn't walked through a twelve-step cleansing program to transform his life from the rowdy to the righteous track. He'd had an experience with God Himself.

It happened one night after talking on the phone with his grandmother. It was the first time he'd truly accepted that Gran'nola's memory was slipping away. He'd suspected it, but he hadn't wanted to admit it. In his eyes, his grandmother would always be the vivacious, plump-cheeked woman who'd jumped down the umpire's throat at his high-school baseball games. She was the grandmother who'd mowed her own lawn on Saturday mornings, even though she had six brothers who offered to do it for her. But that night, he'd had to remind Gran'nola whom she was talking to. One minute, she was telling him about her church's revival, and the next minute, she went off on a tangent about her recipe for bread pudding. She'd called him "Peggy" twice. Peggy was Malachi's aunt. Gran'nola had forgotten other things and people before, but never *him*.

During his phone call with Gran'nola, Krystal—whom he'd called out of loneliness because Alexandria was out of town—had made herself comfortable in his kitchen, using the hibachi grill to prepare a steak dinner. She was a self-taught student in culinary arts who could rival the head chef of any five-star restaurant. But Malachi had lost his appetite and put Krystal out before she had a chance to finish preparing the three-course meal she'd planned. He'd dined alone on a bland microwave dinner, then had taken a shower so hot, the water nearly scalded his skin.

Everything his grandmother had taught him about God had rushed into his mind as the water from the massaging showerhead pulsed across his back: Life was short. Things didn't stay the same. Gran'nola always said she wanted him to get his life right. That he knew better. And now, he needed to let her see him as a changed man. He *wanted* to be a changed man. That Sunday night, his sins were washed away as he cried under the hot, pulsating stream.

And now, Malachi was back in Greensboro. Yes, he wanted to show his face to kick off the summer camp he'd been hoping for years to orchestrate. But his main purpose was to see about Gran'nola.

Malachi pulled down the brim of his baseball cap until it was flush with his eyebrows. He was incognito with the darkest shades he had in his collection. He thought no one would notice him.

But people did.

"Malachi Burke."

Alonzo Jones might as well have announced his name on the airport's intercom system. Every head turned his way, and for a moment, Malachi thought about ducking into the bathroom. But it was pointless. Alonzo, along with the five strangers who had spotted him, would still be standing there when he emerged.

"Man, I knew that was you," Alonzo said when Malachi sent him a peace sign. "You're big-time. I hope you weren't trying to pull off a disguise under those glasses. I've known you since kindergarten, and you look the same as you did when we graduated. But with more money." Alonzo sniffed in the air. "You even smell like money."

Malachi couldn't help but laugh. "You ain't changed a bit, Zo," he said, bumping fists and noticing that his childhood friend was employed by the airport.

Alonzo pulled off his black cap to reveal a shiny bald head.

"Well, except for that," Malachi said.

"Sometimes, you have to know when it's time to let go," Alonzo said. He ran his hand across his smooth dome. "When in doubt, I ask my wife. She doesn't hold her tongue."

"So, can I call you 'Mr. Clean'?"

"I've been called worse," Alonzo said. "We both know that." He flashed a gap-toothed smile.

Alonzo had been caught cheating on so many of his high-school girlfriends that he'd had to find a prom date from another school across town. By the end of the night, his exes had scared that poor girl away, too. He'd ended up catching a ride back home with Malachi, since his date had asked the limo driver to take her home.

Other arriving passengers started to notice Malachi. It was a small airport, nothing like New York's JFK or LaGuardia. Malachi's childhood friend stepped back to give him space to autograph the T-shirt of a man holding his toddler son in his arms. "Get that shoulder ready," the man told him as his son tugged playfully at his father's earlobes. "The team needs you. I need you. I bet my money on you every time."

"I'm trying," Malachi said, accepting a black marker and a magazine from another waiting fan. He scribbled his autograph like it was second nature, barely looking at the page. He'd seen the photo and read the *Sports Illustrated* article speculating about his return next season. He was once the golden boy, but, with his recurring injuries, his stats had lost their shine.

He posed for photo after photo. Signed autograph after autograph.

"How long are you going to be in town?" Alonzo asked Malachi once the crowd was starting to dwindle.

"At least a month," Malachi said as he posed for a picture with an elderly lady who probably didn't even know who he was. She stood beside him, her arms and her smile stiff, after the younger man she was traveling with basically positioned her beside Malachi like she was a statue on display.

That was it. The crowd was gone.

"What's your number, man? We should meet up. And if you need a little security, I'm the man you need to call," Alonzo said. "If the TSA can trust me, you know you can."

"I might do that," Malachi said, meaning it. He didn't come back to Greensboro often; the times he had, he'd flown in one day and returned to New York the next. If Alonzo was as even-keeled as he used to be, he'd make for good company. They'd played together on the high-school baseball team, and although Alonzo hadn't been in the starting lineup, he was always just as committed as the star players, if not more so. Malachi remembered how he used to make up chants and raps to hype up his teammates. One thing that Alonzo didn't lack was heart.

Malachi and Alonzo exchanged numbers.

"Don't forget about me, man," Alonzo said. "I'll show you a good time."

"In Greensboro?"

Alonzo shrugged. "You've got to work with what you've got."

"I'll hit you up tomorrow night. I might want you to help me with this baseball camp. I've got a crew in place here, but an extra hand never hurts. And I don't expect you to work for free."

Alonzo's expression showed that he was in. You could always depend on a man when green was in the picture.

"I'm there. My wife is pregnant with my first son. Some extra padding in my pocket would be helpful right about now. Hit me up."

Malachi picked up his pace and followed the signs to the car rental counters.

"Reservation for Burke," he told the representative. While he waited, he checked the text messages that had been popping up on his phone since the plane had landed. There was one from his personal assistant, Katrene. His physical therapist. His manager. His agent. His publicist. And Alexandria. He hadn't heard her voice in three months; and, two months prior to their last conversation, they'd barely communicated at all. His reason was because she was a temptation he needed to avoid. Hers? She'd been traipsing around Dubai, working and immersing herself in Arabian culture. Every now and then, she'd text him a photo of herself on her latest adventure—riding a camel through the desert or posing in the foyer of a luxurious hotel with golden floors.

But now, she was back in New York, and Malachi was glad he *wasn't*. He couldn't have come to Greensboro at a better time.

Malachi would reply to business contacts only. He'd forgotten about the interview he'd agreed to do, but, as usual, Katrene was on top of things. He definitely wanted publicity and coverage for the summer camp, but he knew that reporters were always out for the inside scoop. They'd bypass his enthusiasm about the children and dig directly into his personal career. Was there hope for his injured shoulder? If baseball was no longer an option, then what? Baseball was all that Malachi knew. He lived it every day, even during the off-season. It was hard to imagine his life without it.

And so he didn't. Not right now. But soon he'd have to. His life was changing.

"Mr. Burke?"

He looked up at the car rental representative.

"Your rental SUV will be outside shortly." She slid a contract in front of him. "If you would just sign here, here, and here," she said, indicating the designated lines with her finger.

Then the agent handed him a blank piece of paper and smiled sheepishly. "And here, for me." She paused. "Well, it's actually for my dad. He's a big fan. You can sign it 'To Wade,' if you don't mind."

"No problem," he said as he did one last John Hancock.

Malachi shoved his folded paperwork into his pocket, then rolled his suitcase out to the curb where his SUV awaited him. The model was top-of-the-line, with a medium tint on the windows. He'd hoped it would be darker, but if the sunlight hit the glass at the perfect angle, no one would be able to see him at all. The last thing he wanted was to be followed.

Malachi slipped a sizeable tip into the hand of the young guy who'd pulled his car around.

He shoved it into his front pocket without a second glance. He'd probably assumed it was a five, so he'd be in for a surprise when he discovered it was a hundred-dollar bill.

"You're blessed to be a blessing," his grandmother had told him once his checks and signing bonuses had begun to roll in.

Behind the wheel, Malachi relaxed. He sank into the plush leather and moved the seat for his lengthy legs. A few more adjustments, and the built-in lumbar support cradled his back. He was too young for aches and pains, even though they were minimal. Professional athletes had more miles added to their bodies than people realized.

Malachi relished the silence. No radio. No one buzzing in his ear to update him about everything he had to do that day. No fellow teammates clowning him when he turned down their invitations to the latest bar hop or club opening. In fact, unless it was Gran'nola, he was shutting out everything and everybody until Wednesday.

Then, he'd give the reporter thirty minutes to get the story. What was the name again? He glanced at the text. Rae Stevens. He? She? Whoever it was had half an hour. That was it.

4

I sat in front of my laptop, scrolling through online images of Malachi Burke and the unending stream of women he kept on his arm. Whether it was for a red-carpet event or a shot the paparazzi caught of a casual evening at a New York restaurant, it seemed Malachi was no stranger to women with long legs, long hair, and a bulging bustline.

"How can one man be seen in public with so many women?" I griped. "Has he no shame?"

"He's a professional athlete," Farrah said. She dotted some white cream under her eyes, a product she swore would eliminate under-eye puffiness and prevent future wrinkles. "To them, women are a dime a dozen. If offered the opportunity, most men are not going to turn it down."

"I'll never understand it," I said, lowering the screen. I'd had enough research for the day. Why would Shelton want a center-spread feature on a womanizer? Some people weren't meant to be glorified.

Farrah had been working on a skin detox concoction in the kitchen before I arrived, and so, for the last twenty minutes, my face had been covered with a mixture of mashed bananas, honey, and sour cream.

She draped a towel around my shoulders. "You don't have to marry the man. You have to write about him."

"It'll be short and sweet. I'm going to include as many photographs as possible so I won't have to worry about content. I know his kind. He's probably doesn't want to be bothered, especially with a small paper like ours."

"He can't be all that bad. He's hosting a free baseball camp that practically everybody in the city is going to want to attend. Give the man a break and try to see some good in him. You might be surprised at what you find."

"It's probably a publicity stunt or a tax write-off." I picked up the nearby hand mirror and studied my reflection.

"Well, if you have big money, you have to do big things," Farrah said. "Why should you be concerned about his personal life, anyway?"

"I'm not concerned." I poked the side of my nose with my pinkie finger. "It's part of my research."

"Well, can you research Malachi later? We need to get this stuff washed off your face."

"That's a good idea, because I'm starting to not be able to move my lips."

"On second thought, I might need to leave it on a little while longer." Farrah walked away and left me sitting at her kitchen table.

"Whatever." I stood up and followed Farrah into the master bathroom, where I plopped down on the vanity seat in front of the mirror. Her makeup collection rivaled the cosmetics counter of any department store, with eye shadows ranging from deep plums to smoky greys, and blushes from amber to rose. The myriad foundations could conceal the imperfections of the fairest of skins to the deepest of chocolate tones.

"You've added to your collection," I remarked.

"I had to. I'm already booked for two brides and their bridal parties this summer. It's a big responsibility, enhancing the beauty of these women on one of the most important days of their lives. My work will live on forever in their bridal albums. 'Till death do us part.' That's a lot of weight for a woman to have on her shoulders."

"You'll do fine," I assured her. "You're already an expert."

I turned on the bathroom faucet and adjusted the handles until the water temperature ran warm across my fingers. I soaked a white washcloth under the stream, then squeezed out the excess water. "Just put my bridal booking on hold," I told her. "I don't care if it's five years from now. I still want the entire package."

"You always have been and always will be my number one client," Farrah said as she took the washcloth from me and wiped it gently across my forehead, removing the hardened mask.

"I saw Trenton today after I left the grocery store," I told her. I'd been withholding that information, trying to push it out of my head. For once, I'd wanted to show up at Farrah's house without bringing a pity party. "We were stopped at the same traffic light."

"I'm sorry." She paused her routine for a moment, as if to see if I needed more than her words, maybe a hug or a shoulder to cry on.

I was fine. I didn't have another tear set aside to cry for Trenton.

I shrugged. "He didn't see me. He was too busy singing a duet with some chick. His new love, I imagine. You know how men operate. They have a new woman on their arm in less than three months. Don't you remember when April and Edward got divorced?"

Farrah frowned at the memory of the ugly details we'd learned about our mutual friend. April had slumped into a deep depression, but after we'd found her a great counselor, we'd banded together to help pull her through tough times. Every Friday morning at six thirty, we connected on a phone conference line for prayer, whether April chose to join us or not. She and Edward had been college sweethearts from the time they toured the campus together during freshman orientation, and then, after ten years of marriage, she became a single mother of two. Six months later, Edward was engaged again, with a baby on the way. Plain and simple, men moved on.

"Who cares about Trenton?" Farrah said, circling the washcloth down the side of my chin, then under my closed eyes. "It's his loss."

"I know. And I finally believe it."

"Well, as long as you believe it, no one can take it away from you."

I opened my eyes and saw the compassion on my friend's face. "Then why did it hurt me to see him? It was a tiny pinch to my heart, but I thought I was completely over him."

"I'm sorry," Farrah said again. "But it'll get better. It didn't hurt as much as it did the first time you saw him, did it?"

"Nothing like the first time," I said, closing my eyes again. The first time he'd shown up at my doorstep after our breakup, his unexpected visit sent my heart racing. Looking through the peephole, I'd seen him standing with his hands stuffed in his pockets. He was coming back to ask for my forgiveness for the way he'd abruptly turned our lives upside down. He still wanted the two of us to become one. Or so I'd thought. What he'd really wanted were the two sports jackets he'd left in the back of my guest room closet.

That night, after he'd left, I'd closed the door and wept like a baby. And for the following three weeks, my anguish had spilled out at the most inconvenient of times. It wasn't until I'd watched him on the eleven o'clock news, smiling like he was living in a perfect world, that I'd found the strength to make it through the day without crying. I figured, if he could smile, so could I.

I leaned forward so Farrah could splash cold water on my face, a trick she'd taught me to prevent my T-zone from becoming too oily.

"You know what they say. Life isn't life without a good heartbreak," Farrah said.

"Who says that?" I asked, reaching blindly for a dry towel. Farrah stuffed one into my hand, and I blotted my face.

"Girl, I don't know. I might have made it up, but it sounded like an old woman's wisdom. Regardless, it's true. Look how much your relationship with God has grown. Your faith, trust, and love for Him have grown immeasurably."

"Now you're speaking truth," I said, as she cleaned the last of her homemade mask from my face.

My rough patch had pushed me to my knees and caused me to seek the strength and peace I needed through my relationship with Christ.

I studied my complexion in the mirror. I was grateful I'd inherited the smooth skin that all the ladies on my mother's side of the family were blessed to have. Save for the occasional pimple, I'd never endured the acne that most people suffered during puberty. And now, I was finally beginning to see the inner glow I'd lost over the past months return and reflect itself on the outside. That was a better result than any beauty product could have produced.

"How does your skin feel?" Farrah asked.

"Remarkable," I said, pinching my cheeks. "It feels fresh."

"It looks it, too," Farrah said, examining my face. "You could stand to spruce up those eyebrows, though. And can I please try one of my new eyeshadow palettes on you?"

I settled back to let Farrah do her thing. "I'm ready to be transformed," I said.

Farrah picked up a stack of pages she'd torn from various beauty magazines and thumbed through them. "Let's see…something a baseball player would be attracted to."

"That won't be necessary. I don't want him, and trust me when I say I'm not his type. My top side is too small, my backside is too flat, and my standards are too high."

Farrah draped a black vinyl cape around my shoulders and fastened it behind my neck. "You never know when and how God will send love your way again. I met my sweetie because of a blown-out tire," she reminded me.

"And that perfectly describes my love life right now." I laughed. "Flat."

5

Malachi

One of these days, Malachi was going to convince Gran'nola to let him hire somebody to pave her driveway. He slowed as he traveled up the gravel drive leading to her house. Brown dust rose and settled on the windshield, and Malachi could hear an occasional pebble ping against the undercarriage of the SUV. He hoped it wouldn't rain anytime soon, or he'd have to mush through the mud and soft grass to get out. There were some things he missed about being in the country versus the concrete jungle of New York, but muddy tires wasn't one of them.

He pulled around to the back and parked close to the carport where Gran'nola kept her sedan. She'd also refused his offer to have a stand-alone two-car garage built for her, but at least her vehicle was somewhat protected from the elements. That woman could be stubborn when she wanted to. She hadn't refused the brand-new car he'd had delivered last year for her birthday, however. She was too smart to be stubborn about that.

Malachi took a deep breath, inhaling the scent of freshly cut grass. He stopped and listened, hearing nothing except the blaring television inside of Gran'nola's house and the buzz of two bees fighting over the bloom of a potted flower at the bottom of the steps.

Malachi opened the screen door, not surprised that it wasn't locked. It never was, despite his insistence. Stubborn. The Burke women were stubborn.

"Gran'nola," he shouted over the television. He found the remote on the side of her favorite sitting chair and hit the mute button to silence the two families feuding on the game show.

"Gran'nola," he called out again.

"Malachi? Malachi, is that you?"

Malachi could hear the shuffle of her feet coming down the hall. "Yes, ma'am, it's me. Come on out, pretty lady."

Gran'nola had dropped a few pounds. The loss was most evident in her face. Her cheeks were nowhere near as plump as they'd always been, like two round apples. She'd aged in the eight months since last he'd seen her, and her knee had stiffened more, judging by her slower gait. Obviously, the arthritis had worsened to the point that popping a couple of pain relievers a day did little to help. He'd suggested an orthopedic specialist, a physical therapist, *and* water aerobics to help. Every time, he'd been shot down with the same phrase: "I'll get around to it." When Gran'nola said that, it meant no.

Malachi had been in her house less than a minute, so he wouldn't dare start rattling off his list of things she needed to do—lock her door, make a doctor's appointment.... It was wise to wait until he'd softened her up with some of his grandson love.

Malachi stooped his six-foot-four frame low enough to hug his grandmother, but it only gave her a better grasp on his ear. She tugged at it like she used to do when he was young.

"Why did you walk in my house without ringing the doorbell? I might've gone to get my friend and shot you dead."

The "friend" Gran'nola was referring to was the outdated pistol she kept locked in the top of her closet. But first, she'd have to find the key, hidden inside an old sardines can in the top drawer of her dresser, then drag over a step stool so that she could reach the top shelf. After that, she'd have to find the bullets, load them, and hope the weapon wasn't too rusty for her to pull the trigger. No one had to worry about Gran'nola's little "friend."

"You need to keep your door locked, Gran'nola," Malachi said, pecking her cheek. He couldn't pass up the opportunity to mention it. "I want you to be safe."

"The good Lord watches over me," she reasoned, shaking her finger in the air. "He who dwells in the secret place of the Most High shall abide under the shadow of the Almighty. I will say of the Lord, He is my refuge and my fortress. My God. My God. My God. In Him will I trust."

When Gran'nola put her finger in the air, she meant business. The conversation was over. Malachi couldn't—and wouldn't—argue with Scripture, but God had sent His Word *and* common sense. It was an argument for another day.

"I thought you were coming later this week," she said.

Malachi followed her into the kitchen. "No, ma'am. I needed to get to town early so I could take care of some things before the camp started."

Gran'nola's eyes lit up whenever Malachi talked about baseball. It was her love of the game and her fascination with Hank Aaron that had sparked his interest in the first place. While all his friends had aspired to earn their fame on the basketball court or the football field, Malachi's field of dreams had always been the baseball diamond. *That* dust he loved.

"They've been announcing it at church every Sunday, and I saw that Trenton man talking about it on the sports part of the news." Gran'nola glanced at the TV screen, clearly wondering what had happened to the sound.

"It was up pretty loud," Malachi said, picking up the remote. He unmuted the television but lowered the volume a tad.

"I like to hear it when I'm back in the bedroom."

"What happened to the television I set up the last time I was here?" Malachi questioned. He'd mounted a fifty-two-inch high-definition television on the wall above the armoire in her bedroom. If one of her brothers or his cousin had come to stake claim to it, there was going to be some trouble.

"There are too many buttons. I can't get that thing to work right half the time," she complained. "And when I do, it looks so big and bright, it hurts my eyes."

"What do you mean, you can't get it to work right? All you have to do is hit the power button. I wanted you to have a larger screen. And it's called HD. It's supposed to look bright."

"I don't like it. Do you know you can see people's cavities when they open their mouths? There's something wrong with that." Gran'nola shook her head disgustedly.

Malachi pulled out a kitchen chair and plopped down on the cushion. It felt good to be home, even with Gran'nola and her funny ways. Part of being home also meant bearing with the blasting television, Gran'nola's habit of rising at the crack of dawn, and the incessant ringing of her telephone.

Sure enough, it wasn't long before the phone was ringing off the hook. Gran'nola was one of fourteen children, and since she was the eldest of the Burke crew, her brothers and sisters called her daily to complain about one another, to update her on happenings at their family-founded church, and to gossip.

"Mimi, guess who's here?" Gran'nola said. "Malachi. Yes, he got here just a little while ago.…Well, I don't know; he just walked in the door.… How long are you staying, Malachi?"

"I'm not sure yet," Malachi said, deciding to check the fridge for Gran'nola's Sunday leftovers. "Tell Aunt Mimi I said hello and to fix me a chocolate chip cake."

Gran'nola passed along the message. Malachi knew he'd have his favorite cake by tomorrow morning, if not before. All the Burke women could burn in the kitchen, but Aunt Mimi had a special talent for whipping up the moistest cakes he'd ever tasted.

Malachi opened the crisper drawers where Gran'nola sometimes kept fruit. There was nothing there but a head of lettuce. Even the freezer, where he'd always been able to find a television dinner, contained only a few bags of unidentifiable meat and two packages of frozen vegetables—spinach and chopped broccoli.

He waited until Gran'nola was off the phone with Aunt Mimi, and then he asked her, "Gran'nola, where's your food? Have you been eating?"

"Now, when have you known me not to eat? Yes, I eat. There's only one of me. How much food do you expect one woman to consume?"

"But there's nothing cooked, and I don't see any leftovers."

"I had a piece of cheese toast and some coffee for breakfast, I had a sweet potato for lunch, and I'll probably have a can of soup for dinner." Gran'nola opened the cabinet above the stove. "There're two cans of beef stew," she said, evidently satisfied. "I can make some rice, and we'll eat good tonight."

Eat good? Malachi's stomach would disagree. He'd go to the grocery store tomorrow. For today, however, he needed another option.

"Let's go out for dinner," he suggested. "I saw a new hibachi place when I was driving in."

Gran'nola frowned. "What's that?"

"It's a Japanese restaurant where they cook the food at the table using the hibachi grill. It's delicious. You'll love it, I promise."

She waved her hand dismissively. "Oh, I've been to that place, for your uncle Ellis's birthday. The chef came out and did all these tricks, throwing eggs in the air and making a volcano with the rice and onions. All the while, I'm thinking to myself, *I wish he'd go ahead and cook so we can eat.*"

Malachi laughed. "Yep. They put on a show. But did you enjoy the food?"

She smiled. "Rice is rice. There's nothing special about that. But the shrimp tasted so good, I dreamed about it for three days."

"Then that's where we're going." Malachi was relieved that he wouldn't have to endure a meal poured from a can. If it came down to it, Malachi could survive on most anything, but he'd grown accustomed to the dishes prepared by his personal cook, Chef Devlin. Even though he was on the disabled list for the season, Malachi had to maintain his athletic build and his proper nutritional intake. When he returned to the roster, he didn't want to have to battle weight gain. *If* he returned to the roster. Most of the decisions in his life had been based on baseball. How could he turn that off? *Could* he learn to live without it?

At the sound of Gran'nola's riding mower, Malachi looked out the window and saw his uncle Bud behind the wheel, wearing an oversized straw hat and oil-soaked gloves.

"Oh, that's Bud, coming to finish up out back. He cut the front and the sides, but by the time he got back around to the utility shed, he'd ran out of gas," Gran'nola said. She swept a broom across Malachi's feet.

"I'm glad he's taking care of the yard for you," Malachi said. "You don't need to be out there."

"That's what y'all think. I know I can do my own yard, but I let Bud do it because he needs something to do. And it helps keep his mind preoccupied, so he has something to do besides turn up beer cans all day."

"Good for Uncle Bud," Malachi said.

His uncle had enjoyed his morning, midday, and evening cold brews, but he'd told Malachi he was cutting back for the sake of his liver. Malachi had wanted to believe him; but, since he'd made the same pledge before and lasted only two or three days, at the most, Malachi hadn't gotten his hopes up. Maybe this time, Uncle Bud's promise would stick.

"His gout started flaring up worse and worse until he couldn't stand it. We went up here to the clinic, and the doctor told him he wouldn't have as many problems if he cut back on the alcohol. So he did. He might drink one a week now. If that."

Malachi went outside to greet his uncle. He cupped his hands over his mouth so that his voice would carry over the rumbling engine of the mower.

Uncle Bud turned off the engine and jumped off the mower with more ease than most seventy-year-olds. He'd lived in the country all his life, and his muscular arms, stout back, and big-calved legs showed that he was no stranger to manual labor. In the wintertime, he still chopped his own wood for his fireplace, and in the summer, he tended a small garden of cucumbers, tomatoes, okra, and bush beans. With his physique, the man could have passed for someone fifteen years his junior. Until he smiled.

In addition to alcohol, Uncle Bud had been addicted to taffy for as long as Malachi could remember. And his fear of the dentist had begun even earlier. The way Gran'nola told the story, Uncle Bud was so traumatized from a cavity he'd had filled when he was seven that he'd sworn never to visit the dentist again. And, as an adult, he hadn't. Malachi was surprised he still had as many teeth as he did.

And the man had no shame.

"My main man," Uncle Bud crooned. "That's you in this big machine?" He gestured toward the black SUV.

"A rental," Malachi said. "I need some wheels to get around while I'm here."

Uncle Bud snatched a handkerchief from his front pocket and wiped the sweat dripping from the tip of his nose and his chin. "I thought that was somebody from the church in there. I know most of them are family, but they get on my nerves," he said, spitting into the bushes. "They brought in a new pastor with his whole family, and now they think they own the church. I don't care whose name is on the sign. That's the Burke family's church. That's our legacy."

Malachi merely nodded, figuring it was futile to disagree. Gran'nola had always said that the Burke family may have founded it, but God owned it. Uncle Bud may have fought a drinking problem, but that had never kept him from shirking his duties at the church. He was responsible for the maintenance—mostly cleaning the baptismal pool once a month and overseeing the groundskeeping. Every Sunday, he was at least an hour late for church, but at least he attended. Back row. Right side. Always.

Malachi picked up a rake and a shovel and propped them against the utility shed. "Uncle Bud, tell me truth. How is Gran'nola doing?"

"She's doing fine. Didn't you see her in there? She's her normal, spry self. Except for that leg, of course. It cuts up on her from time to time."

"She's losing weight."

"That's because she's listening to that doctor on television telling everybody what they should and shouldn't eat. We lived off of pork and grease, and now, all of a sudden, it's a bad thing. I don't buy it. Look at me. I still look good." He punched himself in the chest. "And strong. I bet I could send a baseball flying farther than you."

"I don't doubt it," Malachi said. "Maybe you can help me down at the camp, Unc."

Uncle Bud had taught him how to swing the bat with power. There would be boys there who needed to learn that skill.

"I'm there," Uncle Bud said, climbing back on the mower. "Let me finish this yard so Nola won't try and get out here to do it herself. I still need to run back home for that bag of cucumbers I picked from my garden."

"Good. She needs something more than a head of lettuce in the refrigerator," Malachi said. "We're going out to dinner tonight. Otherwise, I might starve by morning."

"Then I really better get going so I can have time to shower up," Uncle Bud said, inviting himself to dinner.

By mealtime, the word would be out. Malachi figured he had better call for a reservation to account for the rest of the Burke crew who'd show up. He didn't mind. In their own way, each of them had contributed to his success. But there went his plan to shut everybody out for the first few days.

Uncle Bud flew around the tree trunk near the shed like a driver on a racetrack. A rock kicked out behind the mower and hit Malachi on the shoulder. Another one pinged his knee.

He laughed it off. *Welcome home,* he told himself.

6

Malachi

Word that Malachi was in town had spread like the winter flu, and the next morning, he knew it would be nearly impossible to stay incognito. He'd talked so much about his grandmother over the years that everyone knew Nola Burke. And since her contact information had been listed in the city phone directory for half a century, they also knew where she lived. The media hadn't been disrespectful enough to set up camp outside of her home, but they'd called several times that morning already.

Even Gran'nola, the usual chatterbox, had grown tired of their calls.

"If I had a dollar for every time that phone rang, I'd be millionaire," she fussed. "You'd think people would get tired of calling if they didn't get an answer the first time."

"I apologize, Gran'nola. I wish you'd get a private number."

"These calls will stop soon enough. They want you, not me. The hometown hero. From him to whom much has been given, much is required."

"Hero?" Malachi said, locking the house door behind them. "I think that's a bit of a stretch."

"Say what you will, but that's what they called you on the morning news."

The coverage of his return and of the baseball camp had been on every local station, and Gran'nola had flipped triumphantly from channel to channel.

Malachi's publicist, Donna McBride, had reached out to him several times about potential TV interviews, but he'd turned them down, despite her pleading.

"It's for your foundation, Malachi," Donna had insisted during her latest phone call. "And it's for you. You need to keep your name on the media's mind. Stay relevant. If you don't, they'll find another kind-hearted, handsome baseball player to dote on. You know how they love you."

They loved him now, Malachi thought. But all it would take was one mistake, one mishap, or one misunderstanding, and they'd drag him through the mud like they'd done to so many others.

"Then what was the point of uploading that electronic press kit to the foundation's Web site?" Malachi asked as he parked outside the grocery store. "Everything they need is there. The dates, times, location, and requirements. The Q&A, with tons of quotes. The mission statement. High-resolution photos. What else do they need? If they want to hear from me, they can meet me at the baseball field on Friday afternoon. I'll do one press conference, Donna. One. "

Donna sighed. Malachi could tell when she was tired of putting up a fight with him. "So, all you're doing is the interview for the feature in the *Greensboro Ledger*. For all eighteen people who read it."

"That's the only one." Malachi turned off the ignition and reached into the console for his sunglasses. No baseball cap this time. It would give him away. "I'll talk to you later, Donna. I'm out with my grandmother."

"But Trenton Cason is asking for just five minutes. His station has the highest rating in the area, and he's my college friend. We go way back."

"Then he'll understand when you tell him no." Malachi wasn't giving in. "Thank you for all you do. I'll talk to you later."

He hung up before she could start to plead with him again. But before he forgot, he texted Katrene to send Donna a box of her favorite chocolate-covered strawberries. One bite, and she would forgive him.

Gran'nola zipped her purse and hooked it over her shoulder. "Why do we have to come all the way over here to this store?" she wanted to know. "What's wrong with the store down the street from my house?"

"They have a better variety of fresh fruits and vegetables here, plus more organic options."

Gran'nola opened the passenger door and carefully slid down until her feet were firmly on the ground. Malachi ran around to assist her, but she slapped his hand away.

"What do you think I do when you're not here?"

Malachi chuckled. "Can I at least push the grocery cart, or is that asking too much?"

"You can get the cart for me, but when we're in the store, I can handle it."

Malachi pulled a cart from the corral and wheeled it to the store entrance, where he surrendered it to Gran'nola. He watched her maneuver carefully among the displays of fresh vegetables. It was her leg. She needed the cart to keep herself steady.

"Get whatever you want, Gran'nola. I'm going back to the seafood department to check out the selection."

"Uh-huh," she answered, half listening. She'd lost herself in squeezing the cucumbers and thumping the squash to test for ripeness.

Their meal at the Japanese restaurant the night before had Malachi craving seafood. His "food moods," as his personal cook called them, drove Chef Devlin crazy. Every week, his chef planned a menu of dishes with various culinary influences, but Malachi would often throw a wrench in the plan by requesting Italian for the entire week. The next week, he'd binge on Thai, and the next, he'd swear off meat, until finally he let Chef Devlin have his way.

At the restaurant, Uncle Bud hadn't been able to decide what he wanted, so Malachi ordered several options. Gran'nola and Uncle Bud had kept their dinner outing a secret, so no one else in the family had joined them. Even so, the three of them had ordered enough food for eight people as they feasted happily in the private dining area.

As he scanned the seafood selection, Malachi noticed the woman beside him making a sorry attempt to pretend she was scrolling through the apps on her phone, when she was really trying to sneak a photo of him. Without taking his eyes off the jumbo shrimp, he said, "It would be easier to just ask me for a picture."

She covered her mouth with a box of organic oatmeal. "Oh my gosh. I'm so embarrassed. Was I that obvious?"

"Yes," Malachi said. "But it's all good." Then he leaned in so the woman could take a selfie.

She handed him the oatmeal. "Can you sign this?"

He took the pen she handed him. "They might charge you more than four bucks for it if I sign it before you pay for it," he said, scribbling his autograph across the front.

Her eyes widened. "They wouldn't dare. Would they?"

"I'm kidding."

"Thank you so much," the woman said, clutching the oatmeal box to her chest. "My son is going to freak out when he hears that I met you. He's the biggest Malachi Burke fan on the planet."

"Malachi Burke—I knew it! I told my wife it was you."

Malachi hadn't noticed the older couple roaming behind him.

"I don't know if her son is your biggest fan," the man said, nodding to the oatmeal woman. He grabbed his baseball cap by the brim and turned it around to reveal Malachi's number, 44. "You and Hammerin' Hank put this number on lockdown for me. Two of Major League Baseball's finest."

"Thank you, sir," Malachi said, humbled. He was amazed by the number of older men who respected his baseball career.

"May I?" The man pulled a cell phone from his back pocket.

"Certainly," Malachi said, then waited as the gentleman handed his cell phone to the oatmeal woman so she could snap a photo of him and his wife with Malachi.

Before he knew it, the scene from the airport was replaying itself.

It probably wouldn't be the last time. New Yorkers had gotten used to seeing him around the city, and though he was asked for the occasional autograph, it didn't compare to the attention he received in Greensboro. There'd been times in his career when being noticed in public ballooned his ego, times when it had irritated him, and times such as now, when he appreciated the love.

As the line of folks waiting for his autograph dwindled, Malachi noticed a woman watching him from afar. Usually, the women who lingered until last wanted something more than an autograph, but she looked more conservative than most of the ladies who made bold requests of him in the past—sign body parts, meet her later, or have a private baseball game in the middle of the empty stadium. When he made eye contact and gave a little wave, she turned and walked away with no acknowledgment of his friendly gesture.

Must be a Phillies fan.

Finally having made his selection of seafood, Malachi went in search of Gran'nola. He found her wandering the aisle of fruit juice. Standing nearby was the same woman who'd snubbed him from afar. She was easy to notice in her yellow sundress. Observing her up close, he admired her skin. It was golden. Pretty. When did Greensboro start putting them out like this?

"Hey, baby," Gran'nola said. She pointed to the top shelf. "Have you ever had papaya juice?"

The woman in yellow lifted her head, clearly thinking that that his grandmother's question was addressed to her. Then she saw Malachi. And their eyes locked.

She was beautiful in a simple sort of way. No makeup. No manicured nails. No exquisite jewelry. No stilettos. Just the sundress and a pair of sandals with cute pink toenails. He couldn't help but notice. He'd always been into feet.

Malachi smiled at her in an attempt to make himself approachable. "How are you?"

"Great, thanks," she answered blandly. She turned and walked in the opposite direction.

Maybe a Braves fan.

Malachi took two bottles of papaya juice off the shelf and added them to Gran'nola's cart. By now, it was getting heavy to push, so she finally agreed to let him take over pushing it for the rest of their shopping trip. She still gripped the side like a child who'd been warned by her mother not to wander off. Before long, they'd paid for their purchases, somehow having gotten through the checkout lane without anyone else recognizing Malachi, and were bouncing up the driveway to Gran'nola's.

"Look at your aunt Mimi," Gran'nola said as they parked. "I told her about bending over and putting all her best assets in the air."

Minerva "Mimi" Burke was tending the small flower garden on the side of Gran'nola's house. Once upon a time, there had been a hand-built wooden jungle gym that Malachi and his cousins would play on after church or whenever the family got together. Always crafty, Uncle Bud had patterned it after one he'd seen at the overpriced hardware store, even down to the landing beside the swings that was supposed to mimic a pirate's lookout. Like Malachi, his cousins had all attended college out of state or had simply moved from North Carolina to start careers or families elsewhere. Without much use and upkeep, the hot North Carolina summers and icy winters weathered it down until Gran'nola had finally had it hauled off.

"What's Aunt Mimi doing?" Malachi asked, releasing the lever to lift the automatic trunk.

"Planting petunias."

"I hope she brought my chocolate chip cake," he said, his mouth already salivating at the thought of a piece quickly warmed to just the right temperature in the microwave. Sweets were a rare indulgence in Malachi's diet, but he had a weakness for the cakes Aunt Mimi cooked from scratch.

"You know she has your cake," Gran'nola said. "She would've brought it over last night if she didn't have her bowling league. That's the only reason she didn't come to dinner with us. But it was probably for the best. Look how big she's getting. I'm going to buy her a T-shirt that says 'WIDE LOAD' on the back."

Malachi hid his amusement. The older Gran'nola got, the blunter she became.

"That's not nice, Gran'nola."

"Why? I told her that very thing. Tell the truth to shame the devil."

Gran'nola hobbled through the grass and up the steps to the back porch. "Mimi," she hollered. "Didn't you hear me and Malachi drive up? You need to get your hearing checked. Somebody could've snuck up on you, and you wouldn't have even known it."

Aunt Mimi stood, her aging body not allowing her to pop us as quickly as she used to do.

"I can hear fine," she insisted. "And anybody who tries to jump me from behind is going to get a rude awakening." She used her hand to shield her eyes from the sun. "Malachi, you're the only one of my great-nephews who gets more handsome every time I see him. You should see those cousins of yours. Their heads are getting bigger and bigger. They have the Burke head, you know. You should be thankful to God that you take after your mama on that. Both of you have nicely proportioned heads."

"They've always had big heads," Malachi said, hugging his aunt. "That's how they used to be able to beat me up. They'd ram into me and knock me over." It was the family's running joke.

"Go look in there on the kitchen counter," Aunt Mimi said. She pulled off her gardening gloves and beat them against her thigh. Potting soil fell down her pant legs to her shoes, and she stomped them on one of the rocks that lined the flower bed.

"Let me get the groceries unloaded first," he said, hastily heading to the trunk.

Within fifteen minutes, he'd unloaded and unpacked the grocery bags. Besides the papaya juice, Gran'nola's bags were full of her normal pantry and refrigerator staples. Malachi had purchased the items he preferred, telling her she was welcome to it all, but Gran'nola made it clear that avocado chips and meatless burgers weren't to her liking.

Gran'nola worked methodically to shelve her items the way she liked them. Malachi yielded to her perfectionist tendencies and settled down with a piece—make that two pieces—of chocolate chip cake. There were two cakes. One was for family who would undoubtedly begin to swing by during the week. And the other bore a sticker that read "Hello

My Name Is," on which his aunt had written "Malachi" in bold marker. One of the Burke family's unspoken rules was that if your name was on something edible, it was off limits to anyone and everyone else. An extra pan of baked spaghetti was always tagged by Gran'nola for Rhonda. An extra casserole dish of chicken pie was tagged for Kieva by Aunt Suge. And Uncle Mack labeled two containers of his world-famous chicken salad for Nadia. That was how it was, and how it had always been.

"This right here has made my day," Malachi said, licking gooey melted chocolate off his fingers. "I'm telling you, it's turned my whole life around."

"Then my job is done," Aunt Mimi said. "How long are you going to be home?"

Malachi shrugged. "Probably a month or so. I'm in no rush to go back to New York. I need some time away to think. I don't have a reason to run back to an empty place."

"You sure it's empty?" Gran'nola asked.

"Absolutely." Malachi looked her in the eyes. Gran'nola always said that a man who couldn't look you in the eyes was lying. But he knew for a fact that his condo was free of any lipstick tubes, extra toothbrushes, or pairs of earrings. Clear of any evidence of females trying to stake their claim.

That hadn't been the case during Gran'nola's last visit to New York two years ago. Malachi had given his housekeeper, Bahati, specific instructions to clean, box, and seal any items around his place that could've belonged to a woman—anything that hinted at a female's presence. It wasn't until the third day of Gran'nola's visit that she'd discovered a pink pair of yoga pants belonging to Alexandria in the clothes dryer.

There he was, a grown man, getting an hour-long lecture on virginity. Listening to the evils of living with a woman who wasn't his wife.

It was too late. He'd violated all the rules. More than once. Even more than twice.

Alexandria had been Malachi's on-again, off-again girlfriend for almost six years. She wasn't concerned about his money, since she'd gotten a hefty inheritance through a trust fund and also added to her net worth with her own well-paying job as a financial analyst for a pharmaceutical company.

Alexandria was beautiful, spontaneous, and fun. She also didn't like to be pinned down. And after his years as a player—and not just on the baseball diamond—she'd broken his heart. It had ignited his escapades in an attempt to make her jealous, but she never seemed to be peeved. Alexandria would show up in his life when she wanted to and demand his attention. And she'd always gotten it—until recently. Thank God, he was free from her. He used to go to bed thinking about her, but she hadn't even been a thought last night when he'd finally lain down.

Until her risqué text message.

He'd been lying in bed, listening to the sounds of crickets and counting the number of pickup trucks that roared by in the distance. It had taken all his willpower to erase the message without responding. Fighting fleshy urges wasn't for the weak, and so he'd prayed for strength. He'd actually gotten down on his knees beside the full-sized bed in his old room and prayed for strength to stay the course.

"Malachi's a grown man," Aunt Mimi was telling his grandmother. "You should know by now that you can't control his life."

"I don't want to control his life," Gran'nola said. "I want God to control his life."

Malachi stopped when he noticed a carton of whole milk on the top shelf of the cabinet, along with a tub of butter and two containers of yogurt. Aunt Mimi seemed to notice at the same time.

"Gran'nola, I don't think that cabinet is going to stay very cold," he said.

She stared at him, confused.

Malachi pointed. "Your milk, butter, and yogurt didn't make it to the fridge."

She grunted and snatched them off the shelf as the phone started to ring.

"You say I can't hear, but evidently you can't see, if you thought that was the refrigerator," Aunt Mimi joked.

"You know good and well I didn't think the cabinet was the fridge. I was distracted."

"Of course you were." Malachi gave Gran'nola a kiss on the cheek and looked at the caller ID on her cordless phone.

"Who is that? A member of your fan club?" Gran'nola smirked. She turned to Aunt Mimi. "He's been getting calls from reporters day in and day out," she explained.

Malachi wished it was one of the reporters again. They were easy to ignore. But the caller ID showed a New York number that he'd stored in his memory bank six years ago.

Alexandria's.

"Nobody that either of us needs to talk to," Malachi said, letting the call roll over into voice mail. She couldn't leave a message, since Gran'nola's mailbox had reached capacity. That was best. What Alexandria had to say probably wasn't suitable for his grandmother's innocent ears.

7

I pumped my arms to keep up with Farrah's long stride as we lapped the high-school track for a fifth time. We'd started power walking together regularly over a year ago to tone my physique for the wedding and, more important, the honeymoon. Farrah enjoyed the brisk walks, but I preferred swimming. I could already see the muscle tone returning to my arms and legs after my winter hiatus from the rec center. Now that it was summer, I was a regular there, swimming laps as often as three times a week. The swimming pool was my compromise until I could make it to the ocean. But not just any ocean—I wanted to fly to Hawaii and swim in the Pacific.

"You should've seen him," I said to Farrah, recounting my sighting of Malachi at the grocery store. "People were flocking around him. He was eating it up."

Farrah checked the calorie counter on her wristband and upped the speed of her stride again. "He was probably just showing some love to his fans. And how do you think it's going to look when you interview him tomorrow, and he recognizes you? You didn't even speak to the man. Not professional at all."

"I know," I admitted. "That was a totally rude thing to do. I just…I don't know. But why are you taking his side?"

"How can I take his side when I don't even know the brother? What I do know is that as long as you harbor even a pea-sized amount of bitterness in your heart, you're going to look at every man like the enemy."

"That's not true," I protested.

"Believe what you want to believe. This is not a blind date. It's an interview."

Beads of sweat were trickling down my back, and I could feel the moisture starting to gather on my scalp. Curly hair plus sweat always equaled a bundle of frizz on top of my head. I pushed the elastic band around my temples further back to the crown. My interview with Malachi was scheduled for ten o'clock the next morning, and I didn't want to show up looking like a high schooler with my hair in a ponytail, even though that was the easiest option. Farrah was right to call me out. That's why I loved her. I was a professional, and I would treat the interview as such. But I wasn't going to let Farrah do my makeup. It was an interview, not a photo shoot.

Farrah and I passed two teenage girls who were clearly pretending to be at the track for fitness but whose true motive was to catch the attention of the group of boys in the middle of the football field. They'd met with some success, I saw, as one of the boys gave them the universal sign for "Call me," holding his hand to his ear like a phone receiver. Evidently satisfied with his invitation, the shorter of the two girls tied the bottom of her tank top in a knot, baring her midriff. She was too naive to understand now, but I hoped she would soon arrive at the epiphany that things like toned abs might get 'em but wouldn't keep 'em.

"All I'm saying is, 'pro athlete' and 'playboy' are usually synonymous," I said, still trying to prove that point. "Can you just agree with me on that?"

"I refuse to get into this conversation with you," Farrah said. "Get the facts. Get the story. Take care of business. Then you can go on your merry way, and he on his."

"That's my plan."

After two cool-down laps to return our heart rates to normal, we headed back to Farrah's car. With the windows down and the radio on, we sat in the parking lot and enjoyed each other's company. I twisted the cap off a bottle of water and guzzled half of it before taking a break. I hadn't realized how thirsty I was.

"The weather's perfect," Farrah said. "It's a great day for ice cream. Let's go."

I eyed her incredulously. "You just made me power walk a marathon around that track, and now you want me to eat ice cream? You must mean frozen yogurt."

"No. I mean ice cream."

I pulled off my tennis shoes and peeled off my socks. "Chocolate chip *would* be delicious right about now."

"And you know how I love a good waffle cone," Farrah said. "I can already see my double scoop of butter pecan."

"Mmm. And you know else what I can see?" I said, baiting her.

"What?"

"I can see how different we're going to look in our swimsuits when you spend the summer eating ice cream and I spend it drinking fresh fruit smoothies. I have a refrigerator full of apples, bananas, mangos, pineapple, and strawberries. Doesn't that sound even better?"

Farrah started up the car. "You can take the fun out of anything, you know that?"

"The fun *and* the calories. Your thighs will thank me." I reached under the seat for my cell phone. The screen showed a text message from Shelton.

Malachi had to cancel for tomorrow. Meet him at the field Friday night for the opening rally.

"See?" I showed Farrah the text. "Mr. Ego's head is too big for our small-time community paper. And evidently Shelton thinks I have nothing better to do on a Friday night."

"You usually don't—let's keep it real," Farrah said. "And I'm out of commission, anyway, because my baby is coming home tomorrow."

"Another reason why you should stay away from dairy," I said with a chuckle.

Farrah gave me a playful shove in the shoulder. "Get the facts. Get the story. Get going," she reminded me.

That mantra replayed in my head as I pushed through the jostling crowd of eager children and hovering parents at the baseball field on Friday night. I wished I could skip to the "get going" part. I might have been able to conduct an interview if he'd been seated across a table from me, with nothing between us but my digital recorder, tablet, and foldable keyboard. Instead, there were hundreds of zealous young boys wielding baseball gloves. Balls were thrown in the air at random, looking like freshly popped corn kernels. *Pop! Pop! Pop!* Children lifted their heads and raised their arms with synchronized motion, ready to catch a ball, whether or not one had been thrown.

"This is a madhouse," a lady complained as she pushed past me. "All these boys are dressed the same, I'm afraid I'll never find my son."

It was a roaring sea of red and blue. Most of the boys had immediately pulled on the T-shirt they each had been handed as they entered through the gates. One of the shirts had even been stuffed into my hand, despite my insistence that I wasn't a parent.

"There's enough for everybody in Greensboro," the enthusiastic volunteer had assured me as he reached inside a torn cardboard box and produced another stack of red shirts.

"Excuse me sir, sir," shouted another woman, waving enthusiastically. "Can I trade this blue shirt for a red one?"

"No problem, pretty lady," the volunteer said. "It's my pleasure."

The woman who'd favored red over blue now jostled for a position at the front of the crowd of parents and boys. They'd roped off a section in front of a raised metal platform—the spot where I assumed King Malachi would step up in all his glory for his long-awaited appearance.

"Hey, Rae. What's up?"

I turned at the familiar voice. Jared was the *Ledger*'s only student intern from nearby North Carolina A&T State University. He was a journalism major who'd grown up in the city and knew all the best eateries, hangouts, and nuances. When Shelton had discovered that Jared was handy with a camera, he'd given him the title of staff photographer.

"Glad you could make it," I said. "You'll get some pretty good shots out here tonight."

Jared held his camera above his head and took an aerial shot of the crowd of hyper boys, now chanting in unison, "Malachi! Forty-four! Smash that ball and make it roar!" And, of course, a chant wouldn't be complete without an impromptu dance step to accompany it.

"These boys are off the chain," Jared said. "I love it. This is like a dream for them. Shoot, it's like a dream for me. *The* Malachi Burke."

A voice sounded over the intercom system, and the boys went wild when they realized it was Malachi. They started to jump and pump their fists when he appeared from behind the dugout and approached the platform.

"I hope you boys can play as good as you can dance," he began. "I was watching. I saw your moves out there."

There was an eruption of cheers and applause, which Malachi allowed to continue for at least a minute before holding up his hands to quiet the crowd. It took twice as long for a hush to fall over the boys.

Malachi was wearing a T-shirt that touted the name of his charity: Malachi Burke's "Batter Up" Foundation. Of course, I'd researched the history and mission of the organization; I'll admit I was impressed with his commitment to encourage young boys to "step up to the plate" in their academics, extracurricular activities, fitness, and family goals. The foundation was in its fifth year of charitable donations and programs, but this was the first "Batter Up" baseball camp.

"I'm going to get a little closer for some better shots of Malachi," Jared said, resting his zoom lens on his shoulder. "You want to come? I'll lead. You follow."

"No, I'm fine here," I said. "If I don't run into you again, I'll see you at the office later."

"Cool. I'll go through the shots, pick out some of the best, and drop you an e-mail. My summer school schedule is crazy, so I may not be in the office much. My dad doesn't want me on the five-year college plan. The fewer student loans I have, the better."

I held up my hand. "Student loans—never say those words again," I grumbled, having just taken my own out of forbearance. "If I only knew then what I know now."

"You sound just like everybody else," Jared said before going off to join the growing swarm of reporters, photographers, and cameramen. Evidently, the Greensboro media was scratching to tell a feel-good story after a week of bad news, including an exposed coaching scandal at a local high school, a couple of armed robberies, and a tragic car accident that had left an entire family dead.

The city needed a reprieve, and Malachi's visit seemed to be perfectly timed for it.

"Thank you all for coming out," Malachi continued. "It's an honor and privilege to see so many young boys who love the sport of baseball or who want to learn more about it. But the Batter Up Foundation doesn't just want you to be successful on the field; we want you to be successful off the field, too."

This time, it was mostly the parents who cheered. It seemed more mothers than fathers had taken it upon themselves to bring their sons to the opening celebration, and I'd already spotted a few women who looked ready to play a game or two with Malachi. They were the ones in the low tank tops and shorty shorts. The ones who caught the attention of the men who knew they shouldn't be looking but found themselves trying to catch a glimpse, anyway. It was hard trying *not* to catch a glimpse of what they had on full display.

"Tonight, I wanted to come out and greet you all, then give you a chance to meet the other coaches who will be working with you over the next couple of days. Make sure you grab a hot dog, chips, some fruit, and a drink. And take something home to your grandma, too," Malachi said, provoking a wave of laughter. "My grandma Nola is here, somewhere." He scanned the crowd. "She's the one who first introduced me to baseball and took me to all my practices, since my parents were working. You boys are here today because of her commitment to me."

Another round of cheers erupted.

That was sweet, I thought.

"And to you guys over here," Malachi said, pointing to the group of reporters, "stop calling my grandma's house. She can't gossip with her sisters if you're tying up her phone line."

"I know that's right," affirmed an elderly woman dragging along a folding chair. She stopped close to me. "But we're not gossiping; we're sharing news. You wait until I get that boy home."

"Sit down, Nola," said another woman carrying two hot dogs on paper plates. She waited until the older woman was settled in the chair, then set one of the plates on her lap. "This is Malachi's show, so let him run it. You know he's just making a joke."

I stepped to the side so I wouldn't block the women's view.

"Oh, no, you're fine," the older woman assured me. "I've seen that boy all his life. I'm his grandma Nola Burke. Or, as he calls me, Gran'nola."

"Nice to meet you," I said.

"And I'm her sister, Malachi's aunt Minerva Burke. Or, as everybody else calls me, Aunt Mimi," said the other woman, a piece of hot dog stuffed in one cheek. Then she lifted the remaining half of her hot dog. "You should go ahead and get a plate. There's a lot over there, but you know what happens when people see something for free." She leaned forward, as if sharing a secret, "They get greedy."

I laughed, more at the way she basically growled the words than at the words themselves. "I'm fine," I assured her.

Nola ripped open a bag of chips and dumped some on her paper plate. "You must be trying to keep your girlish figure. I don't blame you. Keep it as long as you can, because, one day, it's going to run away from you, and you'll be so out of shape that you couldn't catch it if you tried."

I laughed again. These women were a hoot. The people closest to the platform in front probably thought they had the best seats in the house, being only footsteps away from Malachi; but my quiet corner was vastly more entertaining.

Malachi's voice boomed over the intercom system once more, pulling my attention back to the person I was supposed to be listening to in the first place.

"If anyone has any problems or questions, look for my man Alonzo. He was the one handing out T-shirts at the front gate, and if I know him, he was handing out compliments, too. He'll take care of you." Malachi produced a baseball from beneath the podium, tossed it in the air, then cracked the bat, sending it flying far off into left field, away from the crowd.

I had to give it to him—he had an arm. If he could hit a ball that far with an injured shoulder, there was no telling what he could do when he was at his best.

"Malachi knows he's not supposed to be doing that," Nola fretted.

"Leave him alone," Mimi countered.

The way the Burke sisters carried on reminded me of Farrah and myself. Although they bickered, they would probably never let anyone or anything come between them.

"What's your name, baby?" Nola asked me.

"Rae Stevens. I'm actually supposed to interview your grandson for a feature in the *Greensboro Ledger*."

Nola took a sip from her can of grape soda. "So, you work with Shelton. You're the blessed one, because Malachi hasn't agreed to any other one-on-one interviews. He said he's going to talk to the other reporters as a group." She reached over and patted me on the knee. "I hooked you up. Told him he absolutely had to talk to the folks at the *Ledger*."

That's right. I remembered. The grandma he'd called for the sweet potato pies and ended up getting the inside scoop.

"We certainly appreciate it. You ladies have a wonderful evening. I have a story to write."

I left them so I could wander around and immerse myself in the environment. It was crucial for my story. The aroma of grilled hot dogs, the sight of the freshly painted lines on the field, the sounds of boys cheering with joy—it was all part of the picture I would paint with words in order to capture the life and legacy of Malachi Burke.

As I walked, I looked down and noticed the dirt that had collected on my black and silver tennis shoes. There were other shoes I would've rather worn, but these would clean easily, and I could toss the laces in the wash. I'd almost grappled over what was appropriate to wear for the interview. Farrah had suggested a sundress and strappy sandals, but I had decided that a pair of khaki Bermuda shorts and my green polo with the *Greensboro Ledger* logo was the best option. I was glad I'd followed my instincts. I liked the feel of beach sand between my toes, not dirt.

Malachi was beginning a press conference with the members of the media who remained, so I strolled over to listen in. He'd been media trained, I was sure of it. His words flowed easily and clearly, and he spoke in sound bites. He was captivating. No wonder he had women groveling at his feet.

After several minutes of busily scribbling notes, I looked up and saw his gaze pointed in my direction. He smiled, and I turned around to see who was standing behind me. There was no one there. Was that smile intended for me? Was he flirting? I lost my concentration for a moment, then flipped to a blank page in my notebook.

"Thanks, you guys," Malachi said, ending the conference. "And I'm serious—stop calling my grandma's house. If she roughs you up, I can't be held responsible."

"Show's over," said a voice behind me, loud enough for my ears alone.

I recognized it immediately. That voice had whispered "I love you" in my ear at least a thousand times. It was the voice of the local favorite. The voice of all things sports in Greensboro.

Trenton.

I locked my expression into a poker face before turning around to address my ex-fiancé. I didn't want to let him know what I was—or wasn't—thinking.

"Pretty much. At least for now." I pushed my pen through the wire coil at the top of my notebook. Trenton was in his station's embroidered polo, as well, but with black dress slacks and leather dress shoes. Only Trenton.

"I wanted to talk about his career and see how things are going. This camp is good for the kids and all, but I want the exclusive interview. Supposedly, he's not giving any one-on-ones," Trenton said, as if I needed an update. "His publicist couldn't work her magic for me, so I decided to come out here myself. Sometimes, you can't send a woman to do a man's job."

I couldn't believe he'd just said that. He was looking for a reaction, and I refused to give him one.

"Actually, he's doing one. And just one." I brushed past him, silently thanking Ms. Nola.

"Don't tell me it's for the *Ledger*," Trenton called after me.

But I ignored him. Ignored him like he'd ignored my calls when I was tearful and wanted answers, wanted closure.

For once, Trenton wanted something he couldn't get.

8

Malachi

Simple beauty. That's what Malachi had seen the first time he'd spotted her, at the store, and the same description came to mind tonight. She was pretty, but he detected a bit of an attitude. Her face hadn't cracked with any emotion when he'd smiled at her. And she hadn't given him the slightest hint at the grocery store that she was from the newspaper. Strange. But that was a woman. When a female wore a chip on her shoulder, a man could never figure out the who, what, when, where, or how. But Malachi would crack through that facade. He could feel it.

When he had noticed the logo on her shirt, he'd realized she was the one who would be interviewing him. Rae Stevens. She was nothing like the way he'd pictured her. He hadn't even known if the reporter would be a man or woman. She was definitely all woman. Not rough around the edges. He'd have his time with her after he wrapped things up.

Opening night for the baseball camp had been all of the success Malachi had hoped for, thanks to his team—especially Alonzo. He'd called his buddy on Tuesday night to ask for his help on Wednesday tying up some loose ends and taking care of some of the grunt work, and Alonzo had readily agreed. Malachi had had no choice but to reschedule with Rae. He hadn't realized until later that Alonzo had taken a day off from work, but, as promised, Malachi would compensate him for his time. A man who worked with as much dedication and selflessness as Alonzo deserved to be paid, even more so when he was committed to setting up a future for his family. Malachi admired the change he'd seen in Alonzo. He'd witnessed all his dirt, and then some. If Alonzo could change, anybody could.

Aunt Mimi hurried over to him. "Malachi, have you seen your grandma?"

"Not since we started. There's no telling where she is. You know how she is around people. She probably found some people she knew and started talking their heads off."

"I've looked everywhere," Aunt Mimi said frantically. "Alonzo even called her name over the intercom."

Malachi's radar went up. He didn't like the look of despair on Aunt Mimi's face or the way she was wringing her wrinkled hands. Something was wrong.

"What's your real concern, Aunt Mimi?" Malachi asked, trying not to raise his voice. There were still plenty of boys and their parents hanging around the field and taking pictures in the dugout. "Tell me what happened. Why does it matter if you can't find Gran'nola?"

Aunt Mimi sighed, her brow creased with concern. "About a month ago, your grandma got lost going home from my house."

"What do you mean?" It didn't make sense to Malachi. The sisters had lived just fifteen minutes apart since before he was born. How could Gran'nola get lost?

"She got lost," Aunt Mimi repeated. "Whenever she's at my house past nightfall, she always calls me when she gets home so I know she made it okay. I waited over thirty minutes, and she never called. I thought she must have stopped for gas or groceries, but that wasn't like her. Me and your uncle P.T. drove out looking for her."

Malachi bit his lip. Why was this the first he'd been told about this?

"She pulled into our driveway again an hour later. She got out of the car acting confused and saying things got mixed up in her head, and she couldn't figure out where to go, so she just kept driving around."

Malachi wanted to demand why no one had called him, but now wasn't the time. "Did you check the restrooms?" he asked instead, taking deep breaths to steady his anxiety.

"All of them," Aunt Mimi confirmed. "And I checked our cars and the parking lot."

Malachi noticed Rae Stevens standing over to the side. She approached him cautiously. "Is everything okay?"

"No," Malachi said bluntly. "We can't find my grandmother. I'm sorry, but I can't do an—"

"I'll help look," Rae interrupted him. "Where should I start?"

Malachi didn't know what to tell her. He was typically a quick thinker in times of crisis, but now that the situation affected him personally, he was having trouble putting together a plan. Where could she have gone? And with whom?

"Don't worry about it," Rae said. "I'll ask one of the people on your team to help me, if that's okay."

Malachi nodded. *Hold it together, man. Hold it together,* he kept telling himself.

Alonzo ran over to him after getting the update from Rae. "We're on it, man," Alonzo assured him. "You stay here—"

"No. I can't do that." Malachi fought off his rising panic. "I need to look for her."

He headed toward the rental SUV, unsure of what direction to go in first. Alonzo jumped into the driver's seat before Malachi had a chance to object.

"You ride along," Alonzo said. "I've got this."

Alonzo drove so slowly down the street that Malachi could've walked faster. At five miles per hour, they scanned the streets and the alleys between every building they passed.

"Gran'nola couldn't have gotten this far on foot," Malachi decided once they'd driven nearly half a mile. "Her knee can't handle it."

Alonzo made a U-turn in the middle of the street. "Let's double back," he suggested.

Malachi patted the back pocket of his shorts for his cell phone, then remembered he'd given it to Aunt Mimi for safekeeping.

"Got your phone?" he asked Alonzo. "We should call the police."

Malachi noticed a look of relief wash over his friend's face. "No need. There's Gran'nola."

She was waiting to cross the busy intersection near the park, and Rae Stevens had a guiding hand on her shoulder. As soon as Alonzo turned into the parking lot, Malachi jumped out of the vehicle and bolted to the middle of the crosswalk as the light changed to yellow. He held up his hand to stop the oncoming traffic.

When Gran'nola and Rae were safely on the opposite side, he ran to his grandma.

She frowned at him. "What was that all about? You're gonna mess around and get yourself killed running out in the middle of the street."

"Where have you been?" Malachi asked, trying to sound concerned rather than alarmed. His grandmother hated it when people fretted over her.

"I went to use the restroom," Gran'nola stated matter-of-factly.

"Across the street?"

"Have you seen those nasty bathrooms over here? I went to the women's *and* the men's, and both were downright disgusting. You need to have somebody come in and clean those up before tomorrow morning. I wouldn't want my child using them."

"There's a church down the street," Rae calmly explained, "so she went there to use the restroom. Then she sat down in the sanctuary to listen to the choir rehearsal."

"And I'm telling you, they can sing," Gran'nola said, throwing her hands in the air. "It sounded like melodies from heaven. I mean, our church choir can sing okay, but that choir had something special."

"Thank God you're okay," Malachi said. His heart was slowing to its normal pace. Five minutes more, and he would've lost it.

"Of course I'm okay. Why wouldn't I be? Mimi kept pumping all that water into me, trying to keep me hydrated. Or so she said. I have a seventy-nine-year-old bladder. I can't hold it forever."

Malachi saw Rae cover her mouth to stifle a laugh.

"And I'm sure you're Rae Stevens," Malachi said, taking advantage of the opportunity to formally introduce himself.

"I am," she said, suddenly seeming embarrassed. "At the store the other day...sorry about that. I should've introduced myself."

Malachi shrugged it off. "Today's a new day. Let's start with a clean slate."

"I'd like that," she said with a grin. "Nice to meet you."

It was the first smile she'd ever offered him. He took it and cherished it, because he didn't know when he'd get another one.

"I invited Rae over for breakfast in the morning," Gran'nola announced.

"You did?"

"Yep." She beamed. "I told her if there was anything she needed to know about you, she'd better talk to me, because I know it all. You might as well do the interview in the morning over some biscuits and country-fried steak."

Rae looked unsure as to how to respond. Gran'nola had a way of pushing people to do what she wanted them to, and she was so sweet, most didn't know how to object.

"Ms. Stevens might want to go ahead and take care of the interview tonight," Malachi said, speaking up for her. "She probably has a deadline."

"Rae didn't object when I invited her during our walking back from the church. Did you?"

Malachi looked at her with questioning eyes.

"No, I didn't. But it's up to you," she told him. "I can do the interview now or in the morning, whatever's more convenient. My deadline's not an issue, either way."

"Seven thirty, then," Gran'nola said, barging into the middle of their conversation. She proceeded to give Rae her address.

Malachi hoped Rae was flexible and wouldn't be aggravated by a second delay of the interview. Though, this time, the postponement hadn't been his doing.

"You need to take me to a real grocery store on the way home," Gran'nola said to Malachi, still completely unaware that they'd formed a search party for her.

Everyone on the team resumed his regular assignment when it was learned that Gran'nola had returned unscathed. Malachi sent Alonzo to scope out the bathrooms, asking him to call their emergency contact and request a thorough cleaning by the morning, in the event that the crew of volunteers found the job too overwhelming.

There was still an unfinished discussion with Aunt Mimi hanging over Malachi's head. He was furious that no one ever discussed important issues with him. Not even his parents had mentioned the episode of Gran'nola's getting lost, but Malachi wouldn't be surprised if his father had withheld the information from his mother. Like Malachi, Douglas Burke was generous in his financial support of Gran'nola, but, living in California, he saw her so rarely that he probably didn't realize how much his mother had aged. Malachi's mother had been begging her husband to move back to North Carolina when he retired, and Malachi hoped his father would listen, for once.

It was after ten at night when they returned home, but Malachi decided to call Aunt Mimi anyway. He wanted answers.

He retired to the second bedroom, which he'd claimed as his own as a kid. Growing up, he spent more time than any of his cousins with his grandmother, which was why she'd let him decorate the room to his liking. But the walls had since been stripped of the posters of his baseball hero, Hank Aaron. Gran'nola had replaced them with articles, clippings, and pictures spanning Malachi's entire career, from Little League to the big league.

"Her doctors think it may have been a small seizure that temporarily impaired her judgment," Aunt Mimi explained. "We didn't want to worry you."

"Will I ever be treated like a man and not the baby of the family?" Malachi asked. "If we can make informed decisions together, we can get Gran'nola the help she needs."

"Malachi." Aunt Mimi took a long pause. "Nola is getting old. There's no helping that. You live long enough, and you might find yourself in the same boat."

"What's aging have to do with enjoying a certain quality of life? Or with maintaining one's dignity? That's why they have diagnostic tests and advanced treatments. We shouldn't expect our minds and bodies to break down just because we get older."

"Ummm..."

Malachi could picture his aunt with her lips pressed together in a thin line. He already knew what was coming. The Burkes had always been hesitant to seek intervention from medical professionals. They all held that the reason their mother had died at age forty-nine, leaving their father to struggle to raise his children while working, was that she had been misdiagnosed by a doctor and given medicines she didn't need.

"If you think she might have a problem now, you definitely don't want her taking any medicine," Aunt Mimi said. "If they give you something to help with blood pressure, it causes your arthritis to flare up. And if they give you something to help with your eyes, it throws your hips out of joint. No, Malachi. You're wasting your time. Even if she had medicine to take, you know she would refuse."

Malachi surrendered, but only because he needed sleep. Baseball camp was set to start at ten in the morning, and he planned to arrive at least an hour early. It was only a twenty-minute drive to the site, so he technically could've slept in until at least nine o'clock. At least, that would have been the case if his grandma hadn't arranged for a breakfast guest.

Rae. Beautiful Rae, who had finally given him a smile.

9

I couldn't believe I'd agreed to have breakfast with Malachi and his grandmother so early on a Saturday morning. Seven thirty. Who did that? But Ms. Nola was so sweet that I hadn't been able to turn down the invitation. That, and the fact that I could tell by looking at her that she was the type who would whip up a wonderful spread from scratch. It would be a welcome change from the breakfasts I'd been eating for weeks—fruit smoothies, fruit salad, or a container of nonfat Greek yogurt and a bran muffin.

I had seen the sensitive side of Malachi when he'd thought his grandmother was missing, and I could sense the love he had for her. It was real. Almost tangible. That was why I'd stepped in to help. Plus, the woman had already endeared herself to me.

Having a living grandparent at our age was a blessing. My maternal grandfather had died before I was born, but my maternal grandmother and I had enjoyed a strong bond—even stronger than the tie between myself and my own mother. Nana had bathed me in unconditional love and would have given her last breath if it would mean I would get what I needed. A photograph of her wearing my graduation cap on the day I received my bachelor's degree still sat on my night-stand. It was the last picture taken of us together before her death from a massive heart attack eight days later. My life had never been the same.

That was why I'd sympathized with Malachi's anxiety. I'd felt a huge wave of relief when I found Gran'nola seated in the back pew of that church, swaying to the soul-stirring gospel music with her hands clasped in front of her bosom. I would've sat down beside her to listen, too, but I wanted to end the frantic search as soon as possible. When the song ended, I approached Ms. Nola and quietly whispered, "Your grandson is waiting for you. He's ready to head home."

I have to admit, she looked slightly disoriented for a moment before she responded. But she came willingly, holding my hand as we descended the brick steps in front of the church. One block later, I had been invited to breakfast.

And now I was here at her house, instead of rolled up between my bedsheets.

By the way the cars were parked in the driveway, I assumed they used the back door as the main entrance. Taking my chances, I headed for the back porch and rapped lightly on the screen door.

Malachi appeared, his broad shoulders and tall stature taking up the entire entryway. He was dressed like he was ready to head to the baseball field, in a new, freshly ironed shirt identical to the one he'd worn last night. The hem of his shorts met the tops of his calves. His very muscular calves. I averted my eyes back to his face. His very hand-some face.

"Good morning," he said, pushing the door open and standing aside so I could enter. "I hope you're hungry."

"Starving," I said. "And good morning to you."

A pan of freshly baked buttermilk biscuits, a skillet of country-fried steak with gravy, and a pan of hash brown casserole sat on a cooling rack by the stove. And I could smell bacon—probably sizzling to a perfect, crisp brown in the oven—and cinnamon apples.

"Gran'nola is serious about her food," Malachi told me. "She doesn't eat that much anymore, but she loves to cook for other people. I, for one, want to thank you for giving her a reason to lay it out this morning."

He pulled out a chair at the table, and I sat down.

"What did you make?" I asked, wondering if he had some hidden culinary skills. A man who could cook was always a plus. Not that it mattered in this case.

He grinned. "I was responsible for the drinks."

"Freshly squeezed orange juice?" I joked.

"Not quite. But I did wake up with the sun to give myself time to get the carton out of the fridge and to fill the glasses."

"Impressive," I said. I could feel my guard beginning to fall. Things weren't as awkward as I thought they would be. Ms. Nola's house was quaint and cozy; despite the obvious updates, I could tell she'd made it her home for years. "Ms. Nola is joining us, isn't she?"

"She'll be out in a few minutes," Malachi assured me as he sat down, "but she told me to go ahead and get started with the interview so we won't have to hold you up." He handed me a plate from the stack on the table. "We should eat while the food's still hot," he added. "But I can't promise I won't talk with my mouth full."

"For a meal like this, I think it's worth brushing manners aside," I said.

As I filled my plate, I reminded myself that this was an interview like any other, and that I should act as if we were meeting at a restaurant—where I would have ordered something small and concentrated on my list of questions. But the lure of the white gravy over the biscuits and steak almost made me forget my purpose.

"Is that all you're having?" Malachi asked, eyeing my plate. "You'll offend Gran'nola."

I covered my mouth with my napkin and quickly swallowed my bite of biscuit. "I didn't think I should gorge myself."

"Well, if she can see the bottom of your plate before you've even started eating, she's going to think you don't like her cooking."

"That couldn't be further from the truth," I told him. "I like to start off slow. Build my way up."

Malachi sliced through his biscuit and scooped a spoonful of peach preserves onto the fluffy insides. "Maybe I should take your advice. Especially since I'll be at the field all day."

"Speaking of advice," I said, seeing an open door for the interview, "what's the best advice you've been given? And the best advice you've given to someone else? Oh, wait a minute." I reached into my purse for my digital recorder. "You don't mind if I record this interview, do you? My hands are tied up at the moment." I held up my fork and knife.

"That's fine. It'll keep me on my best behavior, since this could be submitted as evidence in a court of law." He winked.

I pushed the button to start recording. "Ready when you are."

Malachi stretched back in his chair. "The best advice I've been given was to watch my money. My first and only financial advisor told me to set myself up so I wouldn't have to worry about the future, and to live like my money would run out tomorrow."

"Did you listen?"

"I did. Some of my buddies who came into the league around the same time? No. But they wish they would have."

"And the best advice you've given to someone else?" I asked, cutting into my country-fried steak.

Malachi didn't miss a beat. "Stay away from that girl."

I shifted in my seat, not sure how to respond to such an unexpected answer. I'd thought he would say something about following your dreams, pursuing your passions—the textbook answers that athletes gave when they wanted to sound like life coaches and role models.

"You consider yourself a relationship expert?" I asked.

"Far from it."

"Do you take your own advice?"

I doubted it, given the number of images I'd seen online of Malachi with a woman draped over his arm. It would be like an alcoholic teaching lessons on sobriety.

"Not all the time," Malachi admitted. "But I'm getting better at being a judge of character."

At this point, I could have taken the interview in a number of directions, but I doubted anyone in Greensboro wanted to hear about

Malachi's philandering ways. I definitely didn't want to write about them.

"I suppose that helps as you mentor the boys in your Batter Up Foundation," I said. "I've read about it, but I want to hear you talk about it in your own words."

From there, we transitioned into our given roles—I as the journalist, Malachi as the athlete. I tried not to ask the carbon-copy questions that would make for a boring article. But neither was I trying to expose something underhanded. The members of the community who heralded our publication did so because they took pride in their city and in the people who'd been raised there. They honored legacy. Which gave me an interesting twist.

Ms. Nola had suggested it herself. She'd said she was the woman to talk to if I wanted to know anything about Malachi.

I heard the creak of a door opening and closing; a moment later, Ms. Nola appeared. She meandered slowly into the kitchen, her presence bringing with it the scent of lathery soap and baby powder.

I grinned. "Just the woman I need to talk to."

"Good morning, sweetie," Ms. Nola said, her bright eyes dancing with the early morning sunlight that shone through the open kitchen curtains.

"Good morning, Gran'nola," Malachi said, rising to help her to the table.

"I was talking to Rae," she said, patting her grandson on the back. "I've seen you all morning."

I stood and wrapped Ms. Nola in a hug. She was soft and a tad bit mushy. Hers was the kind of body that could soothe a colicky baby to sleep immediately, with a lap where any two-year-old toddler would happily nestle, even if she was a stranger.

"Thank you for the delicious breakfast."

"Did you get enough?"

I glanced at Malachi, who looked down at my plate with a grin.

"I'm just getting started," I admitted, sitting down again. "I wanted to make sure I took care of my interview first."

"Malachi, she's a woman who's about her business," Ms. Nola said. "And pretty, too. I bet if you had somebody like Rae in your life, you'd have a reason to come home more often."

"Probably so," Malachi said. He raised his glass of orange juice to his lips.

I could feel the flush rise in my face, but I ignored their comments. I wasn't about to get sucked into the conversation, because I knew how it would end. Ms. Nola would try to dig into my love life. Or, in my case, the lack thereof. And—let's face it—there would be no way I could lie my way through her interrogation. I didn't want the inquiries turned on me when I was the one who'd come to ask the questions.

Malachi's charm could've easily drawn me in, but I knew the facts. His past relationships with women were sketchy, and I had no plans to be added to his list of pursuits and conquests. I'd seen his type before. I bet he hoped I was gullible, but I wasn't that woman who fell for a man because of fame and fortune.

But my thoughts on him didn't matter. Like Farrah had said, "Get the facts. Get the story. Get going."

Gran'nola sat down at the table with half of a grapefruit that she'd taken from the refrigerator and unwrapped. "Where are your notes?" she asked me. "I want to see if Malachi has been telling the truth."

"I haven't written anything yet," I told her. "I've been recording our conversation."

She eyed my recorder. "And what happens if that thing gets erased?"

I forked the last piece of my country-fried steak into my mouth. After swallowing, I said, "Then I'll have to come back for breakfast again so you can tell me truth."

Nola grinned. "That sounds like a deal. You can come eat with me anytime, whether Malachi is here or not. I especially enjoy company that isn't family. They're always trying to boss me around. Sometimes, they forget I'm the oldest. And the boss."

"*Bossy* is more like it," Malachi mumbled under his breath.

For the rest of our interview, Nola busied herself with scooping out the pulpy segments of her pink grapefruit, listening in and interrupting only twice, to tell me about the time when one of Malachi's cousins had duct-taped him to the back of the basement door for being a tattle-tale, and also to describe how he'd once worked with his uncle Mack for three consecutive Saturdays to earn enough money to pay for the church window he'd broken with a fly ball when he was supposed to be inside for the worship service.

"You were right," I told her. "You have all the juicy stories."

"That's nothing. I haven't even told you the good stuff."

Malachi stood and started clearing the table. "I don't remember any of it. In fact, I think half of the stories you tell are things you've made up."

"Nonsense." She tapped her temple with her finger. "I've got them all stored up here. And if I was a writer like this pretty little lady, I'd write them all down." Ms. Nola handed him her plate of grapefruit rind. "My mind may get foggy on some things, but I remember some stuff as clear as if happened yesterday."

"Then you must remember that we have to be at the field soon, so we need to leave now," Malachi told her. "Are you sure you want to come, Gran'nola? I'll be out there all day, and it's supposed to be hot. The high will be in the eighties."

"Being hot never bothers me. I didn't grow up with air-conditioning. We used to play outside all day, no matter what the temperature was. When my daddy would say that it was hot enough to fry an egg on the sidewalk, do you know what we did? We fried an egg outside. We didn't have a sidewalk, but we put a frying pan on the hood of his car, and guess what?"

"What?" I asked, amused.

"It fried. And we ate it. We used to have *real* fun, my brothers and sisters and I. There are fourteen of us. Boy, did we get into some stuff. I have some stories to tell."

I stopped my digital recorder and dropped it in the side pocket of my purse. "My sister is ten years younger than I am, so we weren't that close growing up. Our relationship didn't really start until she graduated college. She moved to Raleigh for a year, but her job transferred her to Miami a few years ago. Now we hardly see each other at all." Malachi took my empty plate from the table, and I nodded my thanks. "That's why, whenever I have children, I want them to be no more than a couple years apart."

"You see how great Malachi is with those boys?" Gran'nola said. "He wants to have children, too."

"And on that note, it's time for us to go," Malachi said. He suddenly seemed embarrassed.

"Thank you again for inviting me for breakfast," I said. "The food was excellent."

"Do you cook?" Gran'nola asked me. All of a sudden, I felt like she was trying to size me up.

"I do, but it never tastes nearly as good as yours did just now."

"If you ever want lessons, come on by. You know the way to a man's heart is through his stomach. I always fed my husband like he was a king, and he always treated me like I was a queen." She looked over her shoulder. "Malachi, get her some plastic containers to take some home," Gran'nola said. "Look right over there in the cabinet on the side of the sink."

I tried to object, but Gran'nola was insistent, getting up to pack the food herself.

Meanwhile, I looked out the window at the vast acreage behind her house. From what she'd told me during breakfast, the Burke family patriarch—Gran'nola's father—had worked tirelessly to save enough to purchase plots of land throughout Greensboro and the surrounding counties. Some of the land had been sold over the years, but Gran'nola's property was considered to be the family meeting spot, and she doggedly refused to give it up, no matter how much money was offered.

"I'll walk you out," Malachi said when I had my bag of leftovers in hand.

Wearing his baseball cap, he looked more like the man in the professional photo on his team's online roster. Actually, the photo didn't do him justice. It made him look older than he was, but there was all kinds of fineness and gorgeousness under that cap. I didn't want to think about it. I didn't want to notice it. But it had been hard keeping my eyes on the cinnamon apples and country-fried steak when he was seated across the table from me. I would not—could not—let myself go there.

"Did you get everything you needed for the article?" Malachi asked as I followed him down the back patio steps.

"I think so. But if you don't mind I can give you a follow up call after I've written my first draft. Or I maybe I'll call Gran'nola."

"Oh, no. Don't do that," Malachi said with a laugh. "You want your story to be accurate, and *I know* that *you know* that my grandma can exaggerate things."

"She's creative," I said, defending her.

Malachi picked up a stack of orange cones and propped them on his shoulder. "You can call me anytime, whether it's about the story or not."

I'd been expecting him to say something like that. Now I wondered if I'd given off a vibe that I was interested. That hadn't been my intention. It wasn't professional.

"What if I said I wasn't interested?" I decided to say.

Malachi shrugged, as if it didn't matter to him one way or the other. But I knew that when it came to a man and his ego, it always mattered.

"It's your decision. Woman's free will."

"A gentleman would ask a woman if *he* could call *her*."

"Point taken." Malachi nodded. "And you're right. I apologize."

"You should be glad your grandma didn't hear you. She'd set you straight."

Malachi grinned. "You know she would." He opened my door, and I quickly slipped in, trying to block his view of the mess I'd left on the floor in front of the passenger seat—last month's issue of *Essence* magazine, a pair of crew socks, my swimming goggles, and an empty water bottle.

"Let me do it right this time," he said. "I'd like to call you while I'm in town."

"Malachi, I...I don't think it's a good idea. You'll be headed back to New York sooner or later, and I'm sure you have more than your pick of females waiting for you in the Big Apple."

Malachi folded his arms over his chest. "What makes you think that?"

I set the bag of breakfast leftovers on the floor behind my seat. "It isn't so much a matter of thinking as it is something I've seen with my own eyes. What can I say? I'm a digital sleuth. It doesn't take much these days to find out what you need to know."

"So, you wanted to know about me?" Malachi asked with a half smile.

"Research," I said. "That's all. And if a man has choices, he's likely to take them. A lot of them. Women, especially."

Malachi's demeanor shifted from cocky to thoughtful, making me wonder if I'd offended him. I'd stepped on his feet in an area that wasn't my business.

"I'm guilty," he finally said. "But that's part of my past. I can't change the past, but I can change the person who I am now. And I'd like to believe I've done that." He took his hand off the door. "You can call me if you want to set up another time to talk. Or you can come by the field later today."

I felt small enough to walk under my car. Words were how I made a living. Words were what I used to build literary tributes in the newspapers, magazines, and blogs I wrote for. And words were what I'd used to punch Malachi in the gut.

Now I found myself without a single word to say.

10

Malachi

Malachi's past had followed him from New York to Greensboro. He wasn't a fool. He knew the Internet told only half the story, but it was the very story the media wanted to portray. On one side, he was a successful Major League Baseball player; on the other side, he was a playboy. His affinity for beautiful women had never been a secret. He'd love them and leave them. And even though he was no longer that man, the Internet was teeming with images of him with various women, a lasting, indelible evidence of the player he used to be.

It was that indelible evidence on which Rae Stevens must have based her opinion of him. What other reason could she have had for turning him down? No other woman had ever turned him down. Alexandria didn't count, because although she'd been in and out of his life, there was one undeniable fact: She *always* came back.

Rae was different from any of the women who'd been in Malachi's life. He hadn't had to spend a lot of time around her to see that. And if she called for a follow-up interview instead of showing up at the field, he'd probably never see her again. She'd made it clear that there was no other reason for them to stay in contact, but he was determined to convince her otherwise.

All he needed was one date. He knew it was crazy, since she'd already turned him down, but he couldn't ignore the magnetism he felt drawing himself to Rae. It was there for her, too—he could see it in her eyes, even though Rae clearly tried to avoid looking at him as much as possible. If they didn't make a connection, he'd never think about her again. But if he could get her to spend some time with him—time that didn't involve a question-and-answer session—and they hit it off.... In the language of the sport he knew best, it would be a home run. A grand slam.

"Let's go, Malachi." Gran'nola clenched the railing. "I'm up, but my knee needs to wake up. It'll be alright once I get moving." She stepped carefully down the back steps, her floral tote bag draped over her shoulder. She kept it stocked with the same things—a book of crossword puzzles, an issue of *Woman's Day* magazine, a sandwich bag of peppermints, an extra pair of slip-on shoes, a bottle of water, and a small pack of peanuts—and refilled it when necessary.

"You were rushing me, and now you're out here daydreaming?"

"I'm ready," he said.

"You're thinking about that pretty girl Rae, aren't you?" Gran'nola smiled. "She's the sweetest thing. You should get to know her. Invite her back for dinner. I could really put out a spread."

If Malachi did have an opportunity to ask Rae to dinner, he wasn't going to invite her back to his grandma's house. How would that look? Would the three of them cuddle up on the couch to watch the evening news after enjoying their dinner? Not happening. In New York, he had five-star dining and the city's sights right outside the revolving door of his condo complex. In Greensboro, it was what it was.

"I asked her if I could call her, but she turned me down," Malachi confessed.

"You'll see her again," Gran'nola said.

"How can you be so sure?"

"I just know," Gran'nola said, letting Malachi help her into the SUV. "And when I know, I know."

It wasn't a far-fetched statement. Over the years, Gran'nola had put her finger on a lot of things that no one else had predicted or realized. She'd called out his cousin's unexpected teenage pregnancy before she'd revealed it the family. She'd known that Uncle Bud was hiding money in the deep freezer in his basement. And she'd had an inkling that Malachi's mother was considering filing for divorce when she'd told no one else. When Gran'nola knew, she knew.

Malachi just wished she knew when.

Rae never showed up at the field, which was probably best. Against his better judgment, he'd agreed to let fifty-three boys who hadn't pre-registered to participate, and the influx of campers caused no small amount of chaos at the outset of the program. But his team worked quickly to address the issue, and Malachi promised to hold two additional camps the following two weekends. Many of the boys wanted to return for one or both extra sessions, and he wanted to accommodate those who hadn't had the chance to attend. He couldn't bear to turn anyone away.

The day had been almost as grueling as baseball training camp, and by the end of the day, it was all Malachi could do not to crawl up the back steps and into the house. He showered, slipped into some fresh clothes, and found refuge in the living room with a cold glass of water and the TV remote. Gran'nola didn't have the exhaustive network choices that he did or the same access to premium movie channels and sports packages. It was probably for the best. What he needed was peace, anyway, and Gran'nola's house was the place to find it.

The media had finally stopped harassing Gran'nola, but she'd still taken the phone off the hook as soon as she'd walked in the door. She never did that. It was like a sin. Evidently, he looked as tired as he felt for her to chance missing the evening gossip update with Aunt Mimi.

Malachi rotated his left shoulder. It was tight. Sore. He'd done more than he should have today, but he'd felt that the only way to teach the boys the proper techniques for throwing, catching, and hitting was to demonstrate.

"Here you go, baby," Gran'nola said, bringing him a plastic bag of ice and a heating pad. "What else do you need?"

"I'm fine," he said, settling back and pushing a pillow behind his neck. "What I need the most is rest."

"Then I'll leave you alone. You did a lot today." She kneaded the back of his shoulder blade with her hand. It was painful but therapeutic. The touch of a concerned grandma was as skilled as a licensed massage therapist, as far as he was concerned.

"Maybe you should see somebody about your shoulder while you're here," she suggested. "You don't want it to get any worse."

Spoken by the lady with a bad knee, Malachi mused.

"I have the number of a physical therapist in town," he told her. "I'll call and make an appointment for *us* next week."

"Us? Don't worry about me. I'm old. You've still got some mileage left on your joints."

Same battle, different day, Malachi thought.

"My main concern is for you to take care of yourself," Gran'nola continued. "I know you want to get away from it all for right now, but you still need to take care of yourself. If you think it's time to move on from baseball, you'll be fine. Baseball doesn't make you; you make baseball. You've done good for yourself, and good to everybody else. God will honor that. Remember, I know what I know."

Malachi swallowed the lump in his throat. For more than six months—even before his latest shoulder injury—he'd been brooding over the decision of whether to retire from the sport. He still loved the game, he just didn't find the same joy in playing that he always had. He'd waited, figuring it was just a phase. Didn't most people get tired of their careers at some point and begin to ask themselves "What if?" Being a professional athlete was brutal on the body. The rigorous training and round-the-clock practices had begun to wear down the cartilage in his elbows. Torn UCLs, bone spurs...you name it, he'd had it. And because the training occurred during the off-season, too, his body never had proper time to heal.

No one but God knew the thoughts he'd grappled with until now. At least, he hadn't told anyone. But, like Gran'nola had said, she knew what she knew.

She'd left the room so quietly that Malachi hadn't realized she was gone. He turned off the bright overhead light and clicked on the side table lamp, then sat alone with his thoughts, staring at the circle of light the lampshade cast on the wall. He'd done everything that could be done in New York—dined at the finest restaurants, attended Broadway shows on opening night, and walked the red carpet at movie releases with his lady friends. He'd partied with little reserve at the most popular clubs, taking advantage of his VIP status wherever he went. But being a celebrity was overrated. And he didn't even consider himself to be an A-list celebrity.

God had clearly shown him that it was time for him to settle down. Every night during his prayers, the picture became clearer, the desire stronger. He'd once heard it said that a woman meets a man, then wants to settle down; but a man decides to settle down, then looks for a woman. It was true.

Malachi's phone chirped, and he picked it up to check the message. It was from Alexandria.

Miss u. U haven't returned my calls.

Busy, he answered back.

Worried about u.

I'm fine.

I should come to NC.

No. Need time alone.

Or time with somebody else?

Malachi didn't respond. Several minutes later, Alexandria texted him a picture of herself in a black bikini. Her head was tilted upward, her wet bangs falling over her face and partially covering eyes that stared intently into the camera. Her pouty lips were painted red.

When they'd been dating, Alexandria had sent him a selfie every morning whenever they were apart. He'd had hundreds of photos of her stored on his phone. Until last week, when he'd erased them all.

He erased this one, too. Alexandria was girlfriend material. Not wife material.

Malachi had planned on sleeping in the next morning, a Sunday, since camp wasn't scheduled to start until three. But if texts and temptations like that could pop up at any time, his mind needed to be saturated with some good, godly teaching. He'd been making the right choices over the past six months, but he needed to fully rely on God's strength, not his own, to stay on the right path. He had survived lonely days, and lonelier nights; sooner or later, he'd want the warmth of a female body beside him. That was when the Scriptures he'd studied and the prayers he'd prayed would kick in to carry him through.

Malachi's phone rang. He wished he could turn it off, but there was always the possibility that someone on his team needed him for something important. He looked hesitantly at the screen, hoping it wasn't Alexandria.

"What's up, big man?" Malachi said, answering Alonzo's call.

"Whatever you say is up," Alonzo said. "I wanted to check and see if there was anything extra you needed me to handle tomorrow."

"Brother, I can't even tell you. When I got back here, I turned my mind off to the stuff that needs to happen tomorrow. That's why I have help. I'm trusting them to take care of everything so I can just show up. Those boys beat me down. They're on another level."

"I feel you," Alonzo said. "It's called youth." He ended his sentence with a loud yawn.

"You sound as tired as me."

"Man, I'm about to hit this pillow earlier than ever, so I can go to church before heading to the field."

"I was thinking I should go to church, myself." Malachi lifted the melting ice off his shoulder and replacing it with the heating pad.

"You should come with me," Alonzo said. "You know they'll keep you at Ms. Nola's church all day. By three o'clock, the pastor *might* be about to preach, or the choir might be on their twenty-third selection, if you're lucky."

Malachi chuckled. "You're right, you know. Do you remember that time you came to church with me? You were so hungry by the time we left, I thought you were about to pass out." He chuckled.

"Bro, I was so hungry, I was three minutes away from chewing off my right arm."

"You never came with us again after that," Malachi recalled.

"First time, last time," Alonzo affirmed.

Malachi turned his neck until he heard a soft crack. "I'll go with Gran'nola next week."

"Don't tell her I invited you, or I'll never hear the end of it," Alonzo said. "Worse, she might change her mind about making me my favorite chicken pie. Today, she told me I was working so hard, I deserved one."

"If I'm here when she makes it, you'll never even see that chicken pie," Malachi said, suddenly wondering about Sunday dinner. Gran'nola usually spent Saturday night in the kitchen, banging pots and pans around as she whipped up a buffet for after church, but he hadn't heard or smelled anything since he'd retired to the living room. She was probably exhausted, too. Exhausted from talking.

Gran'nola had instructed Alonzo on how to set up her tent near the concession stand so she could man the food service area. But when she wasn't policing the water cooler, she was investigating the family lineage of foundation volunteers and the parents who'd decided to stay around. He even thought she'd found a long-lost cousin.

"Church starts at ten. We'll be out by noon," Alonzo was saying. "That'll give us time to grab a bite to eat so you can visit a little with me and the wife." He cleared his throat. "She's got some cute single friends. I can have her invite one along, if you want me to."

"No, I'm good," Malachi told him. "All I need is food and some place to catch a power nap."

"That's easy. Well, I've got to go. The wife is calling me to rub her feet. Man, between me and you, her toes look like sausages. Pregnancy ain't pretty."

"I'm not responding to that," Malachi said. "See you in the morning. Text me the address."

Malachi dozed off on the living room couch, and when he awakened at nearly three in the morning, he was too beat to take the short walk to the bed. He stretched the length of the couch, using one throw pillow to prop his feet and the other to elevate his shoulder. He slipped quickly back into a tired slumber, and the next time he awoke, it was to the aroma of coffee percolating.

"You know you're too old to fall asleep on the couch," Gran'nola said when Malachi shuffled into the kitchen, scratching the stubble on his chin.

He rubbed the sleep from his eyes and headed directly for the refrigerator. Gran'nola's papaya juice had become his new favorite beverage, and he needed a sip to wash the thick, cottony feel from his mouth.

"First it was my shoulder. Then Uncle Bud hit my knee with a rock. Now, it's my shoulder, my knee, and my back," Malachi said.

"See? What did I tell you? I bet you won't do that again."

Malachi dropped into the seat at the kitchen table and quickly responded to three texts that he'd received overnight. Yes, two thousand flyers were enough to advertise the camp for the next two weeks. No, he couldn't let the commissioner's daughter attend. This camp was for boys only. Maybe another year. Of course, put a rush order on more T-shirts to distribute next week. "I hope you won't take all the attention away from the preacher today," Gran'nola said. She reached for her favorite mug and filled it to the brim with black coffee. No sugar. No cream. "You know how it is when you come to church."

Malachi folded the end of the tablecloth, avoiding her gaze. "I'll see everyone next week. I'm going to another church this morning."

"Another church like what? Where?" She frowned.

"Alonzo's church," Malachi said, realizing that he might just have sacrificed his buddy's chicken pie.

"Is he still at Grace Temple?"

"Yes," Malachi answered, waiting for Gran'nola to give her opinion, which she would undoubtedly do.

"Oh, I like him. I listen to him some Thursday nights on one of the local channels. He can rightly divide the Word. If it's not in the Bible, he doesn't teach it. Not like some of these other preachers who are busy talking about their opinions more than anything else." She slurped her coffee. "Yes, I like him. Funny, too."

"You should come with me," Malachi suggested, relieved that she hadn't compared the pastor to the devil himself.

"Oh, no," she responded quickly. She rubbed her kneecap and reached for a bottle of pain relievers on the table. "I like going to *my own* church on Sundays. The church my family built is good enough for me."

Malachi took the bottle from Gran'nola, twisted off the childproof cap, and tipped two pills into her palm before taking out two more for himself.

"What do you want for breakfast?" Gran'nola asked.

"Whatever you're willing to make," Malachi said as he picked up his buzzing cell phone.

"That thing is like carrying around an oxygen tank," Gran'nola said. "You can't live without it."

"You need your own reality TV show, Gran'nola," Malachi told her with a laugh. "I could make some money off of you."

He glanced at the screen, expecting a wakeup call from Alonzo. He was pleasantly surprised to be proven wrong. It must've been God's gift to him, because the last person Malachi had expected to hear from was Rae.

11

He wasn't as bad as I thought he would be," I told Farrah.

I'd joined her for Sunday brunch following the service, and we'd decided to probe the racks of one of the boutique consignment stores she always raved about. Casey had slept in, taking the morning for rest, since he was getting back on the road the following day.

"Girl, I tired him out," Farrah had bragged with a devious smile over her spinach and egg quiche.

"That's married folks' business."

"I'm just saying. When you're trying to make a baby, you have to practice as much as possible."

Farrah would make an unbelievably amazing mother. She ran her hand across the fabric of a maternity wrap dress as we passed through what I called the "big belly" section.

"Then he asked me out," I told her. "Why would he do that?"

"Why would he not?" Farrah said, stopping to wrap a printed scarf around her neck. "You're a stunner, and you're smart. Your love for God and the care you have for others practically oozes out of your pores. And his grandmother loves you after meeting you just one time. The man knows a good woman when he sees her."

"But to him, I would be nothing but a conquest. We live in two different worlds," I said, pulling the scarf from around Farrah's neck. It was hideous.

Farrah shook her head. "Then you're better than me, because I would've said yes without a second thought. Malachi knows both worlds. He wasn't born with a silver spoon in his mouth, and I bet his spunky little grandma keeps him grounded. You should go out with him. What's the harm in having a little sinless fun? Noticed how I added that 'sinless'?"

"Yes, I noticed. You don't have to worry about that."

Farrah held up a cropped linen jacket and examined it closely. "So, what about the article? Did you finish it?"

"Almost. I wouldn't mind talking to a few of the parents who have kids attending the camp, and to get some time to sit down with Gran'nola. Then I can wrap it up. I have other assignments hanging over my head, including some other stories Shelton wants me to write."

"Bottom line: Story or not, you're interested in getting to know him more." Farrah hung the linen jacket back on the rack. "You're trying to act like you couldn't care less, but I know you. Don't forget that. I. Know. You. Admit it."

I shook the thought away. "Get the facts. Get the story. Get going. Those are your words," I reminded her.

Farrah stopped in the middle of the aisle. "Well, add this to it: Get a life."

I turned my attention to a rack of flowery skirts. I remembered the time when floral prints were reserved for elderly church ladies, but they were making a comeback, and I was ready for the trend. I could feel my girly-girl ways being resurrected. Ms. Bessie would approve.

Maybe I should've agreed to let Malachi take me out. But it was easier said than done. There was still the fear—albeit a small one—that I'd get hurt again. It was probably better to avoid the possibility of the pain. At least for now.

I caught a glance of myself in the mirror on the door of the dressing room. I'd washed and straightened my hair the night before so that it now hung past my shoulders. I was giving Ms. Bessie's curls a run for their money. Maybe I would repeat my entire Sunday ensemble, hairdo and all, for our Monday morning staff meeting. The A-line skirt and tank top I was wearing were part of the wardrobe I'd purchased for my honeymoon, and I'd figured today was as good a time as any to cut off the tags and wear them.

"Get the facts. Get the story. Get going," I said again, turning my attention to a black pencil skirt. Adorable but the wrong size. I shoved it back on the rack.

"No response?" Farrah persisted. "I know why. Because you know you can't lie on a Sunday."

"Don't look for something that's not there," I told her. I pushed my shopping cart to the next row of color-coordinated skirts and headed for the section of summery pastels.

"Oh, it's there." Farrah held up her hand and scrunched her nose. "Do you smell that?"

I inhaled deeply but had no idea what odor she had detected.

"It's the smell of new love in the air," she said, grinning. "And it's real heavy over in your direction."

I groaned. "You're only saying that because Casey is home and he's loved you up. I don't hear from you for four days, and now that you've emerged from your house, you're floating through the leftover romance. I've known Malachi all of two days. There's no love connection."

"I am definitely having a love hangover," Farrah admitted, her face aglow. "But I've always believed in love at first sight. That's how it was for me and my boo. And, speaking of my boo, I need to head home so we can get over to his mom's house."

"How's Ms. Williamson doing? I haven't seen her since Christmas."

Farrah's mother-in-law worked as a seamstress, and she'd tailored my wedding gown and also sewn Farrah's matron of honor dress. We'd haggled over the style until we found the perfect look for her. Unfortunately, she had the perfect dress, but I didn't have the perfect man.

"She's great. Casey's going over there before me to change out the appliances. Remember, he and his siblings gave her money to buy a new stainless-steel everything? Well, it took six months for her to choose the ones she wanted. And then, she didn't want the delivery men to change them out and install them. She wanted Casey to handle it. Him and only him."

"Isn't his brother Corey at her house almost every week?" I asked.

Farrah rolled her eyes. "Yes, he's the spoiled baby who goes to his mama's house all the time to eat, but he can't change a lightbulb without blowing out the entire fuse box." She joined me in scavenging around the skirt rack. "And to think he was almost your husband."

"Wrong. He *wanted* to be my husband."

Corey had tried to use his brother's relationship with me to make sparks fly between us, but I never looked at him as anything more than my best friend's brother-in-law. He hadn't abandoned his quest until I was officially engaged to Trenton, and then, once he'd heard the news of our breakup, he'd gone back on the prowl. I'd turned him down six times already, but he was still averaging one dinner invitation per month.

Farrah held up a skirt that I would've claimed for my own wardrobe, had I found it first. I regretted skimming that section so hastily. It was no surprise she'd found the hidden treasure. She always did at places like this. It was white with blue and yellow flowers embroidered along one side.

"This is adorable," she said, holding it up to her waist as she stepped in front of one of the strategically placed full-length mirrors.

"That should have been mine," I pouted, diving back into the mounds of skirts. "You stole it out from under me."

"No, you're just impatient," Farrah chided me, and not for the first time. "Your eyes take in a group of things, but you've got to look at each piece of clothing individually and touch each piece of fabric. That's how you find these fashion gems."

I pulled another flowery skirt off the rack. It was perfect. For Gran'nola.

"The next cute thing I find is yours," Farrah promised me.

"I'm not worried whether I find a single thing for myself," I told her. "Sooner or later, you'll clean out your closet. And an empty closet for you means a full closet for me. Like you told me: I. Know. You."

After repeated attempts to organize her closet with racks, baskets, and bins, the overflow was almost unmanageable. Casey had finally conceded and let her transform one of their guest bedrooms into a wardrobe room.

"Speaking of a full closet, do you still have that wedding dress crowding everything out? You should bring it here. I think you could get at least seventy percent of what you paid for it. All it's doing at your place is collecting dust and old memories."

"True."

I'd been contemplating trying to sell it, but something about getting rid of the dress of my dreams seemed like acknowledging a failure in my life. I couldn't make that decision until the time was right for me. Besides, one of these days, I would make it down the aisle. I just prayed the gown wouldn't have dry-rotted by then.

Farrah checked her watch. "We'll have to postpone the rest of this shopping escapade for later this week."

We found ourselves in line behind a woman who looked like she'd cleared the boutique out of every size 8.5 shoe in their collection.

"What are your plans for the rest of the day?" Farrah asked me.

"Well...." I hesitated. "I think I'll head back out to the baseball camp to speak to some parents. I'll talk to Ms. Nola, too, if she's there."

"Uh-huh," Farrah said, eyeing me skeptically.

"It's my duty to write the best story possible, whether it's for *Black Enterprise* or the *Ledger*."

"Uh-huh," Farrah said, again. "No wonder you look so cute today. But don't mind me. You're going for the facts."

12

I lifted my skirt to avoid tripping as I climbed to the top row of bleachers, seeking shade from the burning sun under the small awning that jutted out from under the announcer's booth. It was six thirty. The camp's first official weekend would be over in an hour.

"Anybody who can get this many people out to the field on a Sunday afternoon has to be loved by this town," said a woman sitting nearby. She slid over until the shade from the awning cast a shadow across her lap, where she held a book she'd been reading.

"So, you have a son participating?" I asked her.

"Yes, along with his best friend. Kyle wouldn't have missed it for the world. And he's begging for me bring him back next week, too. But I don't know." The woman shook her head. "He's supposed to visit his grandparents in New Jersey, and I need him and his sister out of the house as soon as possible before they drive me completely crazy. What about you?"

"No children. I'm working on a story about Mr. Burke and his foundation. The man behind the baseball bat...all that good stuff."

"Really? Who do you write for?"

Most people who asked me that question expected to hear I was a reporter with the city's main newspaper, the *News & Record*. "The *Greensboro Ledger*," I said.

"I love the *Ledger*," the woman said. "I've read it for years. I can only find it at the library on my side of town, though."

"We have very limited distribution," I explained. "We don't print as many copies as we once did, so we focus on the areas with the highest readership."

"Makes sense to me," the woman said, leaning over and offering me her hand. "I'm Zenja Maxwell."

"Nice to meet you, Zenja. Rae Stevens."

Zenja paused for a moment. "Your face looks familiar."

I wasn't about to ask her if she'd seen the on-air proposal that Trenton had sprung on me during the six o'clock news. He'd had me come to the news station, telling me that they were having a surprise birthday party for his producer, Kate. He knew I adored Kate's twin boys and admired her drive and passion for producing Greensboro's highest-rated news channel.

I had been sitting on a stool behind one of the cameramen during Trenton's sports segment when he'd surprised me by asking me to join him on camera. My heart had jumped into my throat, and I had to use every ounce of self-control to still my trembling hands as I joined him in front of the blaring studio lights. And then, in front of the city's largest viewership, he dropped to one knee. The channel had replayed the proposal for the next two days. I'd even had my fifteen minutes of fame when it had aired on a handful of affiliate stations and then had gone moderately viral on social media.

"You wouldn't happen to go to Grace Temple, would you?" she asked. "Our membership has grown so much in the last year that I don't know everyone by name anymore."

"No, I sure don't," I said, though I knew of the church. Ms. Bessie was a member there, and I had seen their pastor speaking on television.

"Malachi visited our church this morning. He was hiding out in the back pew. Most people didn't know he was there until our pastor called him up to thank him for his contributions to the community and asked him to say a few words. After the service, he stayed until he'd signed an autograph for every single person standing in line. That's the kind of man he is. But you might have known that already, with all the research you've probably done on him."

"I've interviewed him once already, and he's not the kind of person I thought he would be," I admitted. "He's a lot more down-to-earth that I expected."

"Do you know Alonzo Jones?" Zenja asked me. "That's who brought him to church. Him and his precious pregnant wife."

"Was he the guy passing out the T-shirts on Friday night?"

"That's him," Zenja confirmed. "He grew up with Malachi, and he's his biggest fan. I know everybody claims to be, but Alonzo really is." Suddenly Zenja stood, cupped her hands around her mouth like a megaphone, and shouted, "Put some speed behind the ball, Kyle!" Then she sat with a sheepish smile. "Sorry. I guess I'm just another one of those embarrassing moms."

"You're not alone in that," I told her. "On Friday night, some of the parents were acting like there might be Major League scouts in the stands."

"Kyle came with his sitter on Friday night, so I missed that show," Zenja said. "I was off mommy duty to help my closest friend, Caprice, coordinate an event she started called Friday Night Love." She closed her book and set it on the bleacher beside her. "Are you married?"

"No," I said.

"Engaged?"

I wiggled my bare ring finger. Against my sister's advice, I'd given the pear-shaped solitaire back to Trenton.

"I was going to invite you to one our events. We have tons of fun," she said. "We're in the ministry of maintaining and building godly marriages."

"That's fantastic," I said. "Do you have a card or something? I'll pass the information to my best friend, Farrah. She'd love it."

"Is she a newlywed?"

"Three years in," I said, taking the marketing postcard she handed me.

"That card lists all the events for the rest of the year. If she sends a text message to the number at the bottom, she'll get a monthly reminder."

"I'll definitely get it to her." I looked at the postcard. "Friday Night Love," I read aloud. "What God has joined together, let no one separate."

Zenja stretched out her long brown legs and propped them on the bleacher in front of her. "Key word: God. I know you're here for interviews, not for a sermon, but I can't stress it enough. If God ordained it, He'll help you maintain it."

"You should put that on your marketing cards," I told her.

Zenja's expression lit up. "Next print run, I will. I came up with that just now. I guess God dropped those words down on me because I'm sitting beside a journalist. I could use you around more often. We're always trying to generate fresh ways of attracting new people to our events."

I thought about the struggling paper and my promise to Shelton. I wasn't a salesperson. More like the furthest thing from it. But I did have the desire to bring the *Ledger* back up from the ashes.

"You should consider running an ad in the *Ledger*. Our advertising prices are very reasonable, and it would give Friday Night Love a lot more visibility."

"That's not a bad idea," Zenja said, sounding genuinely interested. "What's your number? I'll give you a call."

We logged each other's numbers into our phones, then Zenja happily agreed to let me ask her a few questions for the article. She was my fifth and final parent interviewee, and absolutely the most engaging.

Fifteen minutes later, we were joined by her friend Quinn.

"Good to meet you," Quinn said, steadying herself on the rail as she climbed the bleachers. "And why do you look so familiar?"

"I said the same thing," Zenja said, studying my face. She shook her head. "I know you from somewhere, I just can't place it." She turned to Quinn. "She's a writer with the *Ledger*, and she's working on a story about Malachi Burke."

"He's a hunk," Quinn said. "And you can quote me on that."

Zenja playfully pushed Quinn's shoulder. "What would Levi say about that?"

"My man is very confident in my love for him. Why would I have eyes for him"—she pointed toward the baseball field—"when I'm about to say my vows and forever become Mrs. Leviticus Gray?"

Zenja looked at me, amused. "She's recently engaged. Can you tell?"

"Congratulations," I said, recalling my own excitement. "When's the big day?"

"In three months. For one hundred people, but you'd think it was for one thousand."

I knew the feeling. My guest list had somehow grown to nearly five hundred guests—from the original estimate of two hundred—and the work required to coordinate such a grandiose affair had literally caused my hair to shed. By the time I found a trustworthy and capable wedding coordinator, I no longer needed her services.

"Like I always say," Zenja interjected, "the marriage—not the wedding—is the important thing."

"I agree," Quinn said. "But still, if I could find a makeup artist who could make me beautiful without making me look like a clown, I'd feel a lot better about things. Levi can have chicken wings and fries at the reception, for all I care."

Say no more, I thought.

"Your problem is solved," I said to Quinn. "My best friend, Farrah, is a makeup artist, and she's extraordinary. I wouldn't lie to you."

Quinn's gaze was frozen on me, making me fear I'd said something wrong.

"I do know you," she said, realization dawning in her eyes. "You owe me fifty cents. I almost didn't recognize you without your glasses. And your hair is different. Gorgeous, by the way."

Quinn. It clicked. She was the thoughtful woman who'd saved me from embarrassment in the grocery store checkout line. Now I recognized her smile.

"So that's what you look like behind those sunglasses," I said. "We meet again."

Quinn chuckled at the memory. "I'd just come from the eye doctor, and my pupils were still dilated. Those were some glasses they loaned me from the lost and found. They were hideous."

I looked toward the field and noticed Jared following Malachi with his camera like he was the paparazzi. I guess he hadn't been satisfied with the shots he'd taken on Friday night.

I turned back to Quinn. "Farrah will more than make up for the fifty cents I owe you. She'll have you looking like a million bucks. You can set up a consultation with her."

"I have Rae's number, so you two can connect," Zenja said to Quinn. She gestured toward the field. "I think that guy is trying to get your attention," she told me.

It was Jared.

"Have a good day, ladies," I said, standing up, carefully. "We'll be in touch."

Jared trotted over to me, his camera strap slung over one shoulder, a worn-out camera bag across the other.

"What's up, Rae?" he said. "I didn't know you were coming out again today."

"I hadn't planned on it, but my story needs a little something else."

"I think I'll have some great shots for you," Jared said, taking a step back. He lifted his camera to his eyes and pretended to zoom in on me.

I shielded my face with my hands. "Must you be so close? I don't need a photo documentary of my pores."

"I'm not as close as you think," Jared insisted. "Just look at me and smile. The sun is casting an amazing glow behind you. Trust me."

Not counting selfies, I hadn't had any pictures taken since my engagement photos with Trenton.

"That's enough," I said, smiling with clenched teeth as Jared clicked away. "No more photos, or you're fired."

"Hey, I work for doughnuts and for dinners at Mr. Shelton's house. There's no way he's getting rid of me. I'm cheap labor."

"You're a college student. I'm not surprised," I joked. Lowering my voice, I added, "Now get away from me with that camera, or I won't be held liable for what I'll do next."

Jared held up his hands in surrender and backed away. I didn't like to be the center of attention, and with Jared's impromptu photo session, that was what I'd become. Some of the parents had turned their attention away from the boys and were watching us. And so was Malachi. Or was he? I slid my shades down over my eyes so I could watch him inconspicuously. He had turned back to getting a group of pint-sized players lined up for their turn in the batting cage.

I couldn't help but keep watching him. *It's what you're supposed to be doing,* I told myself. *He's the subject of your article.* And that's all it was. I wasn't attracted to him, personally. I was merely showing appropriate interest in someone I was writing about. Right?

Zenja and Quinn walked down the steps behind me, their cushioned stadium seats in hand. "We've got to drag our sons to the car as soon as they pass out the trophies," Zenja said. "They start a weeklong science camp first thing tomorrow morning."

I grinned. "I wonder how that will compare with this weekend."

"It won't," Quinn said, stepping carefully down the last bleachers. "We'll talk soon."

Jared slid his camera inside his bag and zipped it closed as we walked together toward the parking lot. "I'm heading out now, too. My girl wants to go to the movies later."

"Your girl? Since when do you have a girl?"

"Since last week, when I asked her to be my lady."

"Men still do that, huh?"

"I can't speak for other men. I can only speak for myself."

"Is it the young woman you brought to the office a few months back?"

"Kierra? That's her." He wiped his sweaty brow with his even sweatier forearm.

I remembered being struck by her introverted demeanor. Ms. Bessie had needed to ask her several times to repeat herself. She and Jared had met during one of his late-night sessions at the library, where she'd held a work-study job for the last two years.

"Good for you," I said. "I know you'll do right by her. You'd *better* do right by her."

"Sounds to me like a serious threat," Malachi said, appearing from out of nowhere.

"And I'll take it seriously," Jared said. "Rae may look sweet and innocent, but I heard those are the ones you have to watch out for."

"Thanks for the warning," Malachi said. "And if you don't mind, I'd like to get a file of the photos you've been taking. Before you leave, could you talk to Ally, over there in the yellow shirt? Let her know your fee. As a matter of fact, if I can, I'd like to hire you for next week's camp, too. And don't sell yourself short by undercutting your price."

"Man, wow," Jared nearly sputtered. "Thanks, Mr. Burke." He shook Malachi's hand as if he'd just delivered the best news he'd heard all year. "I really appreciate it. Really."

"No problem," Malachi said, clapping him on the back. "See you next week. Get yourself a staff T-shirt from Alonzo." When Jared had gone, Malachi turned to me. "You look beautiful. Not exactly ready to play baseball, but still cute."

"Thanks. Next time, I'll remember to wear my cleats."

"Next time," Malachi said. "I like the sound of that."

"Where should we talk?"

"We can sit on the bench over there. I guess it's as good a place as any. Unless you want to go somewhere and grab a bite to eat," Malachi suggested.

I wished he would stop looking at me like that. I wished he was arrogant and self-centered, so it would be easier to keep my mind from entertaining thoughts of him. I wished my preconceived notions of him were true. But they weren't.

"Oh, no thanks," I said. "The bench is fine."

We sat down, and I took my digital recorder out of my purse, kicking myself for not accepting his dinner invitation. Again. Farrah was going to flip.

Malachi took off his baseball cap and balanced it on his knee, then changed his mind and put it back on his head again. "Go ahead. Shoot."

All business now, I thought.

"Well, the first weekend camp is finished, and you've decided to launch two more. After that, you'll return to New York. But when will you return to baseball? I never asked about your shoulder because your publicist advised me not to. And I know it's a sensitive issue. But I can't help being curious."

Malachi glanced skyward with a thoughtful look, as if trying to decide whether to answer. Initially, per his publicist's request, I'd steered clear of any questions about his shoulder injury and his future as a professional athlete. But he'd asked me out. Twice. That fact had chipped away at the wall of professionalism between us. I had eaten at his grandma's breakfast table, for goodness' sake. The least he could do was give me a hint.

"Baseball will always be a part of my life, whether I'm playing professionally or coaching young kids. Will I hang up my bat this year, or three years from now? Only God knows. And when He makes it clear to me, I'll let the world know, too."

I perked up at his mention of God. "So, would you say that your faith drives you?"

He nodded. "When I finally came to the realization that I didn't have to do this on my own, and that God was my biggest fan, my life became a lot easier."

"Well, amen to that," I said.

Malachi seemed happy to answer my remaining questions. After that, we veered off track and onto topics that had nothing to do with his baseball career or his charity. Of all things, we shared our favorite soul food. His was macaroni and cheese, mine crab cakes—which, according to Malachi, didn't count as "soul food." He loved chocolate chip cake, and I had a thing for chocolate chip ice cream. Off the field, he liked to fiddle with computers; I told him how, when I had time, and the weather was perfect, I could be found at the nearest pool.

"I'm not much of a swimmer," Malachi confessed. "I mean, I'm comfortable in the deep end, and I can tread water to keep myself afloat; but I wouldn't trust myself to rescue a drowning person. I could save myself, but probably not someone else."

"I was a lifeguard in high school, and I can tell you, it's even hard for swimmers with extensive training to save someone who's drowning. There's always a risk of getting pulled under by the victim."

"Impressive," Malachi said as he walked me to my car. The car I'd cleaned out since last he saw it. We were walking so slowly that we might as well have been standing still. It was as if neither of us wanted the moment to end. As if we knew that when we walked away from each other, that was it.

"I don't know many—"

I cast him a sideways glance. "You don't know many black girls who like to swim, huh?" I laughed. "The whole hair thing. It's no secret."

"Right." He stepped back while I opened my door. "Your hair always looks nice, though. One day, it's curly; another day it's straight. Variety—I like that in a woman. Can I say that, or did I offend you?"

I swept my long tresses over my shoulders. Gosh, I was flirting. That was definitely a calculated move. What was next? Fluttering my eyelashes? "I'm not offended." I got in the car and tossed my purse on the passenger seat. "I'll shoot you a text when this story goes to print. And I'll be sure to mail a few copies to your grandma. I realize this isn't an article for Sports Illustrated, but I know Ms. Nola will be proud."

"As a peacock," Malachi said. "She saves every word that's been written about me, whether it's accurate or not. Hangs it up on the wall." He shook his head.

"Then this feature ought to be one of her favorites, since I wrote about her, too. She brought a lot of things to light. I think I'm going to give her a buzz. She put her number in the bag of food she packed up for me."

Malachi shook his head. "She's too much." He looked at me with an expression I couldn't read.

"Well, thank you again for granting me the interview." I inserted my key in the ignition and tried starting the car. Nothing happened. Frowning, I turned it again. Nothing.

"Great," I muttered. "Won't start."

Malachi stepped back and leaned toward the engine. "Give it one more try," he said, listening closely.

I made one last attempt.

"It's probably your starter. I'm no mechanic, but I'd bet on it."

I was already reaching for my cell phone. "I'll call for the emergency roadside assistance provided by my car insurance company." I tried not to get flustered. I'd padded my rainy-day savings fund for emergencies such as this, but the ordeal was still stressful. The car would have to be towed to my mechanic, and I'd drive a rental for a day or two. Out of all the things that could happen, it wasn't that bad.

"It'll be at least thirty minutes before the tow truck gets here," I told him when I got off the phone.

"I'll wait with you," Malachi offered. "Then I'll drive you home."

I had planned on phoning Farrah to rescue me, but then I remembered that Casey was still home. I didn't want to interrupt the final hours of their weekend together.

"Are you sure you wouldn't mind?" I asked Malachi. "I don't want to inconvenience you. I can give you money for gas."

"It's not an inconvenience," he said, leaning against the car. "And gas money? Really? We aren't in high school."

"Just trying to be courteous," I said, knowing he probably had more money in his pocket right now than I had in my bank account.

"I appreciate the offer, but it's okay."

The thirty minutes passed quickly. Too quickly. We'd escaped the June heat in the cool air-conditioning of Malachi's ride, though he blasted it to the point that I was freezing. But spending some time with a man who hung on my every word warmed me from the inside.

"That's probably your tow coming down the street now," Malachi said. "I'll flag him down."

I collected my belongings from my car before the tow truck driver hitched it to his truck.

"I've got that," Malachi said, taking my tote bag and the travel thermal carrier I stowed in the backseat.

"Thanks."

I handled my business with the tow truck driver, who asked if I needed a ride. There was no way I ever would have climbed in that monstrous machine with a man who looked like he could decapitate me with one slice of a butter knife. Not happening. I politely declined and prayed he wouldn't rummage through my glove compartment to find my address on my registration papers. A single woman couldn't afford not to consider those types of scenarios. Farrah would have called me paranoid, but I called it being cautious.

"All set?" Malachi asked as he helped me back into his vehicle.

"I'm set," I said, buckling in. "Drive safe. I'm precious cargo."

Malachi turned his hat so that the brim was angled to the side, giving him a youthful appearance. "Every now and then, a package doesn't make it to the intended destination. Some packages get delayed...or lost." He wheeled into the street.

"What are you trying to say?" I asked.

"Oh, you know." He fed the car some gas. "Just that it would be really easy to kidnap you right now and hold you against your will."

13

I wasn't least bit worried about Malachi's so-called threat. "I have no qualms about opening this door and jumping out," I told him. "I'm sure I can tuck and roll to safety with no problem."

"I know not to mess with you," he said, flipping on his turn signal and easing into the left lane at my direction. "What's his name—Jared?—he warned me about you."

During the course of the ten-minute drive to my apartment, Malachi's cell phone rang four times. Each time, he ignored it.

"Somebody always wants something. The important people have special ringtones, so I know when I should answer. If I don't think it's important, I deal with it later."

"You can take your calls. I don't mind."

"Why would I want to talk to anybody else when all the conversation I need is riding right beside me?"

Charmer, I thought.

We were only two intersections from my street, and I suddenly wished I lived further away. For the first time in months, I was enjoying the company of a man. But who was I kidding? Malachi was headed back to New York in two weeks, so the question of whether I enjoyed his company didn't matter. I was sure his beautiful entourage of women was anticipating his return. By that time, I would be nothing more than a cute hometown memory.

"Take a right at the second light," I said. "By the gas station."

"Do you mind if I stop first for gas first?" he asked.

"Change your mind about my offer of gas money?" I joked.

"I would never accept an offer to fill my tank from any woman," Malachi said. "What kind of fool would that make me?"

"A very lonely one probably," I said.

"You'd be surprised at the things a man would accept from a woman—and the kind of things a woman would offer," Malachi said.

"Have you seen your share?" I asked, nonchalantly watching a woman power-walking down the sidewalk.

Malachi shifted in his seat. "I'd be lying if I said I didn't. But, let's face it—it came with the territory when I signed my first contract."

He swung into the gas station lot and eased the SUV up to one of the pumps.

"After a while, it gets old. Especially when you realize God has a greater plan for your life, and having a buffet of women isn't part of it."

"A buffet," I repeated. "Never heard it put that way. But at least you know now that one woman is enough."

"One *good* woman is enough," he corrected me.

Malachi hesitated when three men exited the store. Two were carrying bags of ice, the other, a two-liter soda and a jumbo bag of chips. They got in the car on the other side of the gas pump and rumbled away moments later, black exhaust billowing behind them. Malachi watched their departure in the rearview and side mirrors.

I knew what he was doing. Playing low-key. I couldn't imagine how annoying it would be to have people recognizing you wherever you went, hounding you for autographs or asking you to pose with them for pictures. I had yet to witness Malachi turning down a fan's request; but after spending two days in the summer heat, handling hundreds of boys and their parents, he probably needed a break.

"I can pump the gas. I won't hold it against you," I said, placing my hand on his forearm to let him know I was serious. "I can see being a celebrity has its privileges and inconveniences."

"That, too, comes with the territory. I'll handle it."

Malachi peeled off the blue T-shirt with the baseball camp logo in bright red lettering on the front. I turned my head away slightly, not sure if I should be sitting beside him when he was bare-chested with those chiseled muscles popping. I wouldn't look. *God, help me not to look,* I was thinking as he stepped out of the car. And why had he stripped down, anyway?

After setting the gas pump to refuel, Malachi crossed in front of the vehicle and went into the store, and it was then that I realized he'd had a white tank top on underneath. I turned back around and looked in the backseat. It was clean, except for two empty Gatorade bottles and a partially eaten bag of veggie chips. I assumed he'd bought them at the same store where we'd first encountered each other, because I had the same generic store brand in my cabinet. They were disgusting.

Malachi's cell phone rang again, with a noise that sounded like a harp. *It must be one of his VIPs,* I thought. It lit up the console area where he had plugged it in to charge. After what seemed like forever, the harp finally stopped its musical serenade, and a text message popped up on the wide HD screen with an image attached.

A risqué image, at that.

The woman in the photo wore a red bikini, but she wasn't on a beach or by any water at all—ocean, pool, or puddle. She was standing on a balcony with a scenic background of skyscrapers.

Waiting 4 u 2 Come home, the text read.

Home, meaning his place? Or home, meaning New York?

Either way, just as I'd assumed, there was at least one woman anticipating his return. The image dimmed, and the screen went black. Why had I let myself think he was different? Why hadn't I held on to my first instinct?

My mood soured. At this point, I could easily walk the rest of the way home. I would have, too, if I didn't have so many things to carry. Two more people entered and exited the store before Malachi finally emerged, with both his arms cradling brown paper bags. Why he'd decided to go shopping in a convenience store was beyond me.

He opened the back door, secured the bags on the seat, and then got back inside like he'd just had the time of his life perusing the aisles of sour-cream-and-onion potato chips, Butterfinger bars, and cans of over-priced baby formula. "I got you some stuff to eat, since you'll be stranded at home till your car is fixed," he said. "I didn't think to ask if you would rather swing by someplace else, so if you would, just let me know."

"That's fine," I said, curtly. *Just start this car and get me home*, I thought. If I'd had fangs, I would have bared them.

My tone must've caught him off guard. "You alright?" He turned on the interior lights and searched my face.

I turned away to look out the window. "I'm fine."

Malachi yanked the discarded blue T-shirt out from where it was wedged between his back and the seat, slipped it over his head, and started the engine.

"Take this right. Go down half a mile. The complex is on the left," I directed him.

There was a noticeable tension in the air that I tried to pretend didn't exist. I wanted to believe that seeing his text hadn't affected me, but if I'd looked at my face in the visor mirror, I wouldn't have been surprised if it was green with envy. Farrah was going to get an earful. She'd fed me lines from a fairy tale, and I'd fallen for it.

Malachi slowed the car and made the turn into the apartment complex where I'd lived for a little over five years. Plenty of newer places offering more amenities had popped up around town, but I'd never felt the need to relocate. My complex was in the center of the places I frequented the most—the *Ledger* office, my church, and Farrah's house. It provided easy access to the highway, a short drive to the local shopping centers, and an affordable rent. It was also peacefully quiet, since very few families with young children or teenagers lived there. Thank God I was home.

"Circle to the left. I'm in the second building," I told Malachi. "You can pull up to the second breezeway."

"Why don't I park so I can help you inside?"

"Okay," I agreed. "You can use my parking space. It's the one marked two forty-eight."

I normally wouldn't have shared my apartment number, but he was going to see it on my door, anyway.

Malachi eased between two of my neighbors' vehicles—a Harley Davidson motorcycle and an older convertible Corvette.

I fumbled to find my keys as I led the way to my first-floor apartment. I entered the breezeway and stopped, confused. The sight of Trenton standing in front of my door caught me completely off guard.

The three of us stood like we were in a showdown in a Western film, Trenton and me facing each other, with Malachi behind me. I could practically see the wheels spinning in Trenton's head. Here I was, coming home with the baseball star he'd been hounding for an exclusive interview—without success—and he was wondering why I'd been shown preferential treatment. I would let him wonder, because he was already forming an answer in his head.

"There you are," Trenton said. He didn't seem visibly bothered that Malachi was with me.

His eyes took me in from head to toe. Trenton had always loved it when I straightened my naturally curly hair. He used to run his fingers through it and compliment me continuously.

Next, Trenton's gaze went to my skirt. We'd been sitting together on my living room couch when I'd ordered it. "I was just about to knock again," he said. "I thought I heard the TV."

"Why would you expect to find me here with my car not parked out front?"

"I hadn't noticed," he said.

Liar.

"What's up, man?" Trenton finally said to Malachi, as if just noticing him for the first time. But we all knew Malachi wasn't the type of man who was easily overlooked. "Good to see you again."

"You, too," Malachi said, though I doubted he remembered Trenton. "Give me your name one more time?"

I could tell that Trenton had tried to hide the shock on his face, but it hadn't worked. He was used to people knowing him by name.

"Trenton Cason. Lead sports anchor."

"Okay," Malachi said. "I'll have to remember that."

Trenton extended his hand but quickly tucked it inside the pocket of his shorts, clearly having noticed that both of Malachi's were occupied.

"What can I help you with, Trenton?" I asked him, putting my key in the door.

"Well, an interview would be nice," Trenton said, his voice shifting into his on-air tone as he addressed Malachi and now ignored me. "Man, you're in your hometown. You have to agree to at least one more interview beyond those press conferences out on the field. Hook a brother up."

Now Trenton wanted to play the "brother" card? He was hilarious.

Malachi, however, wasn't taking the hand. "Maybe the next time I'm in town."

I shifted my weight from one foot to the other, determined not to let Trenton act like I was invisible. "Why did you really come here?" I asked, my impatience mounting.

"I needed that red canopy you used last Memorial Day."

Correction: The red canopy *we* used last Memorial Day.

I turned the bottom lock, then opened the dead bolt. "Come on in, Malachi," I told him. Then I turned to Trenton. "I'll be back in a minute."

Malachi followed me into the dark apartment. I closed the door behind him, leaving Trenton on the other side. I flipped the nearest light switch, flooding the living room with the soft, understated glow of my lamps.

"You can put those on the kitchen counter," I told Malachi, nodding to the bags of food. "Let me find this oh-so-important canopy."

I unlocked the patio door, slid it open, and went to unlock the storage closet where I kept the items that I didn't use often so they wouldn't clutter my apartment's interior. I was a stickler for open spaces where I could breathe and think freely. Physical clutter clouded my mind. I moved aside a bin of Christmas ornaments, an old box of books that I'd been meaning to donate, and an old torch lamp so I could reach the box containing the red canopy. I'd resealed it so perfectly that it looked like it had never been used.

I lugged it out of the closet and dragged it through the apartment to the front door.

Trenton was leaning against the wall, picking at his cuticles.

"Here you go," I told him, dropping the box at his feet.

He gave me another slow scan. "You look nice," he said. "You did all that for Malachi Burke?"

I walked back inside closed the door in his face with a loud click. That was my answer.

Malachi had made himself comfortable on the couch. He raised his thick eyebrows in perfect arches like question marks.

"Yes, he's an ex," I said, answering his unspoken query.

"Too bad for him," Malachi said with a shrug. "But good for me—it got me in your door. Good for you, too, using me to get to him." His lips turned up in a smile.

I picked up a hair elastic from the end table and pulled my hair into a ponytail, wrapping it in a knot. "That's not what happened at all. You offered to walk me to the door. It just so happened to be perfect timing."

Malachi stood and meandered toward the kitchen to unpack the brown bags that were nearly bursting at the seams. "He's in his car right now, wondering what's going on in here. I bet you he hasn't even left yet. He's staking out the place."

I turned on the extra-bright overhead lamp. The subtle lighting I usually preferred was definitely too romantic.

"He made me his ex. Not the other way around. So, there's no jealousy, if that's what you're saying." I stepped out of my sandals.

"There is," Malachi said, "but he'd never admit it. Trust me on that one."

I didn't know what to say to that, so I just stood there watching him unpack the contents of the bags from the convenience store.

"I picked up a few things for myself, too," Malachi said, dropping the conversation about Trenton. He lifted out an oblong plastic container I immediately recognized, because the hot dogs at the gas station were a guilty pleasure of mine. Through the clear lid, I could see that he'd topped his liberally with slaw, relish, onions, and chili. My mouth watered. I hoped he'd made mine up the same way.

But when he reached inside the bag again, he produced two sub sandwiches neatly wrapped in paper. On the orange labels, I read my dinner options: cold cut combo or turkey and cheese.

"Thanks," I said, trying not to let my disappointment show as I reached for the turkey and cheese. If I wouldn't let Farrah have her ice cream, it was only right that I deny myself of a beef hot dog dripping with chili. I thought about the beach. I thought about my swimsuit. No hot dog.

Malachi took out a small pouch of baked potato chips, then started to return his hot dog to the bag.

"You can eat here if you want to," I told him, snatching two paper towels off the roll. "I'd hate to use you and then run you off."

"And just like that, I'm having dinner with you after all," Malachi said, reclaiming his spot on the sofa. "Tell your boy I owe him one."

He settled back comfortably, as if we'd known each other for years. I had to remind myself that it had been only two days. I'd broken all my rules with this man. Even Trenton hadn't made it inside my apartment until three months of dating had passed. Sure, most of the world knew Malachi Burke, but that was his public persona. In private, he could've had an alter ego. I prayed not.

"You owe Trenton…what? An interview?" I asked, struggling to take a bite of my giant sandwich without opening my mouth like a hungry shark.

Malachi, on the other hand, shoved nearly half his hot dog into his mouth. Relish dripped out the end and onto his fingers.

He shook his head. "Nah. I'm serious about not wanting to talk to the media." He swept a napkin across his mouth. "Not *all* the media, anyway. I owe him one for getting me behind these doors."

I smirked. "Ms. Nola has rubbed off on you." Then I picked up the remote and turned on the television. I needed noise to fill the space between us. It made things more comfortable, for the time being, and helped me to push my other thoughts about Malachi to the back of my mind. I could hear Farrah's voice telling me, "Call on Jesus, girl." Trenton's unexpected appearance had made me forget about Malachi's racy text, but for only a few minutes. I only wondered why it was causing me such irritation. It should have come as no surprise, since I'd called out his character from the beginning. I knew from my research what type of man he was. He could claim to be different, but actions—and, sometimes, text messages—spoke louder than words.

"Speaking of Gran'nola, I should've checked in with her to see if she was hungry," Malachi said, opening his own bag of chips. "She's not big on junk food, though." He patted both of his pant pockets, then wiped his hands before digging with one of them between the couch cushions.

"I think you left your phone charging in the car," I told him. "It buzzed at least once while you were in the store."

He sighed. "I told you, that thing never stops. A cell phone is an electronic leash, and we're all connected to it."

"I'd have to agree," I said, flipping to a channel showing reruns of *The Cosby Show.*

"I used to wish I was Vanessa," I said, remembering how I'd tried to mimic her high-school style even when I was in elementary school. My mom allowed me to wear the baggy sweaters and leg warmers, but she drew the line at the off-the-shoulder shirts and oversized neon earrings. And when I boldly borrowed her lipstick one morning, my teacher, Mrs. Eller, hadn't wasted any time phoning her.

"This was *the* show," Malachi said. He crumpled up his empty chip bag and stuffed it inside the hot dog container. "I was in love with Clair Huxtable."

"Clair?" I laughed, folding my legs and tucking them under my full skirt. "You're kidding me."

"Dead serious. I was attracted to older women back then." He rubbed his chin.

"I guess every boy has his fantasy."

"Like you probably fantasized about Theo."

"Theo and Lionel Richie," I admitted. I put a hand to my forehead, not believing I'd made that confession. Theo, yes. Lionel Richie, no.

"Lionel Richie?" Malachi looked at me in disbelief. "I'll never view you the same way again."

"Whatever," I said. "You're just mad because you didn't have his curly, wavy hair. But it's okay. Maybe someday." I gave him a sympathetic pat on the shoulder.

"A woman with a sense of humor," he said, looking relaxed as he interlocked his fingers behind his head and leaned back against the oversized throw pillows. I'd fallen in love with the orange and gold Moroccan-inspired pattern and had found complementary sheer drapes for windows. He'd been checking out my apartment décor since he walked in.

"Why do you sound surprised?"

"I just didn't expect it from a woman who could've killed me with the looks she was shooting me when we first met. If Gran'nola hadn't come to my rescue by inviting you for breakfast, your article would've been about two paragraphs long."

I collected our trash and carried it into the kitchen. "I judged you prematurely, and I apologize. But don't forget—you said we had a clean slate."

"Apology accepted," Malachi said, joining me in the kitchen. "And that's the last time you'll hear me talk about how mean you were." He purposefully bumped against me.

I smacked his arm, but he grabbed my hand before I could snatch it back.

The world stopped.

It was a moment in time when our hands touched for a reason other than a professional handshake. And it felt natural. It felt right.

But then I thought of the woman in the red bikini, attempting to seduce him from miles away, and I snapped back to reality.

"I appreciate the ride home," I said, ending our night. "And the sandwich. That was thoughtful."

"My pleasure," he said, lingering.

In the confines of the galley-style space, he seemed more like a broad-shouldered football linebacker than a baseball player. We did an awkward dance as Malachi moved past me and lifted the trash bag out of the bin by the handles. "I'll take it out for you," he said. "I saw the receptacle on the way in."

I wanted him to stay, but I needed him to leave.

"If you need anything, give me a call," he said. "I can pick you up. No problem."

"My mechanic is usually pretty quick with repairs," I said. "Vinny's the only man I trust to repair my car without emptying my wallet. I should be up and running again by tomorrow afternoon. And if not, I've got backup."

"Cool." Malachi walked to the door, unlocked it, and peeked out into the breezeway.

"I don't think you need to worry about the paparazzi here," I said, coming up behind him.

"Forget the paparazzi. I'm checking for your boy," he said, pretending to hold a pair of binoculars. "He's probably spying on us right now. Maybe we should give him something to watch, just in case."

I held out my hand, and Malachi took it in his own. He lifted it to his lips and pressed the softest kiss against my skin. *Shivers.* I pulled away.

"Take care, Malachi," I said. Then I gently but quickly closed the door. As I turned the lock to close the space between us, I was still collecting myself from his simple kiss on my hand.

Before I could take a single step, Malachi knocked again.

14

Malachi

Malachi couldn't let Rae get away. He'd never been the kind of man to give up; and, truth be told, he'd never been the kind of man to get rejected, either. Clearly, it was a game. Rae wanted him to chase her, and he was willing to do it. He would run until his legs gave out, and then he'd get up and run again. He'd felt that magnetism again when their hands had touched.

Rae opened the door a fraction, only wide enough to show half her face.

He hadn't thought about what he'd say, but it was now or never.

"One time," he said. "Let me take you out one time. After that, you'll never have to see me again if you don't want to."

"Why?" Rae asked, still not opening the door.

A simple, single word, and yet it was a loaded question. She was trying to make him say something so she could shut him down. He had to think quickly.

"Why not?" Malachi countered.

"You can't throw a question back on me," Rae said. "If you can't answer my simple question, what makes you think I should carve time out of my day for you?"

Snap. She'd pulled out the whip, but Malachi wasn't intimidated. *It's a front*, he told himself.

He studied Rae's face through the six-inch opening of the door, then glanced left and right. The June sun had descended halfway below the horizon, giving the breezeway a purplish glow. And here he was, standing all alone, because the woman he wanted to take out wouldn't open the door wide enough for him to put a foot inside.

"Come on, open the door. Please." Malachi winked at her. Women loved that. It was a tactic Uncle Bud had taught him, and it had yet to fail him. But there was a first time for everything.

Rae turned her head, probably to hide the smile that had started to spread across her face.

Seconds later, she looked back to him, her face serious but with a hint of mischief. "Can't do it," she said.

Two doors down, a neighbor emerged from his apartment carrying two black garbage bags slung over his shoulders like barbell weights. He paused, his eyes narrowing as he stared Malachi down. His door closed behind him with a loud bang.

"How you doing, sir?" Malachi said.

This scene wasn't playing out like he'd planned. He was supposed to knock on the door, have Rae welcome him back inside, and convince her to let him show her the perfect date night. He wanted to smash every stereotype she had of him, and put an image in her mind other than the one she'd formed.

"Rae?" the man yelled. "Are you okay?"

"I'm fine, Perry," Rae said. She poked her head outside, proving that she wasn't in danger.

"Okay. You know I got your back, so just holler if you need me. I'm going to take out the trash, and then I'll be right back. Right back," he emphasized.

Perry eyed Malachi, a scowl forming on his hard, wide face. "What's up, bro?" He looked down at the garbage bag by Malachi's feet. "Do you want me to take that out for you?" He walked over and hoisted the additional bag over his shoulder before Malachi could object.

Then Perry paused, studying Malachi's face. "Do I know you?"

Malachi shrugged.

"You live around here?"

"New York," Malachi said.

"You look familiar. Like ol' boy who plays for the Steelers."

"Naw," Malachi said.

If this guy didn't recognize him, he wasn't about to volunteer any information. Rae cleared her throat to get his attention. She pressed a finger against her lips, and Malachi knew she wouldn't say a word, either.

"Take it easy, man," Perry said, although he still tried to intimidate Malachi with his size. He was significantly taller, wider, and more muscular than Malachi, but that didn't rub Malachi one way or the other.

When Perry disappeared into the parking lot, Malachi took two steps away from Rae's door. "Now I have to look out for your ex *and* Perry. And all I want to do is take you out."

Rae finally opened the door wide enough for him to see her whole body. She leaned against the door frame, playing with the small curls of hair at the nape of her neck. "You can call me in three days. Check your text messages. Sleep on it. And after that, if you still want to take me out, call me. Three days. Not a day earlier."

Then she closed the door again.

Malachi took his bruised ego back to his SUV and immediately checked his phone. What was she going to tell him via text that she couldn't have said to him face-to-face?

He pushed the button to unlock the screen, and a list of notifications popped up. There were several missed calls: one from Gran'nola, one from Alonzo, and two from Alexandria. And then there was the text.

Malachi sighed and let his head fall against the headrest. Rae must have seen the text from Alexandria. Red bikini. New York City. Now it all made sense.

He'd call Alexandria back. Once. He had to make this stop.

"It took you long enough," she answered with a huff. "I was starting to think you'd gone back to North Carolina and fallen in love with one of those country girls."

"You need to stop texting me photos," Malachi said flatly.

"Why? I thought you liked my pictures. You've always liked my pictures. No, make that *loved*."

"I'm around kids all the time. Young, impressionable boys. What if my phone lands in the hands of a seven-year-old? Or a member of my team? Or, God forbid, my grandmother?" *Or Rae?* he thought to himself.

"You're taking away all of my fun," she pouted. "I guess I won't send the ones I took during my bubble bath this evening." She giggled seductively.

Malachi forced his mind not to form a visual based on the statement she'd just made. Alexandria knew exactly what she was doing.

Malachi stopped at the traffic light at the intersection of Rae's street and the main thoroughfare. It was amazing how a term as simple as "bubble bath" could open his mind to memories that went back two and three years. The first time Alexandria had slept over at his place, he'd awakened to a breakfast of smoked salmon and scrambled egg whites, followed by a warm bubble bath that she'd run for him. Of course, she'd joined him in the Jacuzzi.

"Don't you miss me?" she said, barging into his thoughts.

"I'm working, Alexandria. I haven't had time to miss anybody or anything."

"When are you coming back home?"

"I'm not sure," he said. "I'm not in a rush."

"But I'm in a rush to see you," she cooed. "I really miss you. And I'm not just saying that. I haven't seen you in forever. Too long. We're past due for one of our special sessions."

The longer Malachi stayed away from Alexandria, the better. In the past, she'd been like an addiction, and he'd had to go through a veritable detox to rid himself of everything about her—her body. Her scent. Her sex appeal. Even her intelligence. But Alexandria wasn't the one for him.

She may have cost him many sleepless nights, but he would never tie his life to hers forever.

"It's for the best," Malachi finally said. "We've talked about this. We should move on."

"We've moved on before, but we've always come back together," Alexandria countered. "Why is that?"

"We fall back into the familiar. I get lonely. You get lonely."

"Familiar's not a bad thing."

Malachi slowed to a stop at another traffic light. *Stop.* That's what he wanted Alexandria to do. *Stop.* He wanted everybody—his publicist, his agent, his trainer, his coach, his teammates—to stop.

"Alexandria, I have to go," Malachi said. "Stop sending the pictures."

"I know you, babe. You're tired. You're stressed. You have too much on your mind," she said, assessing him.

"I'll be fine," Malachi insisted. "Take care." He disconnected the call before she could pull him deeper into her clutches.

Malachi's two phone calls to Gran'nola went unanswered, unnerving him. He'd been cruising through his old stomping grounds at a leisurely speed, but when he thought of the disappearing act Aunt Mimi had told him about, he picked up his pace. He was so focused on rushing back to Gran'nola's that he hadn't realized he'd been going twenty miles over the speed limit until the blue lights were flashing in his rearview mirror.

Malachi slowed and pulled over to the shoulder of the road. This was one of the times he hoped his name would work in his favor, and get him off the hook. On the other hand, it may be a police officer with a point to prove that celebrity status didn't excuse him from the law.

Malachi let the window down slowly so as not to cause any alarm. He didn't want to be a headline in the news. He watched in the side mirror as the officer approached the car cautiously, a flashlight in his hand.

"License and registration, please, sir," the officer said.

Malachi pulled his license from his wallet and reached into the glove compartment for the car's rental papers. He handed them to the officer—Leviticus Gray, according to his name tag.

"Mr. Burke," Officer Gray said. "If you can hit a baseball at the speed you were driving, you guys might actually make it to the World Series."

Lucky for Malachi, Officer Leviticus Gray was a huge fan. To show his gratitude for the mere verbal warning he'd received, Malachi autographed one of the spare baseballs he'd brought from the field.

Malachi cruised at five miles below the speed limit for the rest of the ride. When he finally turned into the gravel driveway at Gran'nola's, he realized why she had missed his calls. Cars were parked around the perimeter of the yard, leaving the lawn open for several picnic tables and a considerable spread of food.

It was almost nine o'clock on a Sunday night, and the Burkes were partying like it was two o'clock on a Saturday afternoon.

"You've got to be kidding me," Malachi said as he inched between a maple tree and Uncle Bud's beat-up Chevy. He had no words for his uncle, who'd attended the opening session of camp on Friday night but had bailed on him Saturday and Sunday. Bowling tournament, supposedly.

Two of his pint-sized cousins—he honestly didn't know whom they belonged to—ran up to him, holding a wrinkled sign that read "SURPRISE!" They danced in the bright rays of his headlights.

As if on cue, Malachi's car was surrounded with exuberant faces. Family members he hadn't seen in at least five years circled around the SUV, many of them wearing a replica of his jersey, others with his team's cap on their head.

His irritation melted away. He was as tired as the day was long, but he would find the extra energy from somewhere to entertain his family. They'd been his fans before he'd had any.

Uncle Bud opened the driver's door and nearly yanked him out in his excitement. "Boy, do you know how long we've been waiting? The party couldn't get started until you got here."

Malachi looked around at the half-eaten pans of food and the crumpled soda cans left in the middle of the tables for Gran'nola to collect and recycle. He saw the radio sitting on a tree stump near the back porch. It was the same beat-up, battery-operated radio they'd pulled out for family gatherings for years. Once upon a time, his older cousins had saved their money to by the boom box—what it was called back then—to practice their break-dancing movies on a piece of cardboard in the middle of the yard.

Those were the days, Malachi thought as he trekked towards the house.

"It doesn't look like I stopped you from cranking things up," Malachi said. "I know my family. You know how to throw it down."

As he made his way to the house, he was bombarded with hugs, high fives, and words of encouragement.

"I didn't think you'd be gone this long," Gran'nola said, coming to wrap him in a hug. "I did this special, just for you. You know everybody's been wanting to see you, so I told them to go home and take a nap after church, then come back over with a dish."

"I would've been here earlier, but...someone had car trouble," Malachi said. He didn't want to tell her it was Rae. That would just invite a long interrogation he didn't have energy for right now.

"We're just glad you're finally here. Now, go on in and see your cousin Marilyn. She'll be a hundred and three next week. She'll have no idea who you are, and you probably won't know what she's saying, but just nod and smile."

Malachi nodded and smiled.

"Yes, like that," Gran'nola patted him on the shoulder and pushed him toward the den.

Gran'nola was right—Malachi couldn't comprehend a single word from Cousin Marilyn's mouth. But he waited patiently while she held his hand and mumbled incessantly until her daughter, Melissa, stepped in and saved him. When he returned to the kitchen, Aunt Mimi had fixed him a plate, ready to stuff him with fried chicken, potato salad, green beans, dressing, and sweet potato soufflé.

"Had I known this was going on, I would've saved my appetite," he said, certain he couldn't eat another bite. The hot dog from the gas station still sat heavy on his stomach. "Can you wrap it up for later?"

"If you insist," Aunt Mimi said. "And before you ask, yes, there's another chocolate chip cake just for you. It's got your name on it, so not a single slice has been cut."

"But I haven't finished the first one you made," he said. If his family kept this up, they'd have to roll him back to New York.

"This one's fresh. I let everybody else eat the other one."

Malachi would have to buckle down this week if he wanted to keep off the weight. Until now, he'd never truly appreciated how helpful it was to have his meals prepared by Chef Devlin. He made the occasional trip to the grocery store for fresh produce and organic foods, but he was usually either too tired or too preoccupied to cook anything for himself. Gran'nola would make sure he ate heartily while he was here, but not healthily. If a recipe didn't call for vegetable oil, loads of butter, or salt, Gran'nola was clueless.

Malachi ducked into the bathroom long enough to wash his face and freshen up. A shower was out of the question for now. It turned out to be another three hours before he could even think about it.

It was after midnight when the last Burke family member pulled out of the driveway. Other than four commercial-sized garbage bags stuffed with trash, Gran'nola's house looked the same as it had that morning. That was another rule the family didn't budge about: No one could sneak away from a family gathering without lending a hand in the cleanup efforts.

"Gran'nola, I'm headed to bed," Malachi said, growling out a yawn. He was fresh out of the shower and hadn't been able to resist the plate Aunt Mimi had stashed away for him. Or the freshly baked chocolate chip cake. The second time around tasted better than the first. "It's been a long day."

"I know it," she said as she shuffled down the hall to her room.

Malachi followed her. He sat at the bottom of her four-poster bed and watched her pull out a scarf she kept in her top dresser drawer. She untied the simple knot and folded back the edges to reveal a bundle of sponge rollers. Malachi didn't know of any other woman who still rolled her hair with those pink sponges every night.

As Gran'nola carefully wrapped small sections of her hair around the sponges and snapped the rollers into place, he glanced around her room at the television Gran'nola couldn't seem to figure out. The brown stuffed Teddy bear holding a heart that he'd given her for Valentine's

Day during his senior year of college. The oil lamp by her bed. It was a family heirloom, passed down from Gran'nola's great-grandmother. He chuckled to himself, remembering the time he'd almost knocked it off her end table. He'd had to dive like a ninja to keep it from crashing to the floor.

"I'm doing laundry tomorrow, so put your things in the hamper if you want them washed," Gran'nola said.

"I'll check," Malachi said. He definitely had clothes that needed washing, but he wanted to do it himself. Gran'nola shrunk everything. If he gave her an extra-large T-shirt, she'd give him back a newborn-sized onesie. He'd started laundering his own clothes in middle school, so he wouldn't have to endure the taunts of his sixth-grade classmates for wearing high-water jeans.

Malachi's gaze shifted to the phone on the nightstand and the row of sticky notes lined up beside it. He squinted, trying to read her chicken scratch. Each note bore a different phone number. Aunt Mimi. Uncle Bud. The church. Her own home. And others that Gran'nola had known forever. Even Malachi had them memorized. They hadn't changed in over twenty years.

"Gran'nola," he said. "What are these numbers for?"

Gran'nola slid her comb back in the dresser drawer and patted the sides of her hair. "What do you mean, what are they for? To call."

Malachi cleared his throat. "But why do you have them written down? You know them by heart."

"Of course I do," she shot back. "But sometimes my mind gets the numbers mixed up, so I wrote them down to post nearby. If you live long enough, you'll see. Be thankful for your strong mind while you have it."

Malachi had to tread lightly. Gran'nola had always been fiercely independent, and any inference that she couldn't handle things on her own would irritate her. They'd ended the night on a high note, surrounded by the love of their family, and he didn't want to dampen that feeling.

"Are there other things you have trouble remembering?" he asked gently. He leaned over to untie his shoes, wanting to come off casual and unconcerned.

"From time to time." She lifted one shoulder. "Live long enough...."

Malachi tugged off one shoe, then started on the other. "I worry about you," he admitted.

"God's been keeping me all this time. Why would that change now?"

"It won't," Malachi said, pulling on a pair of socks. "But don't you think part of His care includes people who love you and will help you?"

"What kind of help do I need?"

Malachi swallowed. "What kind of help do you want?" he asked, hoping that she'd be real. Hoping that she'd realize she didn't have to be strong.

Gran'nola walked over and stared him down. Her eyes had lightened over the years from a darker brown to a deep, cloudy gray. Her answer was stern. Her answer was final.

"None."

She went into the bathroom and closed the door behind her.

That was the second time tonight that a woman had shut a door in his face. He would sleep. Start over. And hope for a better Monday morning.

Malachi retired to the bedroom and crawled under the covers. He could tell that Gran'nola had changed the linens. The sheets smelled like the lavender dryer sheets she used. The scent battled with the smell of the ointment he'd massaged into his aching shoulder. What he wouldn't do to have a physical therapist and a personal chef for the next two weeks. Gran'nola probably didn't want someone else probing around her kitchen, but she'd adapt. She might even come to enjoy it.

When Malachi closed his eyes, he saw Rae's face and the easy beauty that Jared had caught when he was taking pictures of her at the field. He saw her leaning against the frame of her apartment door, fingering the tendrils of hair on her neck, as she refused to let him back inside.

She'd played him. And he'd liked it.

Three days. She'd said he couldn't call her for three days.

One date. That was all he needed.

15

Malachi

Absolutely nothing happened on Monday, and Malachi wouldn't have had it any other way. No phone calls from the media. No unexpected drop-ins from family members, until Aunt Mimi showed up to cart Gran'nola off to her eye doctor appointment—the one she'd rescheduled after missing one three weeks ago, and still had nearly forgotten about.

Now, with his grandma in the care of her sister, Malachi powered off his cell phone—something he never did. Calls from those who cared about his professional life would be diverted to his voice mail. Calls from those who cared about him, and only him....

There probably wouldn't be any.

For lunch, he exercised self-control and made himself a sauté of zucchini, onion, and red peppers over a bed of brown rice.

"Bon appétit," he said to himself, scooping a huge spoonful into his mouth. Not bad.

Three hours later, Malachi was bored out of his mind, but he still refused to do anything other than bum around on the couch in his boxers. He was used to being on the go, and making the decision to settle down for the day was good for him. He needed to be alone with his thoughts. Needed to contemplate his next move with no input except from the still, small voice.

Shortly before making this latest trip to Greensboro, Malachi had read a Scripture verse that had spoken directly to his life. He'd found it somewhere in Proverbs 19. *"Many are the plans in a person's heart, but it is the LORD's purpose that prevails."*

God, show me Your purpose, Malachi prayed as he stared at the ceiling.

He'd never expected to consider walking away from baseball voluntarily. When he'd first been drafted, he'd dreamed of playing until they dragged him off of the field. He'd thought himself invincible back then. While he'd known that shoulder and arm injuries were common, somehow he'd considered himself immune to the worst wear and tear. But he'd been in his twenties, and, like Gran'nola had always told him, twenty-year-olds didn't know anything.

What would he do if he walked away from the game? Baseball differed from football and basketball in that few retired players found positions as sports commentators or radio announcers. There was always coaching, he supposed. Malachi needed to weigh all that he had to lose and stack it against what he had to gain.

The house phone rang, and Malachi listened for the annoying automated voice that read off the caller ID.

Alonzo Jones.

Zo? What did he want? Malachi pushed himself off the couch. "What's going on?"

"On my break, man. Just checking on you. I called your cell a couple times, but it kept going straight to voice mail. I wanted to make sure you were good."

"I'm good," Malachi said, pulling the sheer curtains closed to shield out some of the afternoon sunlight. "Bored as I don't know what, though. How do y'all make it here?"

"You're a city slicker now, huh? You did just say 'y'all,' though, so you ain't that far from the country. You might've moved, but it's still in you."

Alonzo chuckled. "The key to the good life here is having a good woman by your side. And you can't find her just anywhere. They don't make them everywhere like they do in North Carolina. You need a home-grown country girl. She'll stick with you."

"That's what they all say. New York or North Carolina…ain't a woman a woman?"

"You're more hardheaded than I thought," Alonzo said. "You need to listen to your elders."

Alonzo was older than Malachi by exactly one month, and he had always claimed to be the elder, all-wise one.

"I've already noticed you clocked in on that reporter," Alonzo added. "She's a sweet little honeydew. I've seen you looking at her."

"I notice most women, Zo. I'm a man with eyes."

"Well then, you must've noticed Hakeem's momma in her short shorts and that teeny-tiny, itsy-bitsy tight shirt. Almost broke her neck walking around in those high-heeled sandals. She didn't leave the field for three days, and I don't think you even spoke to her."

"Didn't see her, I guess," Malachi confessed.

"And why do you think that is? Because you couldn't take your eyes off Rae Stevens. Ain't that her name? Whenever she was around, you were mesmerized. And when she wasn't there, I bet you were thinking about her. You know in those old-school Looney Tunes cartoons, when Pepé Le Pew has hearts in his eyes? Yep, that's you." Alonzo cackled.

"Is it that obvious?" Malachi asked. "Too bad the feeling isn't mutual. I asked her out. Three times. And she turned me down. Twice."

Alonzo whistled. "What about the third time?"

Malachi could tell his friend was getting a kick out of this. "She told me to call her in three days."

Alonzo cackled long and loud. "She's stringing you along," he said when he finally caught his breath. "You better hold on to that string with everything you've got. I already told you a North Carolina woman is a good thing. I've seen the pictures of you with plenty of other women on your arm. Just because they have those banging bodies doesn't mean they're your good thing."

"I know. I wish somebody would've told me that a long time ago," Malachi said, listening to a fire truck scream down the street.

"Look, man. I need to get back on this clock. I'll call you in a couple days, but if you need me before then, you know how to reach me."

"You bet," Malachi said.

The clock in the den ticked out one slow minute after another, and Malachi passed the rest of the afternoon dozing in between the sports recaps on ESPN.

He perked up when the chatter focused on him. "A frustrating season is officially over for Malachi Burke, who doesn't seem to be able to shake his repeated shoulder injury," the commentator was saying. "He started out as one of Major League Baseball's elite, but his high-powered arm may not be able to take him much farther in his career."

Click. He wouldn't listen to the speculations.

The crunch of gravel in the driveway announced the return of Gran'nola and Aunt Mimi. At least he'd have company now. He went into the bedroom to put on a pair of basketball shorts and a T-shirt, then walked out onto the porch to greet the two sisters.

As usual, they were bickering.

"They dilated my eyes; they didn't take them out," Gran'nola said, swatting Aunt Mimi's hand away from her elbow. "I can walk fine."

"This isn't about your legs, Nola. It's about your eyes. And, for the record, you don't walk fine. That arthritis in your knee is getting worse and worse."

"Mimi, are you a doctor? No. Hush up."

"I'm not saying another word. Thank God Malachi is here. He can deal with you for the rest of the day."

Malachi watched the exchange with quiet amusement. The sisters were more entertaining than anything he'd seen on television all day. Aunt Mimi waited until Gran'nola had reached the porch—close enough for Malachi to catch her if she stumbled—before heading back to her car.

"I'll be back in the morning to plant some mums," she said over her shoulder.

"Alright. See you then. Love you," Gran'nola said.

That quickly, they were acting as if nothing had happened.

If women could change their minds that quickly, there was no need to worry about Rae. By next week, she'd be in love with him.

16

Being without a vehicle actually made for a more productive Monday than most, even though I would have liked to be able to run out for a new color ink cartridge. Farrah had volunteered to pick me up and take me to Vinny's shop, but I just called a cab. I didn't want to inconvenience her, since she would have had to squeeze in the errand between two of her esthetician classes.

I hadn't told her about my possible date with Malachi. I was still mulling over whether it was a good idea, and I knew Farrah would push me to go out with him.

When I wasn't editing the feature article on him or catching up on my latest freelance articles for *Black Enterprise*, I perused the online montage of photos of him. Maybe he hadn't frolicked in public with as many women as I'd previously thought, but there were at least four recurring faces. The one that appeared the most often, I recognized as the woman who'd texted him the photo of herself in a red bikini. Unlike the others, who looked as if they practiced their statuesque pose in the mirror, she looked comfortable and satisfied on his arm. Her name was Alexandria. And she was waiting for his return.

I thought Malachi would try to call me before Wednesday, but on Tuesday afternoon, he still hadn't contacted me. It gave me more time than I'd anticipated having to think about whether to accept his invitation or turn him down again. I knew I shouldn't go, but I wanted to.

Then again, it was just one date; my heart wasn't tied to it. My prayer since my breakup with Trenton had been that God would guard my heart. I'd even written out Proverbs 4:23 on a piece of paper torn from my journal and taped it to my bathroom mirror: *"Above all else, guard your heart, for everything you do flows from it."*

Our weekly Monday-morning round table at the *Ledger* office had been moved to Tuesday because of a meeting Shelton had with a potential advertiser, but I ended up having to phone in for that one, as well. Ms. Bessie let me listen in to the updates via intercom. She'd procured a new advertiser from her dry cleaner, and Shelton had sold a three-month-run ad to two businesses: a summer tutoring program and a new events center. I was batting zero for zero, though I hoped Zenja would use the paper as an outlet to promote Friday Night Love. She'd called me that morning to ask about our ad rates so that she could pass them along to her partner, Caprice. That alone was promising.

"Ms. Bessie, you would be proud of me," I bragged after Shelton concluded the meeting. "I was cute with a capital C on Sunday."

"You're always cute. But maybe with a lower case C," she teased. "Swing by here when you leave the mechanic's. I want to see your hair before you mess it up in all that chlorine."

Now, Vinny tapped his fingers on the hood of my car, waiting for me to give him the thumbs-up of approval.

"Sounds good," I told Vinny. "And it looks even better." Vinny had thrown in a complimentary detailing package, so my car had been washed and waxed, its interior vacuumed, and the leather seats conditioned. He'd declined my offer for a tip, saying I'd lucked out because of a punishment his fifteen-year-old son had incurred for sneaking out to a party. Apparently, his sentence was working after school at his dad's repair shop. Indefinitely.

"Good seeing you, Vinny," I said. "But, given the circumstances, I don't want to see you again anytime soon."

Vinny stuffed an oil-soaked towel into his back pocket. "See you for an oil change in three thousand miles," he said, waving me off.

My car turned over on the first try and quietly hummed like it was as relieved to be up and running again as I was to have it back. I headed straight for the nearest office supply store for the ink cartridge, swung by my favorite health store for a power green smoothie, then headed over to the *Ledger* office.

The moment I walked in, Ms. Bessie began to coo over my mini-makeover. She summoned Shelton up front to her desk.

"Oh, yes. I know what this is all about," Shelton said, a look of approval on his face. He folded his arms across his midsection. "I think you've found a sudden fascination with baseball. I bet you're glad I assigned that story to you."

"Malachi is not the reason," I said, even though I didn't sound convincing enough to fool even myself.

"As long as that other man is out of your system, I don't mind who got the job done," he told me. "And word has it you went to Ms. Nola's for breakfast."

I knew that was Ms. Nola's doing. I bet she'd called Shelton and Lenora on Saturday morning, probably as soon as I was at the end of her driveway.

"She invited me," I said. "I couldn't turn her down."

"Yes, you could have," Ms. Bessie argued. "You turn me down all the time."

I didn't have an excuse that I could truthfully share. I always declined Ms. Bessie's invitations because her food tasted like she'd cooked it wearing a blindfold, then burned it. Poor Wallace. It was no wonder they ate out so much.

"I was conducting business," I said.

"Oh, that's what they call it these days?" Shelton said. "Carry on." He turned and disappeared down the hallway.

Outside, we heard a car pull into the driveway. Ms. Bessie peeked out the window.

"I'm checking out early today,' she said, cutting her eyes my way. "Me and Wallace have some business to conduct."

"You should come with me to the pool," I told her. "You may need to take a dip and cool off."

Ms. Bessie propped her hands on her hips. "At my age, if something heats up, the last thing I'm going to do is douse it with water." Then she pulled me into a tight hug.

"Have fun," I told her.

I left shortly after to meet Farrah at the recreation center.

Farrah didn't know how to swim, so she was always opposed to working out in the indoor pool. But it was my turn to choose our exercise regimen, so she begrudgingly agreed, as long as I didn't try to drag her into the deep end.

When I arrived at the rec center, I knew it would be at least another thirty minutes until Farrah showed up, so I put on my swimsuit and headed to the lap pool. I didn't understand why Farrah was opposed to learning to swim. Who wouldn't want to experience the feeling of weightlessness it offered? Water wasn't to be feared. It was to be enjoyed. Respected, but enjoyed. I dove in and pushed effortlessly through the water. The coldness was shocking, at first, but I warmed up quickly.

I buoyed to the surface to take a breath, then submerged myself again to swim the length of the pool. I kicked my legs rapidly through the water, propelling myself to the other end as fast as I could go. Three, four, five times. After my workout, my shoulders ached and felt revived at the same time. I dipped back down and treaded water, watching three senior women enjoy the swirling heat of the nearby hot tub.

I'd completed three more laps by the time Farrah arrived. She shuffled in with a towel wrapped so tightly around her that she could barely move.

"Drop that towel and get in the water," I said, swimming over to her side of the pool.

Farrah dipped her big toe in the water, then snatched it back. "Why do I let you do this to me?" she whined. "Walking the track would've been fine."

"We walk the track when it's your choice, and it's your choice all the time. Being in the water is easier on your joints than always pounding on the asphalt."

"If I get in, you better not splash my hair," she warned me.

"Your hair is safely tucked in that swimming cap," I assured her. "And you'll probably pay for your dry hair with a migraine headache. I know it's supposed to be tight, but seriously, I think you're wearing a child's size."

Farrah rolled her eyes and then stepped gingerly down the rungs of the pool ladder into the water, her shoulders shaking until her body adjusted to the temperature. "Let's hurry up and get this over with," she said, taking the water weights I handed her. "And don't try to coax me to the deep end, because I'm not going."

I led Farrah through a series of water exercises using the hand weights, followed by jumping jacks, kickbacks, and water lunges to tone the lower body. I noticed that she wasn't as winded after the repetitions as she'd been when we first committed to our exercise regimen back in the spring.

"You're a lot better than you use to be," I applauded her. "When we first started working out in the pool, you were always panting like you needed oxygen."

"Very funny," Farrah said. "Don't disturb me. I'm in my groove." She blew water from around her mouth. "I'm no Michael Phelps, but I'm getting used to the water. At least more comfortable."

"Comfortable enough that you'll let me help you float on your back?"

Farrah's shoulders tensed.

"Don't let me go under water," she said, agreeing at the same time she warned me.

"I won't," I said easing toward her.

We'd attempted on at least five previous occasions, and each time, Farrah had sunken like a boulder. But I wasn't giving up. If I could teach her how to float, I knew I could teach how her to swim.

Farrah leaned back and kicked out her legs, but her midsection continued to sink. I rested her shoulders against my chest. "You can do it, Farrah. Let your head fall back into the water."

"The water is getting in my ears," she protested in a panicked tone, taking quick gulps of air.

"You're not going under," I assured her. "I'm right here."

I inched backward, letting her feel the movement of the water.

"Lord Jesus, take me now," she sputtered, drops of water popping off her lips.

"Don't say that if you don't mean it," I said. "I don't want to have to explain anything to Casey."

"This is enough. Take me to the edge."

"Farrah, you can get to the edge on your own."

"Don't leave me here, Rae," she said, her body starting to sink again.

"Stand up, girl. It's only four feet deep."

Farrah regained her balance, then splashed me in the face before bouncing over to the side of the pool and climbing out.

I took one final dunk beneath the water. When I resurfaced, I wiped the dripping water from my face and blinked until I could see.

"I'm a very happily married woman, but there's one thing I know for sure," Farrah said, so quietly, I could barely hear her. "There would be a lot more black women learning to swim if men like that would teach them."

I turned and blinked. Blinked again. But, try as I might, I couldn't blink away the sight of Malachi.

17

I turned around, hoping Malachi hadn't seen me. He was standing on the other side of the pool with another man of similar size and stature. Although his companion was fully dressed in workout shorts and a sleeveless shirt, Malachi wore only swimming trunks.

"That's him," I whispered to Farrah.

She leaned down. "Him, who?"

"Malachi Burke." I pulled my hair to the side and squeezed out the water. I searched for my towel, which, of course, was draped across the chair closest to Malachi.

"I guess that made writing your article a lot easier." Farrah glanced his way again. "He looks a lot taller in person than he does in those Internet photos. More muscular, too."

"Will you be quiet and go get my towel?" I said, peeking over my shoulder. Malachi was too preoccupied with stretching out his shoulders to notice me. Even from this distance, I could see him wince as the other man lightly tugged his arm behind him.

"Why do you need your towel?" Farrah asked. "You walk around here without one all the time. Plenty of strangers have seen you in your swimsuit."

"That's the point," I hissed. "Malachi isn't a stranger. It's about being professional."

"You ate his grandmother's country-fried steak. What's professional about that?"

"Towel, please," I said through clenched teeth.

Farrah reached for her own jumbo towel and rewrapped herself like an enchilada before sloshing over to the chair. Wouldn't you know it, she spoke to Malachi. He turned my way with a smile and a wave. The next thing I knew, he had taken my towel from Farrah and was walking my way.

I lowered myself in the water until it made small waves over the tops of my shoulders.

"Hey, you," he said, holding the towel out in front of him. "You can't seem to stay away from me."

"That's funny, seeing how I was here first," I said. I wasn't about to get out of the water. And where had Farrah disappeared to?

"I'm here to work with one of the therapists my guy in New York recommended. I think I overdid it at the camp. Those fastballs did a number on my shoulder." He moved his arm in a circle. "Is this where you always come to swim?"

"Most of the time," I said. "The pool isn't usually crowded, so I have my run of the lanes unless they're having a water aerobics class." I gripped the railing of the pool ladder, then held up my hand for my towel. Malachi tossed it in my direction, and I wrapped it around my waist as I emerged from the water.

His question from Sunday night still hung between us.

"I better get going," he said. "My therapist's next session starts in less than an hour."

Nothing. He'd said nothing. My heart sank. I'd been too standoff-ish. I'd pushed him away, and he was going to keep on walking.

Three days. That was the dumbest idea. I didn't even know why it had come out of my mouth, because we were both too old to be playing games.

"Have a good one," I said. I slipped my feet into my flip-flops and headed for the women's locker room to change. Farrah had already rinsed herself off and peeled away her swimming cap and was now toweling herself dry near the locker we always shared.

"I can't believe you left me out there," I grumbled, taking my shower bag off the hook in the locker.

"It looked like you were in good hands," she said, smiling. "When he took the towel from me, I figured he wanted some privacy. So, are you going to go out with the brother or not?"

"He's not really interested in me," I told her, in case he decided not to call me again. "He's only being persistent because I'm turning him down."

"No man—especially one as eligible as Malachi Burke—would ask out a woman again after an initial rejection unless he was genuinely interested. Maybe one rejection. But not two."

I cushioned my bottom with the damp towel and sat down on the wooden bench. "Well, it doesn't matter. The third time he asked me out, I told him to call me in three days. And it's been that long. Well, almost. Tomorrow will be day three. But he didn't mention it just now."

"Maybe he's just playing by the rules," Farrah pointed out. "Three days is three days, not two and a half. And where did you come up with that nonsense, anyway?"

I shrugged, kicking myself at my own foolishness. "Like I said, it probably doesn't matter. Life goes on."

"You should go out there, confess that you were temporarily insane, and let him know you're available to go out. Tonight."

"I'm not doing that," I said, closing the locker and snapping the combination lock closed.

"Then you better pray one of those senior citizens in the hot tub doesn't snatch him up, because they were whispering and giggling like teenagers when I walked by," Farrah said. "I bet they stay in there until he's finished working out in the pool. They're going to look like prunes."

I laughed. "They already do."

"Bye, girl," Farrah said, blowing me a kiss. "When he calls you tomorrow, and you know he will, do not—I repeat, do not—play games."

After showering, I slipped into a long tube sundress and headed home, where I spent most of the night recounting my conversations with Malachi. The next morning, I dressed and headed to the office, arriving at the *Ledger* at the same time as Ms. Bessie. She was surprised to see me there so early. I was more astonished that she'd arrived with Wallace.

"Some things don't need to be questioned," she said to me as she unlocked the front door, then deactivated the alarm. "Sometimes, you have to let love have its way."

I hadn't asked her anything.

"I hear you, Ms. Bessie," I said.

I set up my work station at my usual desk, then read through the edited draft of my article once more before e-mailing it to Shelton. Even though I hadn't had the chance to speak to Ms. Nola again, I wanted to make sure I was headed in the right direction.

An hour later, Shelton still hadn't showed up.

"Did Shelton say what time he'd be in this morning?" I asked Ms. Bessie.

"I haven't heard from him. He may have taken his wife to breakfast. On Wednesdays, seniors get a fifty percent discount at the spot owned by the Mae sisters. Those sisters can burn in the kitchen."

I was eager for input on my article, particularly the way I'd woven in some of Ms. Nola's recollections of Malachi's childhood. I'd been enraptured by the animated way she'd retold the history of not just her grandson but the entire Burke family, as well. I knew she would appreciate being included.

Ms. Bessie marched into the work area nearly an hour later with a message from Shelton to the staff. "He had to meet with some potential advertisers again," she informed me and Jared.

Jared, still pumped after his offer from Malachi, had stopped in to pick up a chicken casserole Ms. Bessie had cooked for him. It was his first time eating her cooking. He had no idea what he was in for.

"Unfortunately, two of our major accounts pulled their ads. Two in the same week." She tsked. "I know that hurt Shelton to his heart. If we were hanging on by a wing and a prayer before, we have only a tip of a wing now." Ms. Bessie pulled me to the side. "He wanted to tell you this himself, but I thought you should know…he's going to have to reduce our publications to bimonthly."

I was disappointed but not surprised. I knew that the minimal pay I earned as a staff writer would decrease as a result, but I had enough regular freelance assignments that it didn't matter. Work for writers could be abundant if they had the right connections, and I'd been building my network for a long time.

"How do you feel about it?" I asked Ms. Bessie, noticing the wrinkles of worry that were etched in the skin around her eyes.

She sighed. "I'm grateful we've lasted as long as we have, but I don't want to see this newspaper fold. The community needs it, and Shelton needs it."

"Something will come through," I said. "I'm sure of it. I've been busy trying to meet some other deadlines, but by the end of the week, I'll start making some calls."

"Make some calls and say some prayers," Ms. Bessie ordered me. "We need both."

I went back to the desk and closed my laptop. It was only ten o'clock, and I'd planned to busy myself at the office for most of the day so I wouldn't be alone at home, willing my phone to ring like a silly high school girl waiting for her crush to invite her to the prom. I packed up the rest of my things and went up front to find Ms. Bessie with three boxes of files stacked on her desk.

"Do you need a hand?" I asked, hanging my bag inside the coat closet.

"I'll separate, you shred," she said, lifting the lid off the first box.

"Deal."

Ms. Bessie and I sorted, shredded, and organized all three boxes of files before we took a break. "Three down, eleven to go," she said, looking at the mountain of boxes beside her desk. "Everything goes a little faster with help."

"Glad to be of service," I told her. "Do you want me stay? We can tackle two more boxes."

"I've had enough paper cuts for one day," Ms. Bessie said. "Let's close the office. I'm in need of a pedicure."

"Meet you back here in the morning?" I asked.

"If you want to come in, I'm not turning you down."

"Need a ride home?" I asked with a smile.

"No, thanks. Someone's coming to get me," she said, as if I wouldn't know who that person would be.

Someone like Wallace? I wanted to say, but I didn't dare. I didn't want Ms. Bessie to chew me out.

All of the decluttering we'd done at the office inspired me to clean up as soon as I walked in the door at home. I was sitting in my bathroom in a sea of body oils and fragranced lotions when I heard my phone ringing from the living room. I jumped up and vaulted over the scattered bottles to get to the phone before I missed the call. *Please be Malachi,* I thought.

18

Malachi

It was after three o'clock when Malachi went to call Rae, though he'd been ready to phone her from the minute he'd opened his eyes that morning. He would have asked her out again yesterday at the pool, but he hadn't wanted to give her a reason to turn him down. She'd said three days, not two.

Was now a good time? Or would she be busy writing? Had he waited too long?

Just as he was about to make the call, Gran'nola summoned him to her bedroom.

She'd been doing that all day—bellowing for his help every time he sat down. That morning, it was lugging empty flower pots up from the basement. After that, she'd wanted him to mount wall hooks in her storage shed. This time, she wanted to show him the program from the funeral service for his very distant cousin Isaiah Smith. He'd never met the man in his life.

"The service was nice," she reflected. "Lasted too long, but it was nice."

Malachi returned the program to the stack of those she'd collected over the years. "I'm going outside for a minute," he told her.

"Alright, baby," Gran'nola said. "I'll be in the kitchen, seeing what I can put together for dinner."

Finally, he escaped. He'd eat whatever Gran'nola offered tonight, but his assistant, Katrene, had arranged for a local chef to come tomorrow and prepare enough meals to last them a week. Malachi hadn't told Gran'nola yet, and he was leaning toward letting her be surprised when Chef Devlin showed up the next morning.

But Malachi had more important things on his mind. He found Rae's number in his phone's contact list and went to his vehicle, since it was the only place he could talk undisturbed. It reminded him of high school, when he used to take the cordless phone into his beat-up Toyota Tercel to talk to his girlfriends. He'd park close enough to the house for the phone to be in range, but for him to be out of earshot of Gran'nola.

After five rings, he was preparing to leave a voice mail.

Rae answered on the sixth ring. "Hey." She sounded out of breath.

Malachi relaxed. "How are you?" He slid the front seat backward to give himself more leg room.

"I'm great. How about you?"

"No complaints. Gran'nola has been working me like hired help, but I'm good. She's just doing the usual. I've always been the man of her house."

"They won't admit it, but all grandmas have a favorite."

"I'm definitely Gran'nola's favorite," Malachi said, "and she has no problem admitting it."

"She has no problem spoiling you, either. I can tell you always get your way."

"Not all the time," Malachi said. "Not with everybody."

Rae didn't respond. She'd left the ball in his court, so he hit back. He'd been waiting three days to play.

"It's been three days, you know," he said. "I followed your rule. And I thought about it." He paused. "No, take that back. I thought about you. Every day. The text you saw from Alexandria—I know you saw it—means nothing to me. I can't control what other people do, but I can control how I respond."

"And how did you respond?" Rae asked.

"With the delete button," Malachi said. "You can check my phone."

"I wouldn't do that," Rae said. "If you can't take a person at his word, you shouldn't be dealing with him."

That sounded like something Gran'nola would have said.

He took a deep breath. "Rae Stevens, I've truly enjoyed the times we've spent together, and I'd like to take you out. Tomorrow."

"Sure," Rae said. "I'd love to."

"Finally. You made me work for that," Malachi said, releasing a breath he hadn't realized he'd been holding.

"So, where are we going? Choices are few and far between."

Malachi hadn't decided. Dinner and a movie seemed like the default, but it was so ordinary. He wanted to do something that would leave a lasting impression.

"All you have to do is be beautiful, which is easy for you," he decided to say. "Can I pick you up around six?"

"My car is out of the shop, so I can meet you," she suggested.

"I know that's the safe thing for a woman to do on a first date," he acknowledged, "but I already know where you live."

"I just don't want to inconvenience you," Rae said.

"It's not an inconvenience," Malachi insisted. "Trust me."

"Then six o'clock is fine," Rae said.

They both fell silent, and Malachi didn't know what to say next. He'd never faltered in his conversations with women. He'd always known how to captivate the opposite sex. He wouldn't chance complimenting her on how amazing she'd looked in her bathing suit, lest he negate all the progress he'd made. He wouldn't roll the dice.

"How does your shoulder feel?" Rae asked him, breaking the silence.

"Better. Being in the water yesterday helped a lot. If I put in the work, my body will do its part."

"That's what I always tell my best friend, Farrah. She's the one who was with me yesterday."

"Farrah, huh? My physical therapist was checking her out."

"That's too bad for him, because she's happily married," I informed him.

Malachi noticed Gran'nola sticking her head out the open screen door, searching for him. He tapped his horn to let her know where he was before she started to bellow his name. Gran'nola was famous for her strong, heavy voice that everyone said would carry for miles. It had been known to alarm the neighbors and cause a chorus of dogs to howl.

"I hate to cut this short, but Gran'nola is looking for me," he told Rae. "If I don't answer, she'll put out an APB."

"Go ahead. I'll see you tomorrow."

"I'm looking forward to it," Malachi said, meaning it.

"Me, too," Rae told him. "See you at six."

He didn't know what it was about Rae that made her so attractive, but he aimed to find out. Even with the short time he'd known her, it was evident that none of the other women he'd ever dated compared to her. What was it about Rae Stevens?

That's when he heard the still, small voice.

It's the God in her.

Malachi stepped out of the SUV and slammed the door harder than he'd intended to. It was the extra adrenaline.

"What's that crazy smile on your face for?" Gran'nola asked as he stepped back inside the house. "You must've snuck out there to talk to some woman. Stay away from the crazy ones. They don't want you for the right reasons."

"I was talking to Rae Stevens," Malachi admitted. "I'm taking her out tomorrow."

Gran'nola's eyes twinkled. "She finally stopped running away from you?"

"I don't think she's stopped completely, but she slowed down a little."

"Good for her," Gran'nola said. "You know I like her. She's sweet as can be."

Something Rae had said or done must have really impressed Gran'nola. When it came to Malachi, no girl had ever been good enough. And he'd known that without ever bringing one of them home to meet her. Gran'nola was warm and welcoming to those she liked, but her claws came out with those she didn't.

"Any suggestions on where I should take her?" he asked.

"Well, there's the revival at Cedar Grove…starts tomorrow night. The guest speaker is a pastor out of Roanoke, Virginia."

"I'll keep that in mind," he said, not giving it a second thought. Church? Malachi needed Jesus, but that wasn't about to be his first option. Or an option at all.

Malachi had seen the photo albums full of pictures from Gran'nola's youth. She'd worn hot pants and short shorts, and, from the stories Uncle Bud told, she'd been the life of every party. Malachi doubted very seriously that she would have run through the church doors for a date when she was Rae's age. Creativity evaded him, so he did what he always did when he was stuck. When all else failed.

He called Katrene.

Katrene had been his personal assistant and right-hand girl for three years. She was organized and professional, and she never took no for an answer. Katrene didn't make excuses; she made a way. She synched his personal schedule with his professional obligations, coordinated the contractors who came into his condo, and never neglected to send the perfect bouquet of flowers, gourmet basket, or gift when a birthday, anniversary, or job promotion came around for one of his family members, friends, or associates. Whatever he needed, Katrene was on it.

Katrene also knew about the women. She knew, whether they'd been around for three weeks, three months, or three years. And she'd never judged his personal life. "I'm here to work for you," she'd told him. "Unless it affects my check, what goes on in your bedroom is none of my business."

Katrene answered in her usual chipper way.

"Katrene. My ace. My intelligent and all-knowing assistant," Malachi said.

"Oh, so now you want to call me back? For days, all I could get was a text…if I was lucky. You must be in a real bind."

"Forgive me," Malachi said. "You should know by now not to take it personally. Sometimes, I have to shut down. But part of the reason I can do that is because I have you to handle things."

"What do you need?"

Malachi was sure she'd whipped out a notebook and one of her signature purple pens.

"I need somewhere to take a special woman on a date tomorrow. Somewhere other than a restaurant. Can you find me something? A concert, or maybe a play?"

"In Greensboro? On a Thursday night? You've been in New York too long. The Big Apple never sleeps, but other cities do."

"I believe in you, Katrene," he insisted. "Add your special touch. I'm to trying to leave a lasting impression."

"Wow, boss," she said. "This woman must've really caught your eye. You haven't been there that long. Unless she's an old flame."

"None of my old flames live here anymore," Malachi said. He knew. He'd looked them up over the years, and every female worth contacting had moved away and made a life somewhere else, with someone else.

"If I don't call you back tonight, I'll give you a buzz in the morning," Katrene said. "Tell Gran'nola I said hello, and make sure you bring me one of her chicken pies when you come back."

"On the plane? You must be crazy."

"I'd do it for you," Katrene said.

"Okay, Kat," he said, calling her by her childhood name. "Just because it's you. Call me back when everything is in place."

Malachi would have to fulfill her request another way—overnight mail, UPS, FedEx, or mule. He'd pack it up on ice and overnight it, but there was no way he was a taking a chicken pie onboard first class in a 747.

Malachi joined his grandmother in the kitchen, where she was filling a saucepan with water. On the counter was a bag of dried pinto beans and he knew immediately that he would pass on dinner tonight. He swung the fridge door open and found a couple of plums to snack on.

"Did you ever talk to that cute reporter that came out here to interview you?" Gran'nola asked. "What was her name again?"

Malachi frowned. "Rae Stevens. I just told you we were going out tomorrow."

"Oh, that's nice. There's a revival going on at Cedar Grove. She might enjoy hearing the pastor. He's coming in from Roanoke."

Malachi felt like he'd pushed the rewind button on the last ten minutes of his life. Gran'nola continued on like they'd never had the conversation about Rae, asking him if he wanted her to make a pan of corn bread.

Pain clutched his heart. It was more than old age stealing his grandmother's memory. None of the other family members wanted to admit it, but they needed to face reality. Gran'nola knew so much of the family's history and was the most colorful storyteller of all of her siblings. She remembered things that others had long forgotten, and she'd always begged for someone else to pick up the torch and carry on that legacy beyond her living years.

Malachi didn't want to think about it, but it was probable that the grandmother he knew was slowly fading away.

19

Malachi

Malachi pulled into the parking spot in front of Rae's apartment building at 5:47. If she was like most women getting ready for a date, she'd spend every remaining minute perfecting her hair and makeup. He'd give her a few more minutes. He didn't want her to feel rushed, since he wanted their night together to be relaxing and enjoyable.

At 5:55, Malachi couldn't wait any longer; he rapped lightly on her door. He ran his hand down the front of his crisp new button-down shirt, a classic blue fabric with faint red pinstripes so subtle, they were barely visible. He'd taken Alonzo with him to the mall earlier that day for two reasons: He needed another brother's opinion, and he needed someone to run defense on any fans he happened to encounter. His schedule was too tight to allow time for the autographs and photos he was normally happy to give.

He took a deep breath when the first lock clicked. Then the second.

When Rae opened the door, Malachi felt like he'd breathed in a gulp of fresh air. She was wearing a soft pink dress with short sleeves that fluttered like flower petals. He could tell she was wearing makeup, since he knew how fresh her face looked when it had been scrubbed clean. When he'd seen her at the pool, he'd thought she'd never looked more beautiful. No eye shadow, no blush, no mascara. She didn't need all that to impress him.

Until today.

"Hi," she said, almost shyly. Her purse was already on her shoulder, and she was carrying a sweater. "I'm ready if you are."

"Let's ride," Malachi said. "You look gorgeous, just like I knew you would."

Rae brushed her hair aside as she locked the door. She'd straightened it again, and it fell like silk across her shoulders, swaying freely whenever she moved.

They weren't their usual talkative selves on the walk to the car. Nerves, for both of them. Malachi tried to relax.

He opened the passenger door and helped Rae into the SUV. He'd gotten it washed, waxed, and detailed inside to make sure it wouldn't smell like the bags of baseballs and bats he'd been lugging around for a week.

As he started to pull out of the complex, Rae leaned forward and wrapped her sweater around her shoulders.

"Too cold?" Malachi asked, adjusting the air. He flipped up the vent on her side so it wasn't blowing directly on her.

"I always get chilly. That's why I carry a sweater wherever I go. My hands, too," she said. She held them out. "Feel."

Malachi rubbed her fingers and ran his thumb across her palms. It felt like she'd been holding a cup of ice. He squeezed her hands gently before letting go.

"They're super cold."

"And yours are super warm," Rae said, crossing her legs.

"That's from nerves." Malachi checked his watch. He'd worn his Rolex for the occasion, the first expensive accessory he'd bought for himself years ago.

"What are you nervous about? Not me, I'm sure."

Malachi reclined his seat a little, finally starting to relax. "I don't want to do anything to make you swerve this car around and make me take you back home."

"Be on your best behavior, and you'll have nothing to worry about," Rae told him.

"I'll try," Malachi said. They were starting to loosen up.

"What are we doing?" Rae asked. "Dinner and movie?"

Malachi shook his head. "Too predictable."

Katrene had called him early that morning and relayed the plans for the evening. He didn't know how she'd pulled it off, but Rae was in for a memorable evening. Malachi doubted Trenton had ever pulled off anything like it. It was something she never would expect. Malachi had to hand it to Katrene—even on his best day, in his most romantic mood, he wouldn't have come up with the plan she had orchestrated.

"Predictable isn't necessarily bad," Rae said. "It all depends on who you're with."

"I'll remember that for our next date," Malachi said with a wink.

She smiled. "It sure sounds like you've gotten over your nervousness," Rae said.

Malachi shrugged. "You're not intimidating me anymore."

"You expect me to believe you were intimidated?" Rae shook her head. "You're Malachi Burke, the famous baseball player who gets stopped for autographs wherever he goes."

"No, I'm Malachi Burke, the little boy who used to sing off-key solos in the children's choir at church. I don't get caught up just because people know my name."

Malachi listened for the automated voice of the GPS to tell him where to turn next. Over the years, Greensboro had expanded significantly. Shopping centers, subdivisions, and apartment complexes had sprouted up in the areas that had been open fields when he was growing up. The side streets and shortcuts he'd taken as a child were almost nonexistent.

"We're just in time for our dinner reservations," he said, pulling into the entrance of the Tanger Family Bicentennial Garden. He wheeled into a parking space.

"Dinner?" Rae asked.

He gave her an enigmatic grin, though he was almost as curious as she likely was to see what the evening would entail. He'd gotten the basic schedule of events from Katrene, but he still didn't know exactly how the plan would unfold.

"This should be interesting," Rae said, allowing him to help her out of the vehicle. She let her sweater fall from her shoulders. "All this time, I never knew they had a restaurant here. What kind of cuisine do they serve?"

"Rae-merican."

She lifted her eyebrows. "Sounds scrumptious."

They walked side by side past the sundial at the entrance to the gardens, to where Alonzo was waiting, dressed in a black suit and tie.

Alonzo tilted his head without saying a word, acknowledging them as if they were strangers. He held his arm out to the left. "Right this way, sir, madam. I'm Mr. Jones, your host for the evening."

Frowning slightly, Rae pointed at Alonzo, then at Malachi. "Don't you know him? Isn't this your friend?"

"Please follow Mr. Jones," Malachi said with a gentle touch to her back.

Alonzo had jumped at the chance to help Malachi, bragging that he would even wear the suit he'd put on to propose to his wife. Alonzo looked sharp, but Malachi knew the sweat was probably pooling down his back underneath that three-piece ensemble.

Alonzo led them to a clearing in the trees, and Malachi heard Rae catch her breath at the sight of the hot air balloon tethered there, its rainbow pattern resembling a bouquet of flowers in full bloom. Nearby sat a table for two draped in white linen, and a single white wrought-iron bench.

Chef Devlin had taken over Gran'nola's kitchen that morning, preparing five days' worth of meals for Malachi and his grandmother, and now he was holding a silver tray that displayed tonight's dinner.

"You've got to be kidding me," Rae said, her hand pressed over her heart. "I never, ever would've expected this."

As they took their seats at the table, Alonzo served them each a Caesar salad.

"You've outdone yourself," Rae said to Malachi, staring at the hot air balloon. "Are we going up in that thing, or is it just part of the décor?"

"Oh, we're definitely going up," Malachi said.

Rae looked apprehensive, so he quickly added, "Don't worry. We'll be tethered to the ground."

That didn't seem to have eased her anxiety. She gazed wide-eyed at the cords connected to the balloon's basket, prompting Malachi to do the same. All he could do was trust that Katrene had hired a reputable company with the highest safety standards.

But maybe this was a bad idea. Malachi might have pushed Katrene to be a little too ambitious. He hadn't considered the possibility that Rae had a fear of heights. "You don't have to go up at all if you don't want to," he told her, searching her face to gauge her comfort level.

"No," she said, softly resting her hand on his forearm. "You only live once, right? This might be my only chance to experience a hot air balloon ride. Unless, of course, you want to back out."

Malachi rubbed the bottom of his freshly shaven chin. "I've zip-lined in Brazil, ridden a helicopter over the Grand Canyon, and—against my better judgment—tandem jumped out of a plane. I'm going up."

"Excuse me, Mr. Adventurous," Rae said. "I haven't lived a life anywhere near as exciting, or dangerous, as yours."

"That's because you're too beautiful to put your life on the line like that," Malachi told her. "You should play it safe." He nodded slightly to Alonzo, signaling him to serve the main course.

Chef Devlin had prepared a simple yet delectable meal of chicken and risotto with seasonal vegetables. He and Alonzo were a synchronized team, working efficiently and quietly as they served the meal, refilled the drinking glasses, presented dessert, and finally removed their empty plates.

Throughout the meal, Rae was easy to talk to; although she knew his life mostly centered around baseball, she showed genuine interest in other aspects. He told her of his concerns with Gran'nola's memory, and she told him about the *Ledger's* financial woes. And when they began to open up about their personal walks with God, he was able to be more transparent with her than he'd been with anyone else. Rae shared a Scripture—a personal favorite of hers that had helped while she was on the rebound from her experience with Trenton: "*Many are the plans in a man's heart, but it is the* LORD's *purpose that prevails.*"

That fiasco with Trenton was another story. But Malachi now knew why Rae had rejected him as many times as she had. She'd built a guard around her heart. And rightly so.

Rae patted the corners of her mouth with her cloth napkin, then took a sip of water. "So, is this what it's like for you all the time? You just show up to the table and have gourmet meals put in front of you?"

"Most of the time," Malachi admitted. "Food is my weakness, and I need a chef to make sure that my meals are nutritionally balanced, so I can stay fit and perform at my best. The way I see it, eating well is part of my job. But I have my cheat days...sometimes my cheat weeks, too."

"You're not alone in that," Rae said. "It's almost impossible for me to turn down ice cream."

It didn't seem as if Rae had a problem staying fit and maintaining a healthy weight. Not from what he'd seen of her in that bathing suit. And he'd seen a lot.

A man with spiked blond hair was fiddling with the controls. He wore a tie-dyed T-shirt that matched the colors of the balloon. The pilot, presumably.

"I think it's time," Malachi said. He stood, then helped Rae into the sweater she'd brought along. With the sun beginning to set, it was the perfect time to ascend into the cloudless sky.

"Did you save me any of that food?" the pilot asked as they approached the balloon.

"You know, there's probably some left, if you're hungry," Malachi told him.

"Oh, no. I'm kidding," the pilot said, shaking his hand. "Just had the sub sandwich my wife fixed for me. Made with love—the best ingredient. Can't beat that."

"I hear you," Malachi said. "How high are we going up?"

"Probably a hundred feet or so." He handed Malachi a clipboard. "I'll need you both to sign these waivers. I'm Kent, by the way."

Rae laughed nervously. "Should I be concerned, Kent?"

Malachi held the paper so she could scribble her signature across the bottom.

The pilot shook his head. "No worries. I do this all the time. But if you get up there and you're scared, pretty lady, just hold on tight to your man. I can tell by the way he looks at you that he wouldn't let anything happen to you."

Malachi was more than a little pleased that Rae didn't correct the pilot by insisting that he wasn't "her" man. He couldn't speak for the future, and he didn't know what was down the line for them, but he liked the sound of that.

Malachi held his arm out, and Rae tucked her hand in the crook of his elbow. Her grip was tight.

"Here we go," she said, inhaling deeply.

The ascent was slow, smooth, and silent. Malachi wondered what Rae was thinking.

"You doing alright?" he asked her once their skyward climb finally ceased.

"Perfect," she said. "This is so much better than a movie. It's high-definition and surround-sound in the truest sense. God is amazing. Just look at that sunset." She looked toward the west. "Can you imagine being in a hot air balloon in Hawaii, hovering over the island while the sunset paints the sky? One of these days, I'll make it to Hawaii. And this is exactly what I'm going to do."

Home run, Malachi thought.

"This feels higher than a hundred feet," he said, peering down. The buildings, cars, and scenery beneath him looked miniscule.

Rae didn't respond immediately. She seemed lost in thought. "This is how we should feel when we have problems," she finally said. "We rise above it all. Our problems should be small in comparison to a God who sits high and looks low."

Malachi couldn't explain the feeling that came over him at her words. Peace. Contentment. Maybe, an expression of his gratefulness. Rae was right. His stresses and concerns—over his career, over Gran'nola—weren't too big for God to handle. All Malachi had to do was trust Him.

Unexpectedly, Rae leaned into him, wrapping her arm around him and resting her hand on his back. "This has been nice. Even if you go back to New York and forget all about me, I'll always remember this night." Then she dropped her arm at her side again—too soon for Malachi.

Rae's encouraging words about God were right, but she was wrong about one thing.

He wasn't going to forget her.

20

My entire closet was empty, except for two plastic hangers swinging from the bottom rack. After rising early to submit my latest writing assignments before deadline, I called Farrah, as planned, to confirm the "closet conquest," as she called it. She was coming to assist me in a wardrobe overhaul.

I'd forgotten that Farrah was a ruthless purger. She didn't give a second thought to my objections as she tossed my favorite jeans into the box she'd designated for donations.

"I've had those forever," I protested, trying to retrieve them from the cardboard box.

"Exactly." Farrah stood in the way so I couldn't reach them. "You told me you would defer to my decisions."

"That was before I knew you would leave me with no more than three pieces of clothing to my name."

"We're just getting started. I can't help it that things are worse than I thought." Farrah held up the bridesmaid dress I'd worn for my cousin's wedding three years ago.

"It's black," I said. "I'm saving it for a formal event."

"You've been to several black tie functions over the last couple years, and you've never worn it," she pointed out. "And if you ever did, do you know how you would look? Like a woman wearing a bridesmaid dress." She draped it near the head of my bed. "Consignment."

Then Farrah began unclipping all my trousers from their hangers and tossing them on the bed. I tried on each pair, pivoting so she could assess the fit and style.

"You can never have too many black pants," I said, pulling on the fourth pair in a row. "Black goes with everything."

Farrah tossed one pair in the "donate" box, the other on the pile of consignment clothes. "Don't believe every fashion rule you hear. Live your life with a little color. Although, I must admit, you're doing a lot better."

Farrah held up the dress I'd worn on my date with Malachi the night before, nodding approvingly.

I'd figured it wouldn't be long before I went out with a man again, but I hadn't known how I would feel. Thanks to Malachi, I felt refreshed. I felt pretty. I felt wanted. My thoughts about him didn't extend very far into the future, but at least I knew that loving again could be a reality.

"He couldn't keep his eyes off you, could he?" Farrah asked.

"We had a nice time," I affirmed.

"Girlfriend, you went up in a hot air balloon. I don't care if the rope was tied down. How many women can say that they went up in the sky with a man on their first date? None that I know of."

"He was trying to impress me," I said, recalling every minute of the night before. Again.

"And did he?"

"Of course." I voluntarily tossed an ill-fitting blouse with a hideous pattern in the box for items to be trashed. It wasn't worthy of donation. I'd feel like I'd done a disservice to all mankind if I let another woman get ahold of that catastrophe.

"And he was the perfect gentleman. He walked me to the door, left me with a kiss, and called me when he got home to say good night."

Farrah examined the seam of a skirt before setting it aside for the consignment store. "So, where do you go from here?"

"I have no idea," I admitted. "Once he returns to New York, I'm sure we'll talk from time to time. But the first time I hear another woman in the background or see a photo online of him with one draped across his arm, he won't have to worry about hearing from me again."

"That's fair, I guess," Farrah said.

"I know it might be wrong to feel like this, but I'm glad Trenton saw us together."

"I'd feel the same way, if I were you," Farrah said. "And, speaking of Trenton, what do you want to do with this?" She held up the garment bag containing my wedding dress. She unzipped it, revealing the intricately beaded bodice and sweetheart neckline.

"I'm not in love with Trenton anymore, but I'm still in love with that dress," I said, running my hand down the front. I'd dragged Farrah to bridal boutiques in Burlington, Raleigh, and Charlotte in search of the perfect wedding gown. Ironically, I'd found the one I wanted in a bridal shop less than thirty minutes from home.

"Personally, I think you should let it go. This is what you chose for your wedding to Trenton. You might not want the same thing later. A new man, a new dress. A better man, a better dress."

"I see your point, but I'm not ready to let it go. Not yet."

Farrah conceded, hanging it back in the closet. "I'll make an exception on this one."

"Agreed," I said, stopping to study Farrah. "You look different. You have a glow."

"That's called oily skin," Farrah said. "And in the summer, it only gets worse. But I'm working on a product for that." She dropped a pair of run-down heels into the trash. "Forget about my oily face. Tell me more."

Farrah refused to stop talking about Malachi. She seemed happy to see me doing something besides staying cooped up in my apartment writing, taking my weekly trip to the *Ledger* office, or waiting for Casey to leave town so we could romp around together at consignment boutiques and thrift stores.

"When are you going to see him again?" she wanted to know.

"He's in town for only a couple more weeks, and I know he's busy with camp, Gran'nola, and the rest of his family. He doesn't have that much time to spare."

"For you, he'll make time. But do you know what I think you should do?" She tossed two more blouses into the donation bin. "You should go out to the field tomorrow and take him a cold bottle of water or lunch. Something."

"They have plenty of water and food at the field," I said.

"It's not about the water or the food. It's about the thought."

"You know me," I said. "I don't like chasing men."

"You're not chasing him. You're letting him know that you're available. That he's on your mind. And don't try to put up the front that he isn't on your mind. Like you said: I. Know. You."

Every time Malachi had invaded my thoughts since our date, I'd pushed him out. Despite my best efforts to downplay our time together, I'd replayed the evening in my mind, all the way back to the good-night kiss on the cheek. I'd closed the door behind me, half expecting him to knock within a few seconds and ask if he could come in. I imagined that we would talk long into the night about God knows what, until I shooed him off before he got too drowsy. But that hadn't happened. He hadn't knocked.

"You should do it," Farrah insisted. "At least think about it."

Farrah had never steered me wrong, but I was still wondering if it was the right move when I stepped out of my car on Saturday afternoon with two ice-cold bottles of water, the condensation dribbling down my hands.

Although we hadn't been able to coordinate our schedules, Malachi and I talked every evening. We never ran short of things to talk about, and over the past two days, our talks had steered in the direction of how God's grace had been so evident in our lives. God had definitely orchestrated our paths to cross for a reason. Whether it was for friendship, a romantic relationship, or discipleship, I didn't know. But I was thankful to have met Malachi. After my initial hesitation, who could've thought I would reach this point?

"Hey, baby."

I turned toward the female voice and saw Gran'nola staked out beneath a small canopy on a lawn chair beside a red cooler large enough to seat two grown men. She waved me over.

I waved back, and as I walked toward her, I scanned the field. I spotted Alonzo but no Malachi.

"Hi, Ms. Nola," I said, leaning over to greet her with a hug. "You're back for some more action, I see."

"I rode out here with my brother Bud," she said. "He missed the first weekend of camp, so he wanted to come today to help Malachi." She nodded her head in the direction of the concession stand. "The only thing he's been doing most of the day is helping himself to food. He got two bags of baseballs out of the trunk, and I haven't seen him do anything else since then." Gran'nola gestured to the empty chair beside her. "Sit down. He won't be back for a while."

I set down the water bottles and the turkey and cheese wrap that I'd picked up from the deli down the street. I wasn't sure if the wrap was nutritionally acceptable according to his eating plan, but it had to be better than the hot dogs and chips being served to the campers.

"When will you be out to see me again?" she asked. "Malachi doesn't have to be there for you to come hang out. You know I'll feed you real good."

"I know you would, Ms. Nola," I said. "I'll come soon, I promise."

"I'm going to hold you to your word," she said, shaking an arthritic-looking finger at me.

"Yes, ma'am."

I finally spotted Malachi in the middle of the sea of boys. When the crowd parted, he emerged, a bat resting on his shoulder.

"Malachi!" Gran'nola yelled suddenly.

I jumped as every head turned in our direction. Malachi perked up and sprang into action like a nine-year-old summoned for supper.

It wasn't until he'd gotten closer to us that he realized his grandma's urgent summons had had nothing to do with an emergency and everything to do with me.

"Look who's here," Gran'nola said.

I stood, handing Malachi one of the water bottles. "A little something to cool you down."

He twisted the cap off and chugged half the bottle without stopping for a breath. "That was on time," he said, wiping his mouth. "Thank you."

"You're welcome." I was unsure what else to do or say with Gran'nola watching our every move. Should I give him a hug? Should I wait to see if he would hug me?

I waited. He hugged me. Like I was his sister and not the woman he'd carried into the sky.

"Things seem to be going well," I said. "There look to be just as many kids here this week as last week."

"More than half of them are repeaters," Malachi said. He gulped down the rest of his water, so I handed him the second bottle. "But I think they came back with a higher energy level. They must be putting something in the juice boxes these days."

"You were the same way," Gran'nola said. "The only time your motor wasn't running at top speed was when you were asleep. Whenever I watched you, I had to take an aspirin before I went to bed."

"She's exaggerating," Malachi told me.

"Believe what you want to, but you know who's speaking the truth." Gran'nola winked at me, then slid to the edge of her chair and started to push herself up. Malachi jumped to her assistance and waited until she'd gotten her footing before he let go of her arm. "Do you remember that time—"

"Oh, no, Granola," Malachi said. "Don't get started."

"I won't embarrass you. I know you have to look good in front of your lady friend." Granola held on to the side of the canopy to balance on her right foot while she rotated her left ankle. "I'm going to see what Bud is getting into over there."

When she'd hobbled off, Malachi and I were finally alone. Kind of. I could tell we'd tuned out the chaos around us.

Malachi took off his baseball cap, dispelling the shadows that had darkened his face. "What else have you been up to this morning?"

"The usual. I slept in a little. Ran some errands. Nothing special."

"Seeing you is special for me." He scratched the side of his face, where the light stubble of a beard had started to sprout. "I've been thinking about you a lot."

I turned away when I felt myself blush. "You're pretty straightforward."

"No reason not to be. What do I have to lose?"

Alonzo and two other men were corralling the boys into three parallel lines, but it was evident they needed an additional hand. "I don't want to keep you," I told Malachi. "I just stopped by to say hello." I picked up the bag from the deli. "And to bring lunch."

Malachi unfolded the top of the bag, peeled the paper off the turkey wrap, and took a bite so big that I immediately realized I should've brought two.

"Hungry?" I asked.

"Starving. This hit the spot. Thanks for thinking of me."

"It was the least I could do," I said, silently thanking Farrah for the idea.

A chorus of whistles being blown by Alonzo and two of the assistant coaches prompted Malachi to stuff the rest of the turkey wrap in his mouth, his jaws stuffed to capacity. He chewed quickly and, after a final gulp, said, "I'll call you later. I'm staying at the Grandover for a couple days. Needed a break from Gran'nola's house. We've had too many visitors, aka too many requests for money."

Then he gave me another hug, but this time, he didn't hug me like I was his sibling.

He hugged me like a woman he'd been waiting to see, and couldn't wait to see again.

21

Malachi

Malachi stretched out across the king-sized bed in his hotel room. Two weeks on the lumpy mattress in Gran'nola's guest room had done a number on his back. After a hot shower and room service, he would sleep like a baby tonight. He'd thought about asking Rae out to a movie, but he was too exhausted and knew that he'd drift off before the opening credits finished rolling. If he was rejuvenated by tomorrow, he'd try to catch up with her in between church and the start of baseball camp that afternoon. He already knew one change he wanted to make for the camp next year: No Sunday sessions.

He had started to doze off when he heard a knock on his door. Probably a member of the housekeeping staff with the extra towels he'd requested. He needed them to apply wet heat to his shoulder. On Monday, he was scheduled for another physical therapy session. A much-needed one.

Malachi grabbed his wallet off the end table, preparing to drop a tip to the housekeeping staff. "Coming," he yelled out. "I appreciate it," he said as he swung the door open.

Only, instead of a helpful attendant with a stack of fluffy white towels, it was Alexandria who stood there.

"Room service," she said in a sassy singsong voice.

Malachi was too stunned to move, even as she pushed past him and sashayed into the room, her sheer yellow blouse billowing behind her. "Not bad," she said.

Malachi swung around to watch her. As usual, she was dressed impeccably, and she flaunted her long, toned legs in a pair of white shorts that rode high on her thighs. She stopped, as if intending to give Malachi a chance to admire them.

"What are you doing here?" Malachi said, finally finding his voice. He shook his head. "Wait a minute. How did you even know I was *here*? At the Grandover?"

"I called Katrene for your grandmother's address, and she told me she'd booked you here for three nights. I've always loved that girl. She stays on top of her game."

Not on my game, Malachi thought. But Katrene wouldn't have known to keep his whereabouts private. Alexandria had made plenty of spontaneous plans and plotted enough surprises that Katrene probably hadn't thought anything of giving out the information she wanted.

"It's not a good idea for you to be here—in this room, or even in Greensboro," he said, picking up his shoes and tossing them in the corner.

"Oh, I have my own room. Next door. I figured you'd want your own space. But if you need me, I'm just two steps away."

Malachi almost wondered at her nerve. *Almost.* It was Alexandria, after all.

She made her way to the window and peered out at the golf course. There was absolutely no way she could bend over without giving those around her a peep show. And Alexandria was the kind of woman who was well aware of that fact. Which, Malachi knew, was precisely why she chose that moment to bend over and unstrap her shoe.

"I'm exhausted," she said as she slipped her shoes off her feet, then sauntered over to the bed. "I could use a nap." She draped herself across the mattress and patted the space beside her.

"You should go to your own room, then," Malachi told her.

"But naps are so much better when you have someone to cuddle with." She closed her eyes, then opened them slowly as she raised her arms in a seductive stretch above her head, watching for his response.

Malachi was a man, which meant certain things would get to him. It was up to him to turn off the parts of his body that Alexandria was trying to turn on.

"Get up, Alexandria," he said. "You need to go. For real. Get up."

Alexandria made a pouty face and sat up begrudgingly. "I don't like what's happening to us, Malachi. You've been pulling away. But this is what we do. We're together. We leave to handle our business, and then we come back together. It's always worked."

Malachi leaned against the wall. "It used to work. But it doesn't work for me anymore. We've had this talk already."

"But I thought the problems with your shoulder and the team was making you say that. You have a lot weighing on you. That's why I came—to make you feel better. You've always called me when you needed a shoulder to cry on. Or a thigh. Or—"

"Housekeeping." A knock sounded on the door.

Malachi hurried to answer it. He slipped a tip into the woman's hand, accepted the extra towels, and set them on the bathroom vanity. Before he could return to the room, Alexandria had joined him in the bathroom and wrapped her arms around him from behind. She started massaging his midsection. Her hands stopped over his abdominals.

"One, two, three...five, six. Yes, they're all there." She peered over his shoulder and looked at herself in the mirror.

Malachi stared at their reflection. Most men would call him crazy for not accepting everything that Alexandria was ready to offer. But Malachi knew he'd be crazy if he *did* accept it.

He peeled her arms from around him, went to the hotel room door, and opened it.

"I told them not to bring my bags up for another thirty minutes," Alexandria said. "That's enough time for me to run you a hot bath. Did you see the Jacuzzi? It's perfect for two."

He opened the door wider.

Alexandria went to retrieve her shoes that she'd abandoned near the window. "I would be lying if I didn't say I was disappointed," she said. "But I can respect that you need your space." On her way out, she stopped in front of him and trailed her fingertip down his chest to the waistband of his pants.

Malachi grabbed her wrist with a firmness that seemed to surprise her, and he didn't release his grip until she was standing in the hallway.

Malachi closed the door and fastened the lock. At first, he'd wanted a hot shower, but now he felt it might be more appropriate to take a cold one. Either way, he'd probably have to find somewhere else to stay, since going back to Gran'nola's wasn't an option.

Tonight, though, he'd continue with his original plan. He'd shower, get a good night's rest so he could make it to the early worship service with Alonzo, try to catch up with Rae, and then finish out his day at the camp.

As he stepped into the steamy bathroom, Malachi added another item to his Sunday agenda.

Keeping Alexandria away from Rae.

22

Malachi

Alexandria was shielding herself from the sun with an umbrella so wide, it would have kept her dry in a torrential downpour. But Malachi didn't have to see her eyes to know that she was watching his every move. He'd noticed that she'd brought a book along, but, to his knowledge, she hadn't cracked it open since the moment she'd claimed her spot on the bottom bleacher.

She wore a replica of his jersey—the same one she wore for most of the home games she attended. She was wearing shorts again, too, but at least she'd had the decency to opt for a pair that nearly reached her knees. The prepubescent boys would have a hard enough time keeping their attention on their drills while a drop-dead-gorgeous woman looked on.

Malachi had decided on a different approach today. Ignore her. If he did, she'd most likely get bored and find something more productive to do with her time on a Sunday afternoon.

It wasn't long before Alexandria vanished. Just when he thought it was because his plan was working, he saw her return to the bleachers with a jumbo-sized beverage and a container of something she was nibbling from.

With only an hour and a half remaining before the closing ceremony that would end this weekend's camp, he didn't want to think about how the scene would play out when Rae arrived. Her other obligations after church had spoiled his plan to take her out for brunch or a movie, but he still wanted to see her.

He sent her a text: I'll come 2 u. Don't want u to have to drive over.

She responded: No worries. I'll be in the area already.

"You're going to have a problem on your hands," Alonzo said. He picked up a stray baseball from the ground, tossed it in the air, and effortlessly juggled it with the two from his pockets. "Juggling baseballs is a lot like juggling women. You think you've got it under control, but, sooner or later, somebody is going to get dropped."

"Man, I'm serious," Malachi said. "I'm not trying to juggle any women. Alexandria showed up on her own, in Greensboro and at camp. I didn't hear from her all night or this morning, either. If anything, I thought she'd try to corner me when I got back to the hotel. I didn't think she'd come out here."

"She came all the way from New York, and you didn't think she'd drive fifteen minutes out to the field?" Alonzo caught all three baseballs and cradled them in his hands. "Come on, man. You're not thinking. I think one of these pop flies hit you upside your head."

A group of boys flocked over to Malachi, abandoning the others circled around the snack table of bagged apple slices, celery sticks, and water bottles. He'd decided to try something healthier than the usual chips and juice boxes, but it hadn't gone over as well as he'd hoped.

"Mr. Malachi! Are you going to sign our shirts?" asked a boy named Brandon. He was among those whose natural skills Malachi had recognized. The knees of his pants were soiled, and a trail of dust extended up the side of his shirt from his diving attempt to catch a ball, even though it had been blatantly out of reach.

"I'll sign your shirts after camp," Malachi assured him. "I made a promise, and I'm good for my word."

"Told you, big head," Brandon boasted, playfully popping one of his friends on the temple. Then the two ran away, trying to douse each other and some other unsuspecting campers with water.

"Like I said, I'm good for my word," Malachi said to Alonzo. "And I said I'm done with all those women from the past."

"So, it's about Rae? You don't even know her, really."

"I don't," Malachi conceded. He'd thought the same thing a thousand times over. "But I'm drawn to her, and it's more than a physical attraction. Don't get me wrong, though—I think she's beautiful. And three days, three weeks, or three months from now, she could wipe me out of her life like she never knew me. But I won't know unless I try. And right now, I'm not expecting anything more than to build a friendship."

"I'll tell you one thing," Alonzo said. "Back in the day, I never took one of my girls up in a hot air balloon. Heck, I've never taken my wife up one."

Malachi chuckled. "Man, I was disappointed. We didn't get all that high off the ground."

"That's not the point. You did something for Rae that I guarantee no other dude has ever done before, and no dude will ever do. You made it hard for every other man."

"Then I did my job." Malachi blew his whistle, and two hundred seventy-three boys sprang to their feet.

"You better pray that works in your favor," Alonzo said. "And you better drop to your knees now, because Rae has arrived."

Malachi watched her walk from the entrance to the bleachers. Alexandria still sat at her post at the far end. The two women acknowledged each other with a slight nod, then turned their gazes back to the field. Neither of them had no idea who the other was, and Malachi prayed it would stay that way.

Malachi blew his whistle again, prompting the dawdling boys to finish cleaning up their trash and to return to their assigned stations. He was relieved that parents had started showing up to watch the remaining moments of camp. As far as Alexandria knew, Rae was just a mother coming to pick up her son, and vice versa. And Alexandria's outfit wouldn't raise any flags, since there were plenty of parents wearing Malachi's number.

For the remaining time on the field, Malachi sent up a series of urgent prayers for God to get him out of his bind. He'd awakened extra early for church—shouldn't that warrant a little sympathy from the Big Man upstairs?

Apparently not. He wasn't the least bit amused about his situation, but Alonzo had found the humor in it. With only thirty minutes till the end of camp, he started a countdown.

"Thirty more minutes until doom…."

"Fifteen minutes, and it's about to be on…."

"You know you've got only ten minutes, right?"

"Uh-oh. Five minutes left…."

"Man, shut up," Malachi said, throwing a ball at Alonzo, but not with enough force to hurt him. "I ain't worried. What can I do?"

Alonzo tightened the drawstring on his shorts, then folded his arms across his chest and pretended to be in serious thought. "Maybe I can run interference on the New York chick and keep her distracted while you slip away with Rae."

"You see that line of boys waiting to get their shirts signed? And the parents waiting with their cell-phone cameras ready? There is no slipping away. I have nothing to hide. The only reason I'd need to dip was if I'd done something wrong. And I can say with a clear conscience that I haven't."

"I can respect that," Alonzo said. "We all have to man up sometime in our life. Today is your day." He handed Malachi a black permanent marker.

Alonzo turned to the boys. "Alright, fellas. You have to stay in line so we can get you to your parents. I know they're ready to get you home and feed you."

Malachi glanced at the bleachers and saw neither Rae nor Alexandria. As he worked his way down the line of boys, scribbling his name on various items and posing for pictures, he kept sneaking peeks, trying to spot them. Nothing.

Alonzo must've been doing the same thing. "Looks like it's clear," he whispered. "You dodged that one today." He whistled and made a sound like a bomb exploding.

"Let's hope so," Malachi said.

It took twenty minutes for him to wrap up the autographs, then another ten to debrief with his team, updating them on any modified assignments for the third and final baseball camp next weekend. Although his excitement hadn't waned since opening night of the first session, he was happy to have the finish line in sight. Even with an astounding team of volunteers, including local school coaches, it had been more work than he'd expected.

Over the course of both camp sessions, he'd mulled over his career and the possibilities for his future. Should he return to the game and play another year after he recuperated from his injury? That would give him a chance to retire on his own terms, in a blaze of glory. But he wondered if one more year was really worth it. Everyone wanted answers—his agent, his publicist, his coach, his teammates, and the team's owners. He'd put everyone off.

"I'm out, Zo," Malachi said, picking up his duffel bag. He was filthy, covered in dust that felt like it had baked into his skin. He hadn't factored in his need to take a shower before heading out to the movies. He would just ask Rae to come by the hotel, though, knowing her, she'd want to wait in the lobby. That was fine. He'd be in and out in fifteen minutes or less.

Rae was sitting in her car, which was parked beside his rental SUV. She didn't notice his approach, since she was too busy brushing black stuff on her eyelashes in the comfort of the air-conditioning. She looked up just as he was about to knock on her window.

Rae rolled the window down. "You look nice," she said.

"Nice?" Malachi glanced at his dusty cleats.

"Yes. Nice and sweaty. I assume we have a change of plans."

"I'm still good with the movies, but I need to swing by the hotel to shower and change, if that's okay. It'll take me just a few minutes. Follow me over?"

"Sure," she said. "I'll wait in the car."

"That's fine. I'll be quick. We can still make the seven thirty-five show and grab a—"

The *vroom* of the vehicle that pulled into the space on Malachi's right came so suddenly that he instinctively jumped back. Alexandria had sandwiched him between Rae's car and the black sports car she was driving.

"Hey, sweetie," Alexandria said, stepping out. "You headed back to the hotel?" She walked around to the front of the car and leaned over the hood as if posing for a magazine spread. She looked over at Rae like an afterthought.

"Oh, I'm so sorry," she said to Malachi. "I shouldn't have interrupted your conversation with your baseball mom. How rude of me." She craned her neck, trying to peer into the backseat of Rae's car. "Waiting for your son?"

"She isn't a baseball mom, and you know it," Malachi told her flatly. Her behavior disgusted him. She'd always been confident. Overconfident, when it came to Malachi's interactions with women. Something had tipped her off.

"Oh?" Alexandria said. "Well? Aren't you going to introduce me?"

Malachi wouldn't give her the satisfaction.

So she did the honors herself. "Hi. I'm Alexandria." She extended her hand to Rae. "Malachi's girlfriend from New York."

"Hello," Rae said, her voice empty of emotion.

Malachi's jaw tightened. He gave a low chuckle and shook his head. "She isn't my girlfriend," he said to Rae, whose face was deadpan.

Alexandria propped her hands on her hips. "You know how it is when you've been together so long. One day you're off, one day you're on. After a certain point, titles don't matter." She reached over and squeezed Malachi's forearm, then let her hand linger there.

Malachi shrugged her off. "I'm in a conversation right now," he told her.

"I apologize again," Alexandria said, with obvious insincerity. "I wanted to know your plans, but it's no problem. I'll be at the hotel whenever you get there."

Malachi had no words for her. Actually, he did, but he didn't want to unleash his disgust in front of Rae. Instead, he answered Alexandria with silence.

Just as Rae was doing to him, it seemed.

This is jacked up, he thought.

Alexandria returned to the car. She drove away slowly at first, then burned rubber when she reached the far end of the parking lot.

"I think I'll head home," Rae told Malachi.

"Don't let her ruin the evening," Malachi pleaded. "It's nothing, really. Nothing."

"No, I'm good. It sounds like you have some things you need to take care of at the hotel. Handle your business."

"Alexandria's not my business," Malachi said. "She came here on her own. She found out where I was staying and popped up. I have no reason to lie to you."

"I'm not saying you're lying," Rae said, fumbling with the tuner on her radio. "I just think it's best if we change our plans. Maybe call me later this week."

Malachi knew from Rae's stoic expression that nothing he could say would change her mind. As she shifted into drive, Malachi stepped away from the car. "Alright."

Rae smiled as she pulled away, but her usual light didn't shine through.

He couldn't believe it. Alexandria had messed things up—for tonight, and possibly for good.

23

Alexandria was just as beautiful and alluring in person as she was in the selfie she'd texted to Malachi. I couldn't deny that. She deserved her props. I'd spotted her the moment I sat down at the end of the bleachers, decked out in baseball paraphernalia with Malachi's number. At the time, I'd thought nothing of it. I'd assumed she was just another avid fan or an overzealous baseball mom trying to catch his attention.

How wrong I'd been. She'd been trying to catch more than Malachi's attention. When she eased out of her sports car, it came to me. That's when I recognized her, even though she was wearing clothes this time.

I wanted to believe Malachi, but I refused to be the stereotypical naive woman who believed whatever excuse a man threw at her. In this case, I knew what to do—walk away before my heart was fully on the line.

My pulse thumped in my throat. I swallowed, fighting back my tears. It wasn't so much that it was Malachi as much as it was that I'd been stung yet again by a man. Another act of betrayal.

I slowed at the next traffic light, contemplating where I should go. What I should do. Whom I should call. I was watching cars whiz through the intersection when my cell phone rang. It was Malachi. Without a second thought, I sent it to voice mail.

I decided that I would go to the movies as planned, only I'd choose a different theater from the one I was supposed to go to with Malachi. Sweaty and all, he'd probably show up and try to woo me back.

Why had he put so much effort into convincing me to go on a date with him when he was still pouring his affections on someone else? A woman wouldn't just drop what she was doing and show up in another state without good cause. Even if Malachi hadn't known she was coming, he'd given her some reason to pull a surprise. He'd probably sent texts of his own. I'm sure there had been late-night conversations, with whispers of "I miss you."

I stared up at the marquee that listed the movies and times. A thriller? No. A sci-fi? Not my thing. A romance? Definitely not. Comedy.

"One for the seven o'clock showing," I told the ticket agent.

"I saw that one last night," he said, laughing with his mouth open so wide, I could see the little jiggly thing in the back of his throat. "You're gonna roll. I'm gonna tip in on that one again, for sure."

"Great," I said, forcing a smile. "I need a good laugh."

He handed me the single ticket. "Enjoy."

Theater number six was nearly filled to capacity, but I still managed to find a lone seat in the middle—my preferred spot for viewing the big screen. Twenty minutes of previews passed, along with the theater's own animated video instructing all patrons to turn off their cell phones—and encouraging them to visit the concession stand for a buttery popcorn and a bubbly cup of soda. I didn't need either one, but I'd ordered both, so I munched away as the feature film began.

The ticket agent was right. The movie was hilarious. And although I was typically annoyed when other people talked during a movie, the guy behind me offered a truly funny side commentary for all of us.

I stayed seated in the dark theater until the last credit rolled, then watched the extra bloopers and outtakes from the set. Then I stood, pushed my empty popcorn bag and cup into the overflowing trash bin, and scooted past the teenage employees who were hurrying in to sweep the theater. Laughter had lifted my mood.

But the feeling lasted only until I got to my car and checked my text messages. There were two from Malachi. Call me and Breakfast tomorrow? Please? I ignored and erased them both.

The third message, however, caught me off guard. It was from Trenton. Call me ASAP. Need to talk.

Incredible. He still wouldn't give up on trying to get an interview with Malachi. I didn't think it was as serious as he was making it out to be. I was sure there were other things going on in the sports world that were worthy of air time.

I answered him: Find another story.

Trenton must've been right by his phone, because he answered immediately: Not about your boy.

He's not my boy.

Can I drop by?

I have no idea why I typed what I did: Yes. Be there in 20 min.

The second I walked in the door, I opened the refrigerator and poured myself a tall glass from the pitcher of filtered water I'd infused with cucumber slices, lemon, ginger, and mint leaves. I'd been drinking it ever since Farrah had told me it was a good way to detox. I needed it for the junk food I'd just devoured, and also for whatever Trenton was about to say. I was sure I'd have to detox him out of my system by the time he left.

Trenton knocked when I was closing the fridge, and I immediately regretted telling him he could come by.

He walked in wearing his weekend sportscaster gear—a pair of khaki pants and a red polo shirt bearing the station's logo. I watched his gaze whisk around the room like he expected to see evidence of a man's presence.

"So, what's the emergency?" I said, closing the door behind him.

He stood in the middle of my living room, his hands shoved in his pockets, his face bearing an expression that I couldn't quite read. This was the same man who would regularly rifle through my cabinets and refrigerator and cook up a meal for us. This was the same man who'd helped me rearrange my furniture and mount my new television on the wall. This was the same man who'd battled with me over wedding color schemes at my kitchen table. And now he was acting like he was in a strange place.

"Do you want to sit down?" I asked him, motioning toward the living room. All of a sudden, I was concerned. Was he sick? Had he been fired?

He perched on the edge of the sofa. "Aren't you going to join me?"

I shook my head, preferring to stand. "What's up?"

Trenton stood again. He cleared his throat and stepped into my personal space. The last time we'd been this close, he'd ended our engagement.

He reached for both my hands, just like he'd done on *that* night.

I pulled my hands away and took a step back, wondering what in the world was going on.

"I'm not sure if I ever told you I'm sorry," Trenton said. "I mean, truly sorry."

"You did," I said.

"But I mean it. And ever since the last time I saw you, I've realized how sorry I am. I never meant to hurt you."

I waved away his sentiment. "Really, Trenton, I'm over it. I've moved on. It's okay."

"No. It's not okay." He took a deep breath. "Not only am I sorry that I hurt you, but I'm sorry I ever left you."

I tried to get a whiff of his breath, to see if alcohol might be to blame for this sudden rush of sentimental feelings. In the time I'd known him, he'd never even sipped the stuff. He had refused to entertain the thought of having an open bar at our wedding reception, and a champagne toast was out of the question. Ever since his senior year of college, when he'd lost a close friend in a car accident caused by a drunk driver, he hadn't let a drink past his lips. But he'd told me that when he used to drink, alcohol always made him emotional.

I shook my head. "Trenton. Let's not go there. We've both moved on with our lives."

"You've moved on. As you should have." Trenton ran his hand across the top of his freshly barbered hair. "But in my heart, I never did."

I didn't believe him. He was only saying these things because he'd seen me with Malachi, and no man wanted to see his ex-girlfriend in a romantic relationship with someone who had more money, power, status, and better looks. It didn't matter that Malachi and I weren't an item; it was that Trenton *thought* we were.

Silence hung between us. I could almost hear our hearts beating. *Thump. Thump. Thump.* I took another long sip of my cucumber water. I needed to pour a glass for Trenton, too, so that he could detox his mind of these crazy thoughts.

"This is…. You are…." I couldn't complete a sentence. "What are you doing?"

Trenton stepped into my personal space again, and I responded with another step backward.

"I'm telling you that I want a second chance. I *need* a second chance," Trenton said. He touched the side of my face, then trailed his hand down to my neck.

"What you need is a good night's sleep," I said. "And so do I, so you should leave."

Trenton hadn't expected that response. I could tell by the way he furrowed his brow. He'd expected me to fall into his arms and confess that I'd been waiting for him and that I couldn't imagine myself with another man. He'd expected me to cry so hard that the tears would roll down my face and wet my chin. That he would wipe them away, and we'd resume our journey to happily-ever-after.

That wasn't going to happen.

"You don't even want to talk about it?" he asked, sounding dejected.

"There's nothing to talk about," I said. "Except why were you on my doorstep the night Malachi dropped me off? You easily could have called or texted, like you did tonight."

Trenton leaned against the back of one of my kitchen chairs and crossed his arms. "I was at the gas station when I saw you. I noticed him first, when he went inside the store, and then I saw you in the passenger seat."

"And?" I pushed him to tell me more.

"And when he didn't come out of the store for a while, I took my chances and went to your apartment. I figured that's where you were headed. Yes, I wanted my interview, but I wanted to see you more."

"That's creepy," I told him. "Kind of stalker-ish."

"Maybe if I was a stranger," he said.

"You are a stranger, Trenton," I told him. "You aren't the man I fell in love with, because the man I loved promised me the world. I have to admit, though, you put on a good show. I'm just glad the act was over before I committed my life to you."

"It's not like that. You know me better."

I held up my hand to stop him. I didn't care what Trenton had to say. Nine months ago, I might have. Maybe even three months ago. But not today. "You should go," I said. I walked to the door and opened it, signaling that our conversation was over, and so was his attempt to reignite what we'd once had. If he'd walked out once, there was no reason why he wouldn't do it again.

When drama rained, it poured.

24

I'd had a Monday morning like this one before. I didn't enjoy it then, and I certainly would've preferred waking with a better disposition. I hadn't yet seen my reflection in the mirror, but I already knew my eyes were swollen from crying all night. I hadn't been able to control my emotions. Once I was alone in my bed, the tears fell involuntarily.

Sometimes, a woman needs to cry, whether it makes sense or not. A woman needs to cry when she's overjoyed, disgusted, frustrated, and overwhelmed. Sometimes, a woman just needs to cry.

I splashed cold water on my face, and the refreshing sensation made me want to take an early-morning swim. But I'd promised Ms. Bessie that I'd help her tackle the closet full of outdated files and archive the older editions of the *Ledger*. I was bringing fruit and yogurt; she was bringing orange juice.

I turned on the morning news while I dressed. During the overnight hours, a family of four had escaped a fire that raced through their home, two men had been charged in the armed theft of shoes, and a drunken seventeen-year-old had crashed into one of the local post offices. My problems didn't seem that bad anymore.

Ten minutes from my intended departure time, the phone rang. No one ever called me this early. It could be Malachi, calling to convince me that the woman who'd sent him a near-nude selfie wasn't someone he cared about. Or Trenton, calling to retract all that he'd dropped on me the night before. I decided to answer only if it was Farrah. I hadn't spoken to her yet about Alexandria's pop-up appearance. I picked up the phone, ready to spill my heart.

But it wasn't Farrah calling me at eight fifteen in the morning. Nor was it Malachi. Or Trenton.

It was Gran'nola.

It wouldn't have surprised me if she was calling to petition me on her grandson's behalf.

"Hello?"

"Good morning," she sang. It sounded like she'd been gotten up with the sun. "This is Nola E. Burke. Is this Rae?"

"Yes, ma'am, it is." I wedged the phone between my chin and my shoulder while I stuffed my satchel with papers, my laptop, and a bag of trail mix.

"I called Malachi for your number. I hope you don't mind. I was hoping you could come over for dinner tomorrow. I'm making some of Malachi's favorite things. Chicken pie, turnip greens, yams, and potato salad."

My mouth watered just thinking about it, but I couldn't be lured into seeing Malachi again for the sake of soul food, no matter how tempting it sounded.

"I think I'm going to have to pass this time, Miss Nola," I told her. "I have a lot going on."

"You're going to have to stop and eat sooner or later."

"Yes, ma'am, you're right again. But I can't commit to a time, and I wouldn't want to hold you up," I said, fumbling for an excuse. I wished I would've let her call go to voice mail, so I could have had the chance to come up with a reason that she couldn't find a rebuttal for.

"We'll wait," Ms. Nola said. "Well, actually, I'll wait. I can't speak for Malachi. When he smells my food, he likes to dig right in."

"I don't blame him, Ms. Nola," I said. I locked my apartment door behind me and waved at Perry, who was dressed for his job as a security officer at the mall.

"You call me when you're on your way," Gran'nola said.

There was no sense in trying to convince her that she wouldn't see me for dinner. I'd let Malachi handle that. He hadn't tried to contact me, other than sending those two text messages while I was at the movies. I assumed he either had given up or was preoccupied with other things. Or other people.

When I arrived at the *Ledger* office, I walked in on two glum faces.

I set the container of fruit and the containers of yogurt on Ms. Bessie's desk. "Something is going on," I said to them. "You might as well give it to me now."

Shelton pushed his reading glasses to the top of his head. "If you want it straight, I'll give it to you straight. I've made the decision to close the office. We're going under, and there's nothing I can do to stop it. Next week will be our final edition, barring no miracles," he said. He was smiling slightly, but there was hurt in his eyes.

The newspaper publishing business was all he'd ever known. I was losing a few dollars in my pocket that I could replace by picking up more freelance assignments. Shelton, however, was losing his legacy. The history of the paper could never be denied, but Shelton always talked of building something for the next generation. He'd never been able to accept that world news now moved at lightning speed and was accessible with the click of a button. By the time a new edition of the *Greensboro Ledger* came off the press, the news it shared was an afterthought. Shelton's failure to change had cost him.

"I think it will pull through," I said anyway, needing to believe for him. "You may have to take a hiatus for a while, but, knowing this community, you'll be up and running again. Sometimes, people don't realize the value of something until it's gone."

Shelton picked up a container of peach yogurt with a slight frown, as if he longed for a sausage, egg, and cheese biscuit instead.

"I pray you're right," Shelton said. "God knows I don't want to let my baby go. This office has *seen* history and *made* history."

I patted him on the back.

He straightened his shoulders and perked up, seeming to pull himself together for our sake. "We're going to print next week with the final issue."

"The final issue for now," Ms. Bessie added, with tears pooling in the corners of her eyes. "Not forever."

"For now," Shelton said. "Rae, we'll run your piece on Malachi Burke, along with the other stories I've been holding. I'll write a letter from the editor to let the community know what's going on. In the meantime, I'll keeping trying to get new advertisers. The only thing we can do other than that is wait on the Lord."

"They that wait on the Lord will renew their strength," Ms. Bessie recited. "They shall mount up on wings like eagles. They shall run and not get weary. They shall walk and not faint."

"Well, listen to you, Bessie," Shelton said with a laugh. "You went and found Jesus over the weekend."

Ms. Bessie swatted his arm. "I knew Him long before you did."

"That's right," Shelton said, moving out of striking distance from Ms. Bessie. "Didn't you go to school with Him and His brother James?"

"Watch your back, now, Shelton," Ms. Bessie said. "I'm going to get you for that when you least expect it."

I found a paper bowl in our small storage closet, then scooped out three spoonfuls of fruit for my breakfast. "Let it be known that I had nothing to do with this," I said.

Shelton—who'd set the container of yogurt back on the table—poured himself a Styrofoam cup full of orange juice, then picked up a stack of mail. "I saw Nola Burke at church yesterday," he said. "She told me she was going to invite you to dinner on Tuesday. That woman can burn in the kitchen. Did she ever get in touch with you?"

"She called me this morning, but I won't be able to go to dinner," I said. I didn't tell him the real reason I was turning down her offer.

"That's too bad," Shelton said. "She told me that Malachi has his eye on you. I don't know what you did to him during that interview, but it was enough to make him sweet on you."

"I can bet he's spreading his sweetness around on more than just me," I said, stabbing a chunk of pineapple.

"Let's be real," Shelton said, slurping juice from his cup. "He's an athlete. I don't know if women flock to baseball players like they do to football and basketball players, but he's probably had his share of...." He paused. "Choices."

"What makes you think a woman wants to be one of the choices?" Ms. Bessie butted in. "Every God-fearing woman I know wants to be the one and only."

"Like I was saying," Shelton said, "any man has choices. A woman does, too. But Ms. Nola said Malachi is a new man. He's made a choice to live like the man she raised him to be. You know why I believe her? Because of something she always says, and I've never known her to be wrong."

"And what's that?" Ms. Bessie asked, looking at her reflection in the mirror she kept in her desk drawer as she primped and fussed with her curls.

"She knows what she knows."

25

Malachi

Malachi had sent Rae two text messages—two days ago—and still hadn't gotten a response from her. She'd been justified in her feelings about the situation. She hadn't known him long enough to trust his word, and Alexandria's blatant rudeness hadn't made things any better. He hadn't known how to read the look in Rae's eyes, but it lay somewhere between mistrust, anger, and disappointment.

Gran'nola had talked to her, though, and she seemed optimistic about the likelihood of her showing up for dinner tonight, even though she'd claimed she had other plans. Malachi wasn't getting his hopes up. She wasn't coming. He'd even taken a chance and gone by the rec center to swim some laps in the pool, hopeful that she'd show up to do the same.

She hadn't. The only women he'd encountered were three seniors who'd drilled him incessantly about his life and asked if he was looking for a wife. Each of them had a granddaughter or a niece that she thought would be perfect for him.

Malachi pulled out of the parking lot of the Grandover, checking to make sure Alexandria wasn't following him. She hadn't trailed him yet, but he wouldn't put anything past her. Her actions had infuriated him. He'd never truly seen her jealous side until she'd shown it at the baseball field. Every woman had her insecurities, but Alexandria had intentionally tried to give Rae the impression that she was still with him. Malachi had already decided that she wasn't the one, but if there had been even the slightest spark of potential for reconciliation buried deep within him, she'd smothered it. That was the kind of crazy woman Gran'nola had warned him about.

Alonzo's explanation of Alexandria had summed it up pretty well: "You took her power away. That's why she was mad. She's used to being in control. From what you've told me, she always called the shots regarding when she came in and out of your life. This time, she was out, and couldn't get back in. You didn't fold, and you've been rejecting her for three months. Beautiful, powerful women like that don't appreciate being turned down."

"You're right," Malachi had agreed. At that point, he'd been parked on Alonzo's couch for three hours.

While Alonzo had alternately listened to him vent and dissected his problems—of which women was just one—his wife, Deb, had been nestled in beside him. Malachi had watched in admiration as Alonzo rubbed Deb's pregnant belly. She was six months along with Alonzo Jr., and from the time she'd returned home from work that day, Alonzo had tended to her every need. When she wanted water, he jumped up to pour her a glass. When she commented that her feet were swelling, Alonzo pushed the ottoman over and added a pillow to adjust her legs to a comfortable height.

That was what Malachi wanted. No, their life wasn't perfect, but it had the thing that mattered most: Love.

Malachi slowed to turn into Gran'nola's driveway, stopping briefly to check the mail. He thumbed through the stack, just to see if any bills had arrived. There were none. Only an AARP magazine and a sales flyer from the local drugstore. Other than her household expenses, Gran'nola had very little debt. She paid for everything with cash or check, keeping one credit card for emergencies.

Malachi frowned when he noticed that Gran'nola's car wasn't under the carport. He'd spoken to her an hour ago and told her he'd be arriving shortly. He figured she'd taken a quick trip to the grocery store, until he saw that the back door was open. He walked around the corner of the house to the side of the yard, where he had a clear view across the street. Maybe she was making her weekly delivery of a home-cooked meal to her ninety-three-year old neighbor, Ms. Spruill. The old lady complained that the food her family brought her for the week was as bland as white rice.

But the only car in Ms. Spruill's driveway was the gray Lincoln Town Car that she'd always owned, yet hadn't driven for years.

Malachi ran around back again, raced up the steps, and rushed inside. "Gran'nola?" His head whipped left and right as he assessed the empty kitchen. He strode down the hallway, checking the spare bedroom, the hall bathroom, and finally Gran'nola's bedroom. It smelled of the ointment she rubbed on her arthritic knees.

Panic rose in his chest, sending his heart racing.

"Gran'nola," he said again, his voice shaky. He knew she wouldn't answer. She wasn't there. But it made him feel better to say her name.

He scrambled back to the kitchen and grabbed the wireless phone that was mounted above her television stand. Then he paused, hearing the sound of liquid bubbling. He ran to the stove and used an oven mitt to lift the lid off the giant steel pot. A rush of steam hit his face, revealing a mess of corn cobs bobbing in the boiling water. He turned off the burner and didn't waste another moment before calling Aunt Mimi.

"Gran'nola is gone. She's gone, and the car is gone."

Aunt Mimi was too calm. "She probably ran to the store. She said she was cooking dinner for you. What's she having? I might—"

"No!" Malachi exploded. "She didn't go to the store." He was sick of her family making light of Gran'nola's situation. "She left food boiling on the stove. She never does that."

Aunt Mimi was half-listening.

Not knowing what else to do, he ran outside again, still rattling off what he'd found at the house. He looked in both directions, hoping to see Gran'nola's car rounding the curve, trailed by a long line of impatient drivers wishing she'd at least drive the speed limit instead of ten miles under it.

Aunt Mimi seemed oblivious to the urgency of the situation. She was too busy fussing with Uncle P.T. about who'd left the sprinkler on overnight.

"Aunt Mimi," Malachi yelled, shocking her into silence. "Gran'nola's not here. Where is she?"

"Check Ms. Spruill's," Aunt Mimi said.

"She's not there, either."

"She'll be back. She couldn't have gone that far if she left food on the stove."

Why didn't Aunt Mimi get it? Malachi grabbed an empty watering can and slung it against the brick house in frustration. The green plastic cracked as it fell in the grass.

"Should I call the police?" he asked.

"I don't think we have to go to such drastic measures," Aunt Mimi said.

Her voice was sympathetic to him now, but that didn't change the fact that Gran'nola was missing, and he didn't like the looks of her disappearance. *Disappearance.* The word made his insides shudder.

"What are we supposed to do?" Malachi almost whined. He swallowed the lump in his throat. Fear was trying to overtake him. He could feel it. He could taste it.

"I'll be over in twenty minutes," Aunt Mimi told him. "By the time I get there, I'll bet she's already home."

Malachi dropped down on the back porch steps and hung his head between his knees. He took slow, deliberate breaths to calm his racing heart. Aunt Mimi was probably right. Gran'nola would return shortly and offer a perfectly reasonable explanation as to why she'd hurried away in the first place. They'd sit down at the table to enjoy the dinner she'd been working most of the afternoon to prepare, and he'd let her entertain him with news of all the upcoming revivals and appreciation services lined up at the church. She'd share family stories, like she always did.

Five minutes passed.

Malachi called Uncle Bud, at home and then on his cell phone, but got no answer.

He walked across the small plot of land that separated Gran'nola's house from her next-door neighbor's. When he was young, she'd kept a garden of potatoes, corn, cucumbers, and green beans in that exact spot. He'd hated shucking corn because the husks always made his arms itch, and the stringy silk would stick to his clothes. But he loved sinking his teeth into a hot, buttery cob.

Corn boiling on the stove. Gran'nola. Gone.

Malachi rang the doorbell once, twice, three times. After the fourth ring, he finally concluded that the couple who lived there now wasn't home.

Ten minutes had passed when a fire truck blared down the street, heading in the direction of the church. Malachi listened carefully for the siren of a police car or an ambulance. What if Gran'nola had gotten in a car accident? He didn't know whether he should drive around and search the neighborhood or stay close to the house.

He decided on the latter, and paced the house for another fifteen minutes.

Aunt Mimi would be there shortly. She could stay by the phone, in case Gran'nola called while he searched the neighborhood. He would call the police. And he'd enlist the help of family members and fellow church congregants.

Eighteen minutes.

Malachi waited on the front steps, his eyes glued on the street. He and his cousins used to sit there and play punch bug, watching carefully for the next Volkswagen Beetle to rumble down the street so they could pound each other in the arm. Or, they'd each pick a color and earn a point every time a vehicle of that hue passed the house. Malachi always chose red.

Twenty-one minutes.

A car slowed as it approached the driveway. Malachi stood and watched as it made a U-turn and headed in the opposite direction.

"Man, forget this," he grumbled to himself. "I'm calling the police."

"Nine-one-one. What's your emergency?" said the female dispatcher.

"My grandmother, Nola Burke, is missing."

"Sir, how long has she been missing?"

Malachi looked at his watch. "I got to her house about twenty-five minutes ago, and she wasn't here. I'm not sure how long she's been gone in total, though."

The dispatcher briefly paused. "Sir, were there any signs of a struggle in the home?"

Malachi hadn't considered that Gran'nola might have been taken by force. The thought completely rattled the sense of calm he'd almost achieved.

"Sir?"

"No," he said, hoping to feel as confident as he sounded. Gran'nola's home looked as neat and orderly as ever.

"Is there anyone you can think of that she might have left with?"

"Her car isn't here, so I'm fairly sure she left on her own," Malachi said. "She's had at least one prior episode of leaving home and having a memory lapse of some sort," he explained. "I think she might be in the early stages of dementia, but I'm not sure. Even if she left of her own accord, it's possible that she won't be able to find her way back home."

"Sir, I'm sorry to hear that," the dispatcher said, her tone empathetic. "I'll try to get an officer out to help you as soon as possible."

"What do you mean, you'll 'try'?" Malachi said.

"Sir, we'll do all we can to make sure your grandmother returns safely," she clarified. "What's the home address?"

Malachi rattled it off, and the dispatcher promised to send the first police officer available.

"Thank you, ma'am."

He breathed easier when he saw Uncle P.T.'s truck turn into the driveway with Aunt Mimi at the wheel. The tires sent dirt and gravel flying as she barreled toward the house.

"My car battery died," Aunt Mimi said, jumping out. "If it ain't one thing, it's another." She rushed past Malachi and into the house as if her arrival would make Gran'nola magically appear.

Malachi went inside and found her in the kitchen, pacing frantically. "She's not back," she fretted, her brow furrowed with worry lines. "Lord, Gran'nola. Where are you, Sis?"

"I called nine-one-one," Malachi told her. "They're going to send the first available officer out."

Aunt Mimi started searching the house as if she hadn't heard him. The first time, she followed the same route that Malachi had taken when he'd first walked in. The second time, she opened random drawers and cabinets in each room. Malachi didn't know why, but he suspected she felt better when her hands were busy. Waiting was excruciating, and it hadn't even been an hour.

"Did she leave a note?" Aunt Mimi asked. She went to the refrigerator and checked the scribbles on the magnetic notepad, but Malachi had already looked. It was just the phone number for the pharmacy.

"I haven't seen anything out of the ordinary," Malachi said. "I think she probably drove off and got mixed up, like she did the last time you told me about. She wouldn't intentionally go away and leave the stove on, especially when she was expecting company."

Aunt Mimi's shoulders rose and then drooped heavily. "I'll stay here and wait if you want to drive out and look for her."

"I do," Malachi said.

"In the meantime, I know what I'll do," Aunt Mimi said, wringing her hands. "I'm putting a call out to the prayer warriors and the street warriors."

26

Malachi

It had been the longest two hours of Malachi's life.

"Hang in there, man," Alonzo told him. He handed him a bottle of water, but Malachi could stomach only a small sip. His hand shook slightly as he tried to screw the small white cap back on.

"I've got it," Alonzo said, taking the bottle and its lid from him. "Do you want to sit down for a few minutes?"

"No, Zo. I'm good," Malachi said.

But he wasn't. He was a wreck. He couldn't sit. He had too much nervous energy to stop moving. Plus, in his mind, to sit would be an act of surrender, as if he'd tired of the search for Gran'nola and was giving up hope. He would never tire of looking, whether it took him two hours, two weeks, two months, or two decades to find her.

Malachi swallowed his fear. He couldn't think like that. Before the night was over, Gran'nola would be tucked safely in her bed, and Malachi would be making do on the lumpy mattress in the other bedroom. By the end of the night, all his family members and Gran'nola's church friends would be back in the comfort of their own homes, having been cleared to abandon their search for her.

He stared blindly into the whirring blue light on top of the squad car now parked in the driveway. The police officer, Leviticus Gray, had taken down a description down of Gran'nola—every detail but her clothes, since Malachi had no idea what she was wearing—and had dispatched her car make, model, and license plate number. Still nothing.

Officer Gray was the same police officer who had let him off with a warning after a traffic stop just two weeks ago. Malachi had never dreamed their paths would cross again, especially under these circumstances.

Malachi almost wished Gran'nola had left on foot, because there was very little ground an elderly woman with a bad knee could cover in the amount of time he estimated she'd been gone. But with the car missing, too, he couldn't guess how far she might have driven, or in which direction.

They'd checked her usual spots and posted a lookout person at each one: the grocery store, the church, the pharmacy, and each of her siblings' houses. Malachi had even sent two employees from his foundation to stake out the parking lot at the baseball field, in case she ended up there. Where else could she be? Only God knew.

God, bring my grandma home, Malachi prayed silently. *Bring her home safe*. He'd probably prayed more in the last two hours than he'd prayed in a lifetime.

Malachi had watched his aunt Mimi go in and out of Gran'nola's house more times than he could count. She'd walked the perimeter of the property, wringing her hands and praying quietly—first alone, and then accompanied by a group once the other members of the church started arriving. Malachi was sure that their prayers were the only reason he was still able to stand. Without them, he surely would have collapsed by now.

Malachi jumped at the sound of his cell phone ringing in the console of his SUV, where it was charging. He'd set it at the maximum volume so he would be sure to hear if any calls came in, and he nearly dove in the window to answer it.

But the caller wasn't Gran'nola. He almost didn't pick up, but, under the circumstances, he was ready to enlist the help of anyone and everyone. Even Alexandria.

"Hey, baby," she said before Malachi had a chance to speak a single word. "You up for company?"

"I could use your help," Malachi said. This was business. All business.

"Sure," Alexandria purred. "Anything."

"My grandmother is missing," Malachi said. "We could use as many people as possible to help look for her."

"Did you call the police?" she asked, the seductive tone gone from her voice.

"Yes. There's an officer here now," Malachi said, feeling irritated. He didn't need her questions. All he needed was her help. Alexandria was accustomed to running the show and managing people, so it was second nature for her to drill him. But today wasn't the day.

"Alexandria, I don't need you to run things," he told her. "I need you to be here. Can you do that?"

"Uh…sure, I can. What's the address?"

He told her, then ended the call, feeling more helpless than ever before. Maybe, if he'd arrived just a few minutes earlier, Gran'nola wouldn't have gone missing. If only he'd continued staying here instead of checking in at the hotel. If only Alexandria hadn't shown up on Sunday, then maybe he and Rae both would've been here for dinner.

Rae. He hadn't called her yet. He should. She would want to know.

Malachi scrolled through his phone contacts until he found her number. *Answer, Rae,* he pleaded silently. *Answer the phone.* She'd ignored his latest attempts to contact her, but he needed her to answer, just this once. Maybe she'd called Gran'nola to decline the dinner invitation. Maybe she had a clue as to where Gran'nola might be.

"Hello?"

Rae's voice filled him with hope.

"Rae. This is Malachi. Have you talked to my grandma today?" He cut to the chase.

"I'm sorry," Rae said, her voice apologetic. "I should've called, but I couldn't come for dinner. I...I didn't want to. I didn't think it was a good idea."

"Gran'nola is missing," Malachi said, straining to steady his voice. "I came to her house for dinner, and she wasn't here. Neither was her car. It's been over two hours since I got here, and she hasn't come back."

"Oh, no." Rae gasped. "I haven't talked to her since yesterday."

"Okay," Malachi said, feeling deflated. "Thanks, anyway."

"What can I do to help?" Rae asked. "Do you have people looking for her? I can come over."

"Your choice." Malachi briefly wondered at the wisdom in having Rae and Alexandria in such close proximity again. But, at this point, what did it matter? Rae had already written him off, he'd written Alexandria off, and the woman he cared about most, besides his mother, was driving around aimlessly, waiting to be found.

"Is there anything you need?" Rae asked, her voice sounding small.

"Prayers," Malachi said.

"Of course, Malachi. See you in a bit."

Every vehicle that slowed in front of Gran'nola's house was torture. Malachi was grateful that so many people thought enough of Gran'nola to rush to his side, but there was only one car he wanted to see bumping up the gravel driveway. He had to see his grandmother climb out of her car, making a fuss at all the ruckus going on around her house all because she'd simply gone to the store for a bag of sugar.

The latest car to arrive parked next to Officer Gray, and a male driver climbed out, along with two female passengers.

Officer Gray approached them, shaking hands with the couple who'd been sitting in the front seats, then giving a tight squeeze to the woman who'd been riding in back.

Moments later, Alonzo joined the group who'd just arrived. He turned, scanning the yard.

Malachi could tell his friend was searching for him, so he headed in their direction. Alonzo had taken charge the moment he'd arrived, stepping up to direct the family members who were so stricken with worry that they weren't thinking clearly.

"Malachi, meet Roman and Zenja Maxwell, good friends of mine from church, and Quinn Montgomery, Officer Gray's fiancée," Alonzo said. "They're here to help you and your family. Just let them know what you need. Or I can just send them out driving, if you'd prefer."

Malachi didn't know what he needed until he watched his Uncle Bud stumble by. He couldn't blame him for having popped open one beer can after another. His uncle was reverting to the way he'd long dealt with stress.

"Somebody should keep an eye on Uncle Bud," he suggested. "Maybe keep him company and steer him away from the beer."

"I can handle that," Roman said. "After what you've done for my son and other boys in the city, it would be a pleasure."

"Thank you," Malachi said, humbled that he'd left a positive impression on this man he didn't even know.

They shook hands with a strong, sturdy grasp that conveyed Roman's support and Malachi's acceptance of it.

"Don't worry about your uncle. I'm on him," Roman assured him.

Roman followed Uncle Bud, staying a few cautious steps behind him. It wasn't long before Uncle Bud noticed he had company. Roman said something to him, and then Uncle Bud produced another beer from the waistband of his pants and held it out. Roman shook his head, then fell into step with Uncle Bud's slow, shuffling gait as he moved about the yard. When they disappeared into the darkness of the trees surrounding the house, Malachi went back inside.

All heads turned when he opened the door, but their expressions drooped when they saw that he was alone.

Aunt Mimi, looking tired and disheveled, approached him, her arms wide and ready to embrace him. She wrapped them around Malachi's waist and let her head rest on his chest. He couldn't hear her weeping, but he could feel the shudder of her body against his. He wanted to break, but for everyone else, he had to stand strong.

Pastor Hunter, the newly hired minister from their family church, walked over to comfort them.

"Hold on. God is in control. He sees what we can't see, and I believe Ms. Nola will come home safely."

Malachi hoped he was right.

27

I'd replayed the possible scenarios in my head too many times to count, wondering if Ms. Nola might not have gone missing if I'd agreed to come to dinner. If I had been there, maybe she wouldn't have wandered away. Maybe I would've arrived just as she was about to pull out of the driveway.

Malachi had been haunted by the same kind of thinking. I sat next to him on his grandma's bed, listening as he berated himself for not arriving earlier.

"There's no way you could've known," I told him. They were the same words I'd tried using to reassure myself.

Malachi pressed his thumbs against his temples.

"Headache?"

He nodded.

I nodded to the tiny bathroom attached to Ms. Nola's bedroom. "Can I go in there?" I asked.

He nodded again.

To the side of the sink was a small wicker basket of pill bottles. I rummaged through them, examining each one. A prescription for high blood pressure. Fish oil tablets. Antacid tablets. A daily vitamin with extra calcium. I picked up another bottle with a red cap. Ibuprofen. I opened it, shook two caplets into my hand, and took them to Malachi.

He popped them in his mouth and swallowed them dry. "Thanks," he said. "And thanks for coming. It means a lot."

I nodded. "I really don't know Ms. Nola that well, but I know how much you love her. I know how I'd feel it if was my grandmother. I hate that this is happening, but there's a yard full of people out there, and around the city, too, working hard to bring her home. She hasn't seen the story I wrote about the two of you, so she has to hurry up and get back to read it," I said gently.

"Gran'nola has plenty of stories to tell," Malachi said, "and it hurts me to realize they may soon slip away from her. Her memory has always been so keen. She never used to forget anything. I believed that God would preserve her mind. What quality of life can a person have if she can't remember anything or anyone? Or even her own identity?"

I had no answers for him. I'd never personally dealt with anyone with dementia or Alzheimer's. And even if I had, it probably wouldn't have given me much to say or do to console him right now.

I reached over to rub his shoulder and felt the tension tightening his muscles.

"My parents were going to jump on the first plane here, but I told them to wait until morning," Malachi told me. "Why did I do that?"

"You have a lot on your mind," I empathized. "It's probably best, anyway. She'll be back, and they can come to visit her."

"We have some decisions to make," Malachi said. "Gran'nola won't like it, but it has to be done. She won't leave here without a fight."

"You could have someone come and live with her," I suggested. He had the money, and I knew he would have paid his last dime to make sure she was safe and well taken care of, even if Ms. Nola fussed about it.

"Like me," he said. "I could come back home."

This wasn't my family, so I had no reason to offer my opinion; but I was sure that being a full-time caregiver brought more pressure and responsibilities than Malachi realized. It was his love for his grandma that was speaking right now, but he would need someone to help him weigh the options with a healthy dose of realism. He was fortunate to have other options available.

"Everything's going to work out," I told him. "You have to hold on to your faith in God."

"Trust me, I'm trying," Malachi said. "Right about now, that's all I've got."

He stood up, tossed his baseball cap on the bed, and stretched his hands high above his head. "I guess I better get back out here and find some way to keep busy. I can't keep watching the clock. I might ride out again."

"Do you want company?" I asked.

He dropped his hands at his sides. "Yes."

Our gazes locked, and as I looked into his dark brown eyes, I could see the depth of his worry.

I could also sense our attraction to each other, in spite of all that had happened.

"I know this isn't the time to talk about this," Malachi said, "but Sunday was nothing. *She* is nothing. Not anymore."

"You have to understand that I don't do drama," I told him. "I could tell that's what she was coming with, and I didn't want to be connected to that in any way."

Malachi averted his eyes for a moment, then turned back to me. "Alexandria may be coming over to help with the search."

I smoothed back the hair that had fallen from my bun. "You're entitled to any help you can get," I said, meaning it. "This isn't about me or her. It's about Ms. Nola."

I could see the relief wash across his face. I reached out for his muscular hand, took it in my own, and gave it a soft squeeze before we returned to the kitchen. People were crammed into every square foot and empty corner of the home, speaking in hushed tones and hugging one another for support.

"I'll be back, Pastor Hunter," Malachi told a man with a commanding presence.

The pastor used his handkerchief to wipe the sweat beads from his nose, then stuck it in his back pocket.

"Let me give you a verse before you leave, Son," he said to Malachi. "'*Whoever dwells in the shelter of the Most High will rest in the shadow of the Almighty. I will say of the* LORD, "*He is my refuge and my fortress, my God, in whom I trust.*"'"

"Amen," I whispered.

Malachi reached behind him, and my hand naturally went into his grasp.

We went outside, hand in hand. The lawn was still buzzing with people who, like the rest of us, looked unsure about what they should do. On the way to his SUV, Malachi took a detour to speak with an additional police officer who had arrived on the scene.

"I'll be back," he said, apparently not having noticed the TV crew setting up at the end of the driveway.

Knowing Malachi, he would probably shun the attention. But this was one of those times when having a household name could work in his favor. I checked the passenger door of his SUV and, finding it unlocked, took the liberty of climbing inside to wait for him.

Five minutes later, he jumped behind the wheel. "Alonzo's rounding up the people whose cars have me blocked in," Malachi said as he started the engine. He rolled down all the windows, letting in the pleasant heat of the summer evening. Off in the distance, the tiny glows of fireflies dotted the darkness. And if I listened carefully, over the conversations and the sounds of cars going down the street, I could hear the faint chirp of a family of crickets.

"Did you see the news crew at the end of the driveway?" I asked him.

Malachi nodded. "Alonzo told them to stay at the end of the street."

"You should give a statement," I told him. "They'll air it on the eleven o'clock news. You never know who might see it. Greensboro loves you. You'll have everyone in the city watching out for Ms. Nola."

He leaned back against the headrest and thought for a moment. "But what about the person who might take advantage of the situation because she's my grandmother? You never know what a person might do."

He made a valid point. There was always the possibility that someone with evil intentions would seek to profit from Ms. Nola's disappearance. But, even then, at least they'd know something.

"Back it up," Alonzo yelled. He blinked a flashlight in the direction
of the truck, signaling to Malachi that there was enough room for him
to squeeze past the remaining cars parked nearby.

"There are more for you than there are against you," I told him.
"Speaking to the media could make a world of difference."

Malachi shifted into reverse without answering. He eased the vehicle backward while tapping lightly on the horn to warn anyone who
might step into its path.

I spotted a pair of headlights approaching. "Hold on," I told him.
"Someone's coming."

We both watched in the rearview mirror as the car came to a stop
behind us. I could hear Alonzo telling the driver to move out of the way,
to no avail.

Malachi leaned out the window to get a better view. "That's
Alexandria," he said dryly.

"Does she always have to make an entrance like that?" I asked, buckling my seat belt. "I guess she thinks she has something to prove."

"The only thing she's proving right now is that she's crazy," Malachi
said.

"And I don't do crazy," I reminded him.

He shifted into park and opened his door before looking back at me.
"You don't have to worry about her."

"Trust me, I'm not worried," I told him. *Annoyed, but not worried.*

Alexandria rushed over to Malachi like a toddler who'd gotten separated from her daddy in the grocery store. She threw her arms around
him and looked straight at me as she buried her face in his neck.

My cheeks burned, but I didn't flinch.

"Baby, I'm so sorry," she crooned, cupping the sides of his face in her
hands.

Malachi grabbed her wrists and peeled her hands off of him.

That didn't stop her from putting them back on his shoulders. "Has
there been any news? Please tell me you know something."

"Not yet," he said, removing her hands from his body once again.

"What can I do? Are you leaving? I'll come with you."

I'm not sure what kind of help Alexandria was expecting to offer, since she was dressed appropriately for a girls' night out on the town. Her makeup appeared to have been freshly applied, and her eyebrows were impeccably shaped. Farrah would have been impressed.

"Ask Alonzo," Malachi told Alexandria. "The guy back there in the white shirt and camouflage shorts. He'll let you know what you can do."

"But I'd rather come with you," she said, dropping her voice as if she didn't want me to hear her pleading.

"Rae's coming with me," Malachi said.

"Who's he?"

"She," I corrected her loudly.

Malachi spun around at the sound of my voice.

I'd surprised even myself with my abrupt interjection, but I didn't regret it. This may be Malachi's territory, and I had no doubt that he could handle his business; but I wasn't going to sit there passively while Alexandria blatantly disrespected me.

"Oh, I'm so sorry," Alexandria said, batting her oversized false eyelashes in a show of apology I knew better than to take seriously. "We've met before, haven't we?"

"We most definitely have," I said, offering her a smile as fake as the one she'd given me. "Are you ready, Malachi?"

"Absolutely." He slid back into the vehicle and slammed the door. "Thanks for coming, Alexandria. Can you move your car, please?"

Her perfectly lined lips were parted slightly, as if she was trying to think of something to say to keep Malachi by her side instead of driving off with me.

She would be thinking a long time.

"Alexandria." Malachi cleared his throat. "Your car."

She finally retreated.

"Sorry about that," Malachi said as he shifted into reverse yet again.

"Stop apologizing for her," I told him.

"So, we're good?" he asked.

"We're good." I touched his shoulder. "We're great."

Malachi slowed to a stop at the end of the driveway. The bright light of a TV camera shone into the car, and a brunette reporter shoved a microphone in Malachi's face. "Mr. Burke, I understand that your grandmother has been reported missing," she said. "Is there anything you can tell us regarding her disappearance?"

Malachi glanced over at me, and I nodded reassuringly.

He turned to the reporter again. "This evening, I arrived at the home of my grandmother, Nola Burke, to find her missing, along with her car. I would appreciate the public's help in getting her home safely. If you see an elderly woman driving a car, or walking, who looks lost, please call the police."

"It sounds as if you suspect your grandmother may be suffering from memory loss," the reporter probed him. "Is this the first episode she's exhibited? Has she gone missing before?"

"My concern right now is the safe return of my grandmother, Nola Burke," he reiterated.

I rested my hand on his right knee, a gesture intended to let him know he was handling the reporter exactly as he should. The woman was only doing her job as a journalist and digging for the story behind the story. It was her job to speculate.

"Mr. Burke, do you have any suspicion that someone may have broken into the home and taken your grandmother against her will?"

"It doesn't appear that way," Malachi said. "But, again, if anyone sees anything, we're asking that they call the police. Thank you."

Malachi put up his window, and I followed suit with mine. We rode in silence behind the tinted windows until we reached the main thoroughfare.

Where are you, Ms. Nola? I thought. *Please come home.*

28

I hope Gran'nola invites me for dinner again," I said, trying to lighten the mood.

Malachi gave a slight smile. "I don't think she'll have a problem doing that."

I glanced at the odometer. He was driving ten miles per hour under the speed limit. "I could go for a smothered pork chop with some mac and cheese," I added.

"No wonder you swim so much," he teased. "You don't really like eating all that healthy stuff, do you?"

"Who does?" I said, peering into the car stopped beside us at the traffic light. "But that's the price you pay if you're planning on a long life of good health."

I had no idea where Malachi was going, and it was clear that he didn't, either.

"I know it sounds crazy, but I needed to get away," Malachi said. "For ten minutes."

"It doesn't sound crazy. It sounds like you're human. And there are plenty of people back at the house who can handle things in your absence."

Malachi flipped the turn signal. "I forgot to tell Alonzo to give the media a photo of Gran'nola."

I lifted his cell phone from the console. "May I?"

"Sure."

I found Alonzo's number on the list of recent calls, and I shot him a text asking him to give all the local stations a photo of Gran'nola.

Malachi pulled into the parking lot of a small shopping center just as the lights inside the combination deli and ice cream shop turned off. Closed.

"I almost forgot what it's like to be in a city that shuts down at night," he said, parking beneath a streetlight.

"Late-night food is in short supply around here," I acknowledged.

"Don't say 'food.' I'm starving."

I reached inside my purse and produced a granola bar.

"No, thanks," Malachi said. "I'm waiting for Gran'nola to come home so we can eat dinner together."

He looped around the parking lot, merged onto the street, and headed back in the direction of Gran'nola's house, driving ten miles per hour over the limit instead of under. He turned on the radio but didn't appear to pay much attention to it. I figured he was trying to drown out his fears. I could only imagine the scenarios running through his mind. If it was my grandmother, I didn't think I'd have the presence of mind to drive a motor vehicle. We ventured down several driveways and unmarked roads, slowing near a small lake to see if her car had accidentally veered down the embankment. The brush was undisturbed.

Everything seemed to be in order. Behind closed doors, women were peeking in on their sleeping children, and men were peeking into the fridge for a late-night snack. Someone was climbing into bed without worries.

But Gran'nola was still missing.

As we rumbled back into her overcrowded driveway, I couldn't help but notice that Alexandria's car was nowhere in sight. I wondered how long it would take for Malachi to realize that she'd gone MIA. I could've been wrong, but she didn't seem like the type to volunteer for the search committee. And not just because she didn't know the ins and outs of the city.

"When you go back inside, it's going to be hard not to feel overwhelmed," I told him. "You're going to have to find that inner peace, despite what you see around you."

"Faith," Malachi said. "The substance of things hoped for and the evidence of things not seen." He turned off the headlights, and we climbed out of the SUV.

Malachi hadn't taken two steps before he was rushed by his aunt Mimi and a younger woman who was her spitting image.

"Have you talked to your dad yet?" his aunt asked.

"What's the plan?" the other woman pressed him. "We can't just keep sitting around here."

"Hush, Juanita," Aunt Mimi said. Then she turned back to Malachi. "Your uncle Bud passed out by the utility shed. The man who was with him had to pick him up and lay him in the back of his car. I'm so embarrassed."

"I gave Alonzo the picture of Gran'nola that she submitted for the family reunion booklet a couple years ago," the other woman told him. "Was that okay?"

Malachi held up his hand. "I need a minute, Aunt Mimi. Everything is fine. Everything." He'd answered both their questions with a single phrase.

"Hi, sweetie," Mimi said to me. She gently grabbed my hand and patted the back of it. "Thank you for coming. Especially for Malachi. He needs somebody by his side who is real and not just for show. I know who came to make an entrance and who didn't." She lowered her voice and added, "She was gone as quick as she came."

I squeezed her hand in response, then followed Malachi into the house. The same faces were there as before, along with a few newcomers; of those, Shelton was the only one I recognized.

I'd never seen him wearing anything other than creased pants and a heavily starched oxford shirt, so it took a moment for my mind to register that he was the man dressed in a pair of jeans, a plaid short-sleeved shirt, and a pair of tennis shoes. I wasn't even aware he owned tennis shoes. He didn't look surprised to see me.

"Rae," he said, eyeing me over the rim of his glasses. He took them off and hung them from an empty buttonhole.

"Shelton."

"How's he doing?"

"About as well as can be expected. It's a waiting game, you know. That's the hardest part."

Shelton crunched on a piece of peppermint that he'd been rolling around in his mouth. Then he smiled, and I ignored the knowing glint in his eyes. The next time I was in the office, he'd be giving Ms. Bessie a play-by-play. I was sure of it.

"We'll talk later," I said, disappearing between the people standing shoulder to shoulder.

I found a quiet corner to wait while Malachi went into Gran'nola's room with Pastor Hunter and Alonzo, closing the door behind them. When they emerged, I could tell by the red tint of Malachi's eyes that he'd been crying. He'd needed that. He'd needed those tears.

Alonzo motioned for me. "Would you mind fixing Malachi a plate?"

"He told me he doesn't want to eat."

"I know. He told me the same thing. But he needs to. He'll babysit the plate for a while, but eventually he'll eat."

Alonzo knew his friend. Sure enough, Malachi initially refused the meal and the glass of ginger ale that I offered him; but after a few minutes, he begin to pick around the plate with his fork. Small bite by small bite, he polished it off. It was nearly one thirty in the morning before Gran'nola's fellow church members began to leave, with promises to return early in the morning after getting some rest. But I don't think they expected to sleep.

Malachi and I retreated to the living room, lit only by a lamp on the end table. The curtains were drawn back so that the large window framed the night sky.

"I want this to be over," Malachi said, wiping his palm down the front of his face. "I want Gran'nola to fuss at me for drinking her papaya juice. I want her to wake me up early, cackling on the phone with her sisters or Uncle Bud. I want things...." He paused. "Normal."

I placed a comforting arm around him. He rested his head on the back of the sofa, and after some time, his breathing slowed to a steady pace. He was asleep.

I'd nearly dozed off myself when the vibration of my phone awakened me. It was a text from Farrah.

Just saw u on the news recap. Pls tell me they've found her.

I answered: Nothing yet. Prayers needed.

How is Malachi?

Holding up. BTW, didn't know the camera could see me.

It did. U 2 look cute together. Sorry. Bad timing. Had to say it.

U need Jesus. Call u ltr.

Malachi's snore was barely audible, but I knew that his slumber was light. I was careful not to make even the slightest move while he rested, lest I disturb him.

Soon, however, I laid my head against the back of the sofa as drowsiness overtook me. My eyelids grew too heavy to hold open, and I let myself succumb to my fatigue.

I wasn't sure how long we'd been asleep when Alonzo burst into the room with three words that pushed both me and Malachi to our feet.

"They found her."

29

Malachi

"What?" Shocked from his sleep, Malachi flailed his arms. He looked around. It took a few seconds for his blurry vision to adjust, and a few more for him to realize where he was, and why there were so many people gathered at Gran'nola's house. It hadn't been a bad dream. She was really missing. But what had happened? What had Alonzo said?

Rae grabbed his arm. Her eyes were misty. "They found Ms. Nola."

"Where is she?" Malachi said, running into the kitchen. He half expected her to be sitting in her favorite chair, sipping a cup of dark coffee and nibbling at a piece of cheese toast. "Where's Gran'nola?"

"She's with the police," Alonzo told him. "They're bringing her home." His friend's eyes were dark and rimmed with heavy bags. He must not have slept, either; at most, he'd caught just a few z's.

Tears of relief flowed down Malachi's face. His legs weakened to the point that he had to grab ahold of the counter.

"It's been a long night," Alonzo said.

"An endless night," Malachi said. He scratched the itchiness of his beard. He hadn't checked himself in a mirror recently, but if he looked as exhausted as the family members who remained, he was in obvious need of a shave, a hot shower, and some sleep.

Rae put a hand on his back.

He turned toward her and pulled her into his arms. They held each other for a brief moment, until he felt her slightly pull away. Everyone was watching. He couldn't have cared less, but he figured she would be uncomfortable with the even the smallest public display of affection.

"What time is it?" he asked her.

"Five thirty six," she said, guiding him to an empty chair at the table. She sat in the one beside him. "God answered your prayer. Ms. Nola's coming home to fuss again, just like you wanted."

"I'll take it," he said. "Bring it on. I'm not leaving this house. At all."

But there was one problem. Everything he'd brought with him to North Carolina was at the Grandover.

"I'll send Alonzo to the hotel to pick up my things."

"I'll go get them for you," Rae offered, standing up again. She'd pulled her hair back into a ponytail, and Malachi realized for the first time that she was wearing the T-shirt from his camp.

He grabbed her hand. "Don't worry about it. You've done enough just being here."

"I don't mind. Really." She held out her open palm and wiggled her fingers. "Give me your key, and stop being stubborn. I'll be back before you know it."

Malachi wondered if this was how she looked every morning—so bright-eyed and fresh. Ever a simple beauty.

"Should I bring all of it?" she asked.

Malachi conjured a mental image of the state of his room. Because he'd been raised by neatniks—his parents and Gran'nola alike—he'd never been one to leave his things in disarray, even after all these years. Although he had a weekly housekeeping service to help with the routine stuff now, the women he'd brought home had always commented on his tidiness. It was rare for a bachelor, especially, to be so organized. He was thankful Rae wouldn't have to worry about picking up his dirty underwear and socks. He'd been keeping his dirty clothes in a plastic bag with the intent to wash them later.

"All of it," he confirmed. "There's my toiletry bag in the bathroom and two pieces of luggage from the closet. It might take you two trips." He stood. "I'll walk you out."

In the driveway, everyone erupted into cheers and applause when they noticed Malachi, as if he'd done something. He pounded his chest, then pointed his forefinger up at the sky. "Nobody but God," he said. "Nobody but God." He cleared his throat. "I know you all want to hang around until Gran'nola gets here, but everybody knows I can't let that happen. She'd pitch a fit on me and everyone else. I love you. And I appreciate your support. Now, get out of here." He made a sweeping motion with his arms.

When almost everyone had gone, including Rae, a man whom Malachi had seen her speaking with the night before approached him.

"I'm Shelton Hayes. I go to your grandma's church. Let me know if there's anything you need, and I'll get the men together to handle it."

Malachi moved to shake the man's hand. "Thank you, sir. I recognize the name, but I don't think I've ever seen your face. You weren't at the church when I was growing up."

"No," Shelton said, his thick round fingers still covering Malachi's. "My wife and I have been attending there about six years. We always knew about your family's church from all the community service and worship events that they publicized in our newspaper, and so, when we ended up having to look for a new church home, my wife told me she already knew where she wanted to attend."

Newspaper? That piqued Malachi's attention. "What paper is that?"

"The *Greensboro Ledger*."

"Okay, now I'm putting it together," Malachi said with a nod.

"Thanks for agreeing to the interview," Shelton said. "We're giving you the center spread for our latest issue—also our last issue."

"Last issue?" Rae had mentioned that the paper was having problems, but he hadn't realized it was folding.

Malachi propped his foot on the edge of one of Gran'nola's flowerpots and rocked it gently back and forth. Two black bugs scurried out from underneath it.

Shelton leaned back on his heels and scratched his stomach. Malachi thought he heard it grumble. The man had been hanging around since last night, so no doubt he was hungry.

"Advertising is down, and we've never charged our readers," Shelton explained. "Without sufficient ads, there's not enough money to keep it going. We'll be back, though. I'm not going down without a fight. I just have to retreat to the corner for a minute and work on some things."

"That's too bad," Malachi said. "I know you have some good writers." He had thrown the bait out on purpose, to see if he could catch anything.

Shelton snagged it immediately. "Rae? Yep, she's serious about her work. She does as much for us as she does for the other people she writes for, and we can't pay her half of what they do." He was scratching his stomach again.

Malachi looked away. "There's something special about her," he said. "Gran'nola loves her. She'd even invited her over for dinner last night, but she declined."

"And yet she ended up out here, anyway," Shelton said. "Take note of that, Malachi. A woman's actions say a lot."

A *whole lot*, Malachi thought. He'd certainly taken note of Alexandria's disappearing act. She'd sent him a text around two o'clock in the morning that he hadn't bothered to answer. Supposedly, she'd had a headache. His grandmother had gone missing, and she'd flaked out because of something as small as a headache.

"I want to get to know her better. But only time will tell." And if his baseball career went the route he thought it would, he'd have extra time on his hands.

"And time is what she needs," Shelton said. "She's been hurt, but she's not beyond loving again one day. I have to tell you, though: I'm not sure how much leeway you'll make from up in New York."

Malachi braced himself. This would be the first time he made this confession aloud. "I'm not sure if I'm going back to stay," he said. "The way I've been feeling, I might be back down South for good."

"Then, no matter where you land on the East Coast, make sure you do right by Rae Stevens. She deserves the best. And if you find that you can't give it to her, leave her alone so she'll be ready for the man who can."

"Yes, sir," Malachi said, realizing how much Rae meant to Mr. Shelton. "I can respect that."

"Excuse me, gentlemen." Officer Gray politely interrupted them. "Mr. Burke, your grandmother is about thirty-five minutes away."

Officer Gray's shift had ended an hour ago, but he'd graciously decided to hang around longer. Malachi hadn't had the chance to thank his fiancé, Quinn, or Roman and his wife for their sacrifice. He had so many people who deserved his gratitude.

"Thirty-five minutes? Where was she found? How's she's doing?" Exhaustion and elation had kept him from asking any questions earlier. Now, tons of them ran through his mind.

"A couple found her asleep in her car at a truck stop in Winston-Salem," Officer Gray told him. "They said she was slightly disoriented at first. Then, slowly but surely, she came around to herself. She gave them a hard time about not being able to drive her car back."

Malachi chuckled. "They definitely found the right woman."

"I'm staying here until the other officers drop her off," Office Gray said.

"But I'll be leaving," Shelton said, covering a yawn with his hand. "It's been years since I've pulled an all-nighter of any kind. This old man's not cut out for it."

"Are you going to be okay driving back home?" Malachi asked. The last thing he wanted to hear about was a misfortune befalling someone who'd been helping his family.

"I won't fall asleep until my head hits the pillow," Mr. Shelton said confidently.

"As soon as my grandma gets home, I won't be far behind you," Malachi said. His headache was starting to return. He knew it was the result of hunger and exhaustion.

"Let me get out of here," Mr. Shelton said. "I'll make sure to get you extra copies of the paper."

"Do that," Malachi said, then went to search for Uncle Bud.

He hadn't laid eyes on him since he'd stumbled into the darkness with Roman. He was sure they'd dragged him out of Roman's car and deposited him somewhere he could sleep off the alcohol.

Malachi found him in the spare bedroom he'd been staying in. The stench of alcohol reeked from Uncle Bud's pores, imparting the same putrid smell to the entire room. Malachi muscled the window open, then went to the hall bath and returned with a can of vanilla-scented air freshener. He sprayed until a cloud misted over the room.

Uncle Bud rolled over and grunted, but he didn't awaken. Malachi left him alone. He needed to sleep it off. He was going to have a serious hangover later.

Aunt Mimi walked up behind him. "What a night," she said, her hair standing on edge. "Worst ten hours of my life."

Malachi pulled his aunt into an embrace and could tell by the slight shivering of her body that she was crying again. He held her.

"I don't know what I'd do if something had happened to my sister," she sobbed. "I was taking her problems too lightly, and this has made it all too real for me. I should've done something the first time."

"We can't go back," Malachi said. "All we can do is prepare for the future."

Uncle Bud stirred again, flinging his arm over the edge of the bed. It dangled there like a loose cord.

"And look at this fool," Aunt Mimi said, sniffing. She stepped back and wiped her eyes. "He can't help an ant get a crumb."

Malachi patted his aunt on the shoulder. "He'll get it together. We all have things to work on. The stress pushed him overboard. That's all."

"I'd like to push him overboard somewhere myself," Aunt Mimi said, then turned away with a huff. "I'm going to cook my sister breakfast."

"Make enough for three," Malachi told her.

"The way I'm feeling, it'll be enough for fifteen. You know I have to cook when I'm stressed."

The house was quieting. Malachi stared out the window and watched the cars leaving the driveway one by one. Evidently, Shelton had done his job. Alonzo was at the end of the driveway, speaking to a reporter sitting in a news van. Gran'nola didn't need to see that, either. She would flip.

In fact, Malachi needed to make sure she didn't get near the television for the next forty-eight hours. The news stories were bound to make her upset, embarrassed, or a combination of both. Gran'nola didn't need to know that her private business had been aired to the entire city of Greensboro.

The wait for Gran'nola to return home seemed as long as the time that she'd been away. The minutes couldn't have ticked by any slower. Malachi stole tiny samples from the pans of food Aunt Mimi was preparing for breakfast. He couldn't find any other way to preoccupy himself.

Despite Alonzo's initial objections, Malachi finally convinced his friend to return home to his pregnant wife. Alonzo had already called off work for the day, and Malachi felt what he needed more than anything was sleep and quality time with his family. He'd been his right-hand man for the first two sessions of baseball camp, and he'd insisted on fulfilling the same role for the third. In just two days, they'd start it all over again.

And in five days, Malachi would make the calls to the most important players of his career. On Monday morning, they'd know that he was hanging up his baseball cleats to walk a new journey in life.

30

I walked into Malachi's hotel room as the door closed behind me with a soft click. The comforter on the king-sized bed was slightly rustled, as if he'd napped on it last evening before heading to his grandmother's house. Just as he'd said, there were two pieces of luggage in the closet. I zipped up the front pocket of the smaller suitcase, then went into the bathroom to collect his toiletries.

The smell of his cologne still lingered in the air. My, that man smelled good. Looked good, too. Two weeks ago, I never would've imagined that I'd be napping on the arm of a baseball celebrity while the city searched for his missing grandmother. I'd cried when I heard that she had been found, not only because I thought that Ms. Nola was the sweetest, feistiest woman I'd ever met, but also because of the priceless look of love on Malachi's face.

"He's gotta keep those teeth minty fresh," I said, dropping his toothbrush and toothpaste into his toiletry bag.

I scanned the bedroom one more time, then pulled up the handle of his small roller bag and started for the door, halting when someone knocked. It was too early in the morning for housekeeping—in my experience, at least. Perhaps the protocol was different at these five-star locations.

I peeked through the peephole. Alexandria. She was draped in a long red silk robe tied loosely at the waist. Very loosely. And she wore heels. I should've known.

There was only one way in. One way out. But I had nothing to hide.

I swung the door open, and Alexandria stepped back in surprise. She pulled the belt tighter when she saw me, then tossed her hair over her shoulder in a show of nonchalance.

"Where's Malachi?" I could tell she was acting civilly just in case he was within earshot. "How is his grandmother?"

I cleared my throat. "Ms. Nola is on her way home, and Malachi's there waiting for her."

"Oh." Now Alexandria's fangs began to show. "And what are you doing here?" Her gaze traveled from the toiletry bag in my hand to the luggage at my feet. "You're his hired help now? That's cute," she sneered.

"You don't have to be that way," I told her. "It's very unattractive, and you're too beautiful a woman to act so ugly."

"I don't need your advice, sweetheart," Alexandria scoffed. "You, on the other hand, could use mine. Let's start with some fashion advice, boo, because you're looking rather country from head to toe."

I swallowed. She was going there. I'd decided to take the high road and throw in a compliment, and she, in turn, wanted to be nasty. She wouldn't take me there. I'd still be the bigger woman. Some battles weren't worth fighting.

I took the privacy tag from the inside of the door and hung it on the door handle. "Excuse me," I said, pushing past her. "Malachi is waiting for me. For me."

I walked down the hall with a swing in my step, like I was wearing a ball gown and stilettos instead of a navy T-shirt, comfort-fit jeans, and tennis shoes. I didn't have to glance behind me to know that she was fuming. *Run your car up on that*, I thought.

From the car, I called Farrah. "When did my life become so dramatic?" I asked when she picked up.

"What happened now?" she said, her voice groggy. "Wait. Please tell me they found Malachi's grandma."

"They found Ms. Nola," I affirmed. "I don't know the details, only that she's on her way back home."

She exhaled a sigh of relief. "Thank You, Jesus. I was praying for her. Prayed so much, I fell asleep. That's good news to wake up to."

"Excellent news," I said. "But, in the meantime, I ran into Malachi's ex-girlfriend again when I went over to the Grandover to pick up his things. I was on my way out of his room when she showed up at his door. In lingerie."

"I'm not surprised," Farrah said. "Some women will do anything for attention. But if that's how she wants to run her life, that's her business."

"At first, I was bothered by her being in town," I said, slamming my trunk shut. "But, honestly, I think Malachi is through with her. And whatever happens, I refuse to let it steal my joy."

"That's right," Farrah affirmed. "The joy of the Lord is your strength. And you're becoming one strong sister."

I couldn't have agreed more. Day by day, I was reclaiming my life, living my life, and becoming more aware of God ordering my steps.

"Oh, by the way, did I tell you that the lady you referred to me for a makeup consultation for her wedding called?"

"Quinn?" I was happy to hear that she'd followed through.

"Quinn. Right. We're going to meet next week at her friend's house. I told her I'd bring you along. Hope you don't mind."

"That's fine by me," I said. "I love watching the transformation process. Besides, my name is on the line. I already told her you'd make her look like a million bucks."

Farrah laughed. "You were wrong. You should've said two million."

My fifth wind kicked in as I headed back to Gran'nola's house. Farrah was like Gran'nola in the way she had of spinning colorful, entertaining stories. By the time I was parking beside Malachi's truck, Farrah had recounted her latest experience at her mother-in-law's, the spat between one of her classmates and their esthetician instructors, and the hilarious incident when she'd awakened to her neighbor watering his flower garden wearing nothing but a Speedo.

Malachi met me at my car and relieved me of his belongings. "Come in," he said, holding the door open. "Somebody's waiting for you."

I stepped inside and experienced a moment of déjà vu. It looked like I would be having breakfast with Malachi and Ms. Nola again, this time joined by Aunt Mimi and Uncle Bud, as well. Uncle Bud's eyes were so red, it looked like he'd used food coloring for eyedrops.

"You still owe me a visit for dinner," Ms. Nola said when she turned around and saw me. "It's in the refrigerator. All we have to do is warm it up." She patted the empty chair beside her. "But, in the meantime, have a seat. Mimi cooked all of this. I guess she thought I wasn't coming back. She always cooks when she's upset."

"I know one thing," Mimi said, untying the apron from around her waist and slinging it over her shoulder. "We're not letting you out of our sight again."

"You might as well put me in jail," Ms. Nola told her. "I'm fine. I'm back home, safe and sound, aren't I?" She looked at me like I would be her saving grace, "Please tell them they're overreacting."

Malachi handed me a plate.

"It never hurts to have somebody looking out for you," I said.

"See, there? Malachi's been in your ear already," Gran'nola said. "But, as far as I'm concerned, that's a good thing. I expect to see you around a lot. I know what I know."

I'd learned it was best to keep your comments to yourself once Ms. Nola made a declaration. I'd also learned that a girl had to throw her healthy eating plan out of the window when dining with the Burkes'. So, I did. There was nothing piled on my plate that a few extra laps in the pool wouldn't burn.

Ms. Nola held out her mug so Mimi could fill it with coffee. "I know you're probably finished with that story you're writing, but did I ever tell you about—"

"Oh, no," Malachi cut her off. "Not that again. Do you have to tell all of the Burke family's business?"

"Yes. That again," I said, reaching over to cover his mouth with my hand. "Tell it all, Ms. Nola." I never traveled without my digital recorder, and I didn't hesitate to pull it out of my purse and position it in the middle of the table, propped beside a platter of bacon.

And then, her stories began. They lasted two hours. Ms. Nola would've relived her childhood for twenty more if Malachi hadn't finally put his foot down and convinced her that she needed her rest.

I helped Malachi prepare Ms. Nola's room, pulling her blackout draperies closed. Once she was in bed, he closed her door.

"You should do the same thing," I told him as we stepped out into the midday sunshine. "You still have the camp this weekend. You're going to need some extra sleep."

I hadn't bothered telling him about my encounter with Alexandria at the hotel. He had enough on his mind. Besides, she'd already shown her true colors.

Malachi handed me a bag of leftovers from breakfast *and* dinner, which Mimi had packed up, despite my objections. Not only did you not put up a fight with Ms. Nola; her sister was a force to be reckoned with. Suddenly, those five extra laps in the pool had been upped to ten.

"I'll call you this week," Malachi told me. "I can do that, right?"

"Of course you can," I said. "In fact, I'd love it if you would."

"You aren't going to give me a hard time about it?" Malachi said.

I shrugged. "Ms. Nola's home. That put me in a good mood. You'll have to roll the dice."

"For you, Rae Stevens, I will."

31

"What do you mean, the *Ledger* is saved?" I said, looking back and forth between Shelton and Ms. Bessie. They had met me at the front door to deliver the news. "Don't get me wrong. I'm ecstatic. But what happened? Who got us out of the hole?"

I picked up the latest issue of the *Greensboro Ledger*. The one with Malachi's story—rather, the story of Malachi and Gran'nola—as the featured center spread. The one I'd thought would be the last edition, for a few months or forever.

My hair was knotted into a high bun, but it was still wet from my swim at the rec center before coming into the newspaper office. A drop of water landed on the middle of the front page, spreading slightly and blurring the ink.

"Mr. Malachi Burke," Shelton said, fanning a check in the air.

The heavy disposition he'd been carrying for the last week had been replaced by his usual lighthearted, good-humored personality. His recently acquired wrinkles of worry had all but disappeared.

"And, just so you know, we're in a good place for a *very* long time. We could go back to being a weekly paper, but I'm still going to take it slow and use this money wisely."

Ms. Bessie threw her hands in the air. "It feels like we hit the lottery."

I wanted to snatch the check from Shelton and see how many zeroes and commas we were celebrating, but it wasn't my business. Nor was that the point. The point was that our community would continue to have its own voice.

"I had no idea," I said, when Ms. Bessie asked me why I hadn't said anything about it. "We've both been so busy. Maybe he forgot to mention it."

"Or maybe he didn't want to mention it," Shelton said.

I hadn't seen Malachi all week. After two days and nights with Ms. Nola, he'd spent the rest of the week preparing for the final session of camp. In that time, the carpal tunnel syndrome that sometimes plagued my wrists had flared up because I'd been writing almost without stopping, trying to complete as many assignments as possible. I was a woman on a mission to make it to Hawaii by the end of the year.

Although we hadn't seen each other, his had been the last voice I'd heard every night and the first one I heard in the morning.

Shelton shrugged. "I don't know if I was supposed to say anything or not. All I know is, he came to church with Ms. Nola yesterday and handed me an envelope with instructions to open it when I got home. I almost fainted. In fact, I think I did."

"Fool," Ms. Bessie said. "You would know if you fainted." She pouted her tomato-red lips.

"I just hope I don't faint when I take this check to the bank," Shelton said.

"We'll go as soon as the lunch crowd gets off the street," Ms. Bessie told him. "I'm coming with you. You'll need a bodyguard."

"She's a wise choice," I told Shelton. "Have you ever tried to pick up Ms. Bessie's purse? She can knock a person out cold with one swing of that thing."

"You've got that right," Ms. Bessie affirmed.

I unfolded the paper I was holding. "Let's see how this center spread turned out," I said, flipping to the middle. My feature story—framed by some of the photos Jared had taken—filled the entire page, with a tag line at the bottom indicating it continued on the next one. I'd been satisfied with my final draft, and I hoped Malachi and Ms. Nola would be, too.

"This looks nice. Jared did an excellent job," I said, admiring the shots he'd captured. He'd even included a photo of me talking to Malachi, as well as him interacting with Ms. Nola and his aunt, Mimi.

"I set aside twenty copies for Ms. Nola," Shelton told me. "That should give her enough to spare after she's passed them out to all her brother and sisters. Can you get them to her? I'm sure you'll see her before I do."

"I'm sure I'll see Malachi, but I don't know about Ms. Nola."

"Well, listen to you," Ms. Bessie exclaimed. "I think somebody is trying to throw herself back in the dating game."

"Don't start with me today, Ms. Bessie." I said. I felt my face blush. "It's only Monday."

"Monday is the best day of the week," she said. "Especially for you. Keep turning those pages, sweetheart."

"What are you talking about?" I said, thumbing through the issue. Past the community events calendar. Past Shelton's story on the mayor's forum and his editorial on police accountability.

"One more," Ms. Bessie said, looking over my shoulder. "Inside back page."

The entire page featured a full-color ad for the Hawaii Board of Tourism. Why they'd chosen to advertise in the *Greensboro Ledger* was beyond me, but I was sure Shelton would accept all the advertising dollars he could get, despite Malachi's sizable check.

"Why the Hawaii Board of Tourism would want to advertise in our paper is beyond me, but God must be sending me a sign. Who pulled this off? I've been itching to get to Hawaii for a while."

"Well, itch no further," Shelton said. He opened the door of the closet behind Ms. Bessie's desk. We'd cleared it completely of boxes last week.

And gave Malachi just enough room to fit inside.

He stepped out, holding a vase of tropical flowers with blossoms so huge that they covered half his face. Even though his face was obscured, I would recognize those biceps anywhere. *God, help me.*

"What's going on?" I asked, my heart fluttering.

Ms. Bessie slid the flowers from Malachi's grasp and set them on the corner of her desk.

"I had to come by and bring you your gift," Malachi said.

With the exception of our first date, I was accustomed to seeing him in a T-shirt and a pair of athletic shorts. Now, he wore a designer button-down shirt and black slacks, making me feel underdressed in my denim leggings, drapey tank top, and pool flip-flops.

"The flowers are beautiful," I said, beaming. "But you didn't have to do that. It was my pleasure to write the story about you *and* Ms. Nola."

"It's not just for the story. It's for being Rae Stevens."

My heart thumped. I heard Ms. Bessie catch her breath. She'd always been addicted to soap operas, and I was sure she felt that Malachi's words had dropped her in the middle of a real-life romance story.

"You, Rae Stevens, are a beautiful woman. It would be my pleasure if you let me send you—and a friend, of course—to Hawaii."

"Hawaii? Malachi—" The water from damp hair trickled down the back of my neck. I reached up to wipe it off.

"Shhhh," Ms. Bessie shushed me. "Listen to the man."

"When we were in the hot air balloon, you said you wanted to watch the sun set over Hawaii. So, I'm sending you there to watch five of them."

"Are you serious?" I said, looking over to Shelton for confirmation. He nodded.

"I don't know what to say, Malachi."

Malachi stepped closer to me. "Say you'll go. Say you'll have a good time. And say that when you come back, you'll give me a chance to show you how a woman like you should be treated."

"Shoot, if she won't, I will," Ms. Bessie said, shoving her nose in the middle of my vase of blooms.

"You need to worry about Wallace," Shelton reminded her.

I wanted Malachi Burke to kiss me, but I didn't want the spectators. We looked at each other, seemingly sharing the same desire.

"What are you waiting for?" Ms. Bessie demanded. "Go ahead and kiss the man!"

Malachi leaned down and pressed his lips to mine before I could change my mind. I closed my eyes and pretended that we were alone again in the hot air balloon, this time floating over the Pacific Ocean.

"Alright, that's enough," Shelton butted in. "God is watching you, and Ms. Bessie is over here looking all googly-eyed."

"You can't fault me for admiring young love," Ms. Bessie said.

Malachi reached over and snapped one of the flowering blooms off the tip of the stem, then tucked it behind my ear. I wrapped my arms around his waist and swore I could feel every memory of Trenton Cason leaving my mind and being replaced by a growing affection for Malachi Burke.

For the first time in my years of dating, I knew for sure that I'd hit a home run.

Epilogue

Zenja Maxwell's back patio was magazine-worthy, with painstaking attention to detail, from the torch lighting and serenity fountain to the swinging hammocks that matched the custom-designed furniture with coordinating cushions and accent pillows. If I had an oasis like hers, I would never leave home.

Zenja slid open the back door off her kitchen and emerged with a platter of assorted cheeses and crackers. Farrah followed with a tray of tumblers filled with ice and a pitcher of sweet tea. Quinn came out last, with her makeup perfectly applied, as if she were about to walk down the aisle any minute. I wasn't surprised that Farrah had done an impeccable job, or that Quinn had booked her for the job on the spot.

"I can't stop looking at myself," Quinn confessed. "How vain is that? It's like you've turned a duckling to a swan," she told Farrah.

"Believe me, I've worked on some ducklings," Farrah said as she began to pour tea into the glasses. "And you are far from one of those. It makes my job easy when the bride is beautiful to begin with."

"That's sweet of you," Quinn said. "I'm telling you, if Zenja hadn't talked to Rae at the baseball field, I don't know what I would've done."

Zenja bit into a cracker. "That's why I always say, God is so good at what He does. He just orchestrates things and puts them in place exactly the way we need them."

I used a toothpick to spear a cube of cheddar. "But what gets me is that I didn't even realize you two, and your husbands, had come out to Ms. Nola's house the night she went missing. It was all such a flurry of activity that I guess I wasn't focusing on anyone around me."

"Understandable," Zenja said. "But I didn't see you, either. I think we'd already left to go ride through the city by the time you arrived. Roman was there, but he was too busy running behind Uncle Bud."

"Then he had his work cut out for him," I said. Even after breakfast the next morning, Uncle Bud had still been recovering from his intoxicating night.

"Roman told me that man cussed him up one side and down the other." Zenja laughed. "But he could take it. The only time Roman tried to get him under control was when Uncle Bud had some choice words for some woman who was running around claiming to be Malachi's girlfriend from New York. Evidently, Bud embarrassed her so much that she sped down that driveway on two wheels."

"No," I said. My jaw dropped.

"Yes," Zenja said. "He got rid of her, and every intention that she had for showing up in the first place."

"I knew I liked Uncle Bud," I said.

Zenja and Quinn sat down, and the four of us resumed the heart-to-heart we'd been having for the past hour. What had started as a makeup consultation had flowed into a relationship counseling session. Our conversation floated between talks of concealing and contouring, to confessions of love lost and love restored.

It had all started with Farrah's question to Zenja as she applied Quinn's false mink eyelashes: "What's the most important lesson marriage has taught you?"

"Forgiveness," Zenja had answered without hesitation. "If God hadn't shown me the power of forgiveness, I never would've believed that He could restore my marriage after my husband's infidelity. The forgiveness wasn't just about Roman. In fact, it was more about me and the transformation God was doing in my heart."

Infidelity? From the interaction I'd seen between Zenja and her husband when we'd arrived at their home that evening, I was amazed that their marriage had endured that type of trial. They'd gone through the fire and emerged without any smell of smoke.

"Forgiveness is, I'd have to agree," Quinn said now, picking up the conversation where we'd left off. "There was a time when the only reason I wore makeup was to cover up the bruises and scratches after one of my ex-husband's tirades. But even after our marriage ended, and I grew to love Levi, God showed me that I had to forgive my ex. Forgiveness can be painful, but the end result is worth it. You have to put your heart in God's hand, and trust that He has the best intentions for your life." Quinn picked up the handheld mirror and blinked slowly. "If only my eyelashes naturally looked this way."

"I heard on the news today that Malachi is hanging up his baseball glove, so to speak," Zenja said.

"He has his whole life ahead of him," I said, repeating what he'd told me the night before. "Baseball has been at the center of his existence for so long, and now he's ready to see what else there is. At first, I thought it was just because his grandmother was getting older, but it seems he's entering a new season of his own life."

"So, what does that mean for you and Malachi?" Quinn asked. "I know you said you just met, but there seems to be something there that neither of you can deny."

I looked at Farrah. She'd said nearly the same thing on our drive over to Zenja's.

"I can't imagine that he'd pick up his entire life and move to North Carolina instantly," I mused. "Like we keep saying, the only thing I can do is trust that God is ordering my steps. Whether Malachi and I will end up walking this life together...only time will tell." I took a sip of my sweet tea. "The last time I saw Ms. Nola, I recorded the stories she told us while we were sitting around her breakfast table. My plan is to transcribe them and make them into a journal for Malachi so he'll always have those memories to cherish."

"So sweet," Farrah nearly swooned. She'd always been a hopeless romantic.

"But there was a single thread that ran through every one of her stories. And that was love."

Zenja nodded her head and smiled. "And love never fails."

I felt my cell phone vibrate in my pocket. I checked it and saw that it was Malachi. "Excuse me. I need to take this, if that's okay."

Farrah crossed her legs. "Oh, I know who that is. Ladies, was it just me, or could you tell how her entire countenance changed?"

"Undeniable," Zenja said.

"Without a doubt," Quinn added. "That's her boo on the phone."

"Her main squeeze," Zenja put in.

"Her baby daddy." Quinn giggled, then waved her hands in the air. "Oh, wait. That's not a good one."

They erupted into laughter as I stepped inside the house, but not before hearing Farrah's shout, "I've got a better one: her future."

I slid the door closed behind me.

"Hey, pretty lady," Malachi said when I answered. "I've been thinking about you."

I had been thinking about him, too. And I was beginning to realize that Gran'nola had a point when she claimed, "I know what I know."

I did, too.

About the Author

Tia McCollors used to dream of being a television news anchor, but her destiny led her behind the pages instead of in front of the cameras. After earning a degree in journalism and mass communications from UNC–Chapel Hill, she went on to build a successful career in the public relations industry. In 1999, a job layoff prompted her to explore writing and pursue a career as an author. Following the birth of her son in 2006, she left the corporate arena to focus on her family and her expanding writing and speaking business.

Tia's first novel, *A Heart of Devotion*, was an *Essence* magazine best seller. She followed her popular debut with four other inspirational novels: *Zora's Cry*, *The Truth about Love*, *The Last Woman Standing*, and *Steppin' Into the Good Life*. In 2012, she released her first devotional book, *If These Shoes Could Talk: Devotional Messages for a Woman's Daily Walk*. *Monday Morning Joy* follows *Sunday Morning Song* and *Friday Night Love* in Days of Grace, her first series with Whitaker House.

In addition to being an author, Tia is an inspirational speaker, as well as an instructor for writing workshops. She particularly enjoys coaching women of faith, female entrepreneurs, and stay-at-home mothers. Her speaking engagements and literary works have been spotlighted in a growing number of publications, including *Black Enterprise* magazine, *Who's Who in Black Atlanta*, *The Good Life* magazine, and the *Atlanta Journal-Constitution*.

Tia currently resides in the Atlanta, Georgia, area with her husband and their three children. Readers can learn more about Tia at www.tiamccollors.com or connect with her on social media at www.facebook.com/fansoftia or @tiamccollors.

Welcome to Our House!

We Have a Special Gift for You ...

It is our privilege and pleasure to share in your love of Christian fiction by publishing books that enrich your life and encourage your faith.

To show our appreciation, we invite you to sign up to receive a specially selected **Reader Appreciation Gift**, with our compliments. Just go to the Web address at the bottom of this page.

God bless you as you seek a deeper walk with Him!

WE HAVE A GIFT FOR YOU. VISIT:

whpub.me/fictionthx

WHITAKER HOUSE